Blue Tyson

Also by Terry Dowling

RYNOSSEROS
WORMWOOD

Blue Tyson

Terry Dowling

Aphelion Publications

First published in 1992 by Aphelion Publications
3 Pepper Tree Lane, North Adelaide, South Australia. 5006

Postal Address:
P.O. Box 619, North Adelaide, South Australia. 5006

© Terry Dowling 1992

Printed in Australia by The Book Printer, Melbourne

Cataloguing in Publication Data

National Library of Australia

Dowling, Terry, 1947 –
    Blue Tyson.

    ISBN 1 875346 05 8.

    I. Science Fiction, Australian. I. Title.

A823.3

Acknowledgements

"A Dragon Between His Fingers" originally appeared in *Omega Science Digest*, May 1986, Philip Gore (Ed).

"Vanities" originally appeared in *Glass Reptile Breakout*, Van Ikin (Ed), Centre for Studies in Australian Literature, 1991.

Introduction © Jack Vance 1992

The Author would like to thank those who helped make these voyages possible:

Nick Stathopoulos	Katherine Cummings	Kerrie R. Hanlon
Norma Vance	Peter McNamara	Sean McMullen
Harlan Ellison	Keira McKenzie	Jack Vance
Jonathan Strahan	Van Ikin	Nicole Mason
Carey Handfield	Philip Gore	Jeremy G. Byrne
Alastair Kerr	Janet Gluckstern	

Acknowledgements

By way of pirates, gliders, jazz and porcelain rabbits, too much good food, hours at the kiln and the ancient scribes of Ebla, this book could be for none other than my dear friends:

Jack, Norma and John Vance

Contents

Introduction

To avoid confusion and to quiet rumours, I admit from the start that I have been acquainted with Terry Dowling for many years. He has been my friend, accomplice, and fellow vagabond. Together we have roamed and plundered, romanced both fair and brunette maidens, looted their possessions — usually cold cans of Foster's beer from their refrigerators, occasionally a ham sandwich.

Therefore, this introduction is not necessarily dispassionate, although it may be relied upon as a character reference.

In regard to *Blue Tyson*: the culture native to Australia is extremely sophisticated despite its apparent crudity. It goes without saying that the Aboriginal mental patterns and constructs of imagery cannot be translated into our own terms. To understand such lore and emotion, one must be born an Aborigine. Still, a few Aboriginal concepts affect us as if they were archetypal truths, notably 'Dreamtime', which resonates like a gong at some deep level of the mind.

The usual story of the future is based, more or less implicitly, upon contemporary Caucasian ideas, then elaborating upon these to formulate the societies which the writer hopes will seem plausible. There is nothing wrong with this procedure, since all of us swim in the same cultural soup.

Terry has attempted a far more difficult work; he has started with a culture essentially incommensurable with our own and has developed therefrom a new culture of extremely elaborate textures. There are too many details to be mentioned here, although it may be pointed out that the parapsychic abilities of the present-day Aborigines have not been neglected in Terry's extrapolations. For us Long-noses it is a cheerless prospect. The Ab'Os, exploiting their special abilities, have imposed their world-view upon Australia. The details are haunting; each story projects a special mood. Terry writes with verve and flair; his imagination never stops.

So there you have it. Tom Tyson, the Blue Captain of the sand-ship *Rynosseros*, the linking character in each of these stories, will be familiar by reason of his appearance in a previous collection, and apparently Terry is not done with him yet.

Jack Vance

"This is the task of man always . . . not to illuminate the ancient truths, the ancient intimations of the unconscious, the ancient intimations of the soul, but . . . to make them immediate and contemporary, to give them a meaning in the here and now."

Carl Gustav Jung.

Breaking Through
to the Heroes

Three of us from *Rynosseros* were sitting on the long terrace of the Gaza Hotel, enjoying one of the slow twilights we have now and watching a dozen or so patrons playing fire-chess.

We sat near the Promenade, Shannon, Rimmon and I, looking out over the balustrade to the brilliantly-lit Pier and the darkening ocean. One moment we were caught up in the sound of the long swells that crashed on the beach and by the intent expressions on the faces of the players, so many ghostly masks lit by their flickering pieces, then there were two people standing near us.

"Hello, Tom?"

I couldn't place the voice in the windy darkness, though something about it was familiar.

"Tobas?"

Next to me, Shannon laughed.

"It's the Welshman. Cromarthy," he said.

"Right on. Tad Cromarthy, an'doing a job. I've someone fer ya ta meet, Tom. This is Anna Kemp."

People who have never seen haldane Ab'O just cannot appreciate that moment on the terrace at the Gaza, the presence suddenly there, the inherent power, the surprise of recognition that is never that.

When Anna Kemp stepped forward into the light from the party lanterns, pushing back the hood of her dark robe, I saw a very tall tribal woman, uncommonly black, like sculpted night herself, yet with little of the old Koori physiotype about her. As her features resolved, it was hard to tell what was natural, cosmetically altered or haldane legacy, but even in the half-light I could see she was a beauty. The flash of scintillants on the inside of her robe when she pushed it back heightened the effect.

"This, m'am, is Tom Rynosseros hisself. As promised. Or Blue Tyson. Or Tom Tyson. Or Tom O'Bedlam, dependin' on who..."

"Enough, Tad. Be a gentleman and give us room."

The little man took the money I handed him and slipped off along the terrace to one of the bars. Shannon and Rim saw it was business, sensed it was probably one to one and confidential at this point, and got up to go.

"We'll head back to *Rynosseros*," Shannon said. "See if Ben needs help with the new boss housing." They excused themselves and moved off among the tables.

I was left to find words, feeling that eerie sense of recognition again. An Ab'O woman here of all places, unaccompanied, radiating such presence.

Anna Kemp saved me the effort. The twinkling black lamia spoke first, softly, from the seat Rim had vacated.

"I waited for darkness, Captain. I needed darkness. Please, you know what berking is?"

The question surprised me. "Yes. When you draw on the Dreamtime parts of your personalities."

"What we agree to call haldanes."

"We try to be as scientific about it as we can, Ms Kemp. It helps us live with it. I know what — iceberging — is. The current theories anyway. National theories."

"Good. And my name is Anna. Tom."

We exchanged smiles. Hers was a little wintry. She was trying to be relaxed and calm but something was troubling her.

"My father is Arredeni."

I made the connection at once. Of course. *The* Arredeni. Arredeni Paxton Kemp, the Ab'O scientist.

"He has discovered something about berking he wishes to share with you Nationals. A gift. An official benefice. He needs you to go to him at Heart-and-Hand before he is killed."

She stood up, over six foot, her form shimmering in the glow from the terrace lamps and the burning pieces on the boards

2

nearby. "Can we walk please? I would hate to be found here."

"Someone is intent on stopping you?"

"Please. Walk. Along the terrace."

She took my arm and we passed the bright flickering boards, moved before the lit doorways and grand lobbies of the Gaza, eventually joined the dozens of other couples on the Promenade that reached by the Pier and the gardens and followed the dunes and the seawall around by the ocean, out towards Mirajan, Castanelle and the souling colonies. Their lights twinkled in the distance.

I felt absurdly like one of the Dashiell Hammett characters I'd seen in the film festival the week before, right down to having this dark mysterious woman on my arm, here seeking help in what had to be a desperate and dangerous enterprise judging by her manner. But the flashing, sequined shape beside me was real — the pressure of her hand, the recognition I felt as a permanent déjà-vu, so strange and disorienting.

As we walked, I tried to remember what I knew of current disputes and alliances among the different States, hoping to recall Arredeni's present status there. Normally it would have been easy, but not now.

Berking.

Iceberging. Reaching beyond the known to what was beneath.

All I could think of was the Princes and their Clever Men lined up, not moving, fighting a battle on a different plane of reality, breaking through to the heroes that they also were, that we all were to hear sceptics like Arredeni tell it — Colte and Ashbiani and Marduk, so many others. Those wars never stopped, and just as well. The energies were contained, directed inward. The status quo between the Ab'O States and Nation remained intact.

It was wonderfully cool on the Promenade. The further we went, the more the crowds thinned out until we were the only couple and the Gaza and Twilight Beach were so much shimmering gold and black treeline filigree behind us and we were in the terminator dunes between the desert and the ocean. We could hear the waves crashing on our right, and all around us the hiss and whisper of seagrass. The moon was up at last and ahead on the dunes stood the nine-foot iron rod of a belltree, stripped of its higher functions long ago but thrumming in the wind all the same. The diligent in the crown still had a glimmering of life; now and then there was a sad chiming of the dim-recall rods way down in the shaft, below the empty arms.

Seeing the old tree may have done it.

"The stories are true?" she said.

"I'm sorry?"

"You were given Blue by a rogue tree?"

She had to know better than to ask, though she was Ab'O. It did make a difference.

"I don't discuss it, Anna."

"Arredeni said. But you and the other Coloured Captains performed some service for the tree. Something important."

I allowed that much. "Yes."

"You got your ships that way. The Hero Colours. All of you."

"Anna..."

"Tom, see it as I do. I'm about to tell something very important to someone who came out of the Madhouse at Cape Bedlam. Arredeni said that I should read you, that finally I should be the one to decide. I'm doing that now."

"I don't discuss it."

"I know, but it's important. Why were you sent there? Who were you? So little is known. You came out hating the dream machines set to watch over you. No clear memories, just a few half-remembered images..."

I felt a rush of panic. "Anna!"

"...a woman's face, a star and a ship. Correct?"

And surging, irrational anger. "How..?"

"You have been going to a dreamlock for some time now. Mercy Simotee. She has been working on those images; you suspect there might be others."

"She would not give you that..."

"I'm the daughter of a Prince, Tom. By law, Mercy Simotee could not refuse."

"Listen..."

"From our viewpoint, I said! No sooner are you released than a famous oracle tree, possibly the greatest of the Iseult-Darrian

AIs, arranges for you to win *Rynosseros* in the ship-lotteries. It gives you Blue, a Hero Colour..."

"Six other Nationals had Colours and ships already. I wasn't the first."

"A tribal Madhouse, Tom. Why would this tree choose such a person, a man with no past? Why?"

"You have access to Mercy's records. You know about the Captains. Are you going to tell me?"

Incredibly, I really thought she might. Perhaps it was the recognition, the sense of the familiar that attended particularly powerful Clever Men, that flowed from Anna with such undeniable force.

"Me? No. Arredeni may, it occurs to me now. He specified you — not just any of the Seven. The last Captain, he said."

Arredeni may! The words held me, the knowledge that there were tribal people who did know, who could reveal such things. Again, it made all the difference in the world.

"There's so little. The images you said. The ship — possibly *Rynosseros*, I can't be sure. The star is a point I sometimes see, a sharp point of light in my mind. Very bright. The face is Ab'O, quite beautiful, with a triangle of golden lace set into the forehead. An Arete triangle. I do not know the face. But Ab'O. That's all, just the three. Sometimes hints of others. Memories of the dream machines in the darkness. Conversations. I trusted them. Your father really asked for me..?"

"Insisted on it. The Blue Captain. He said to try the Gaza."

"You didn't ask why?"

"Of course I did. He would not say. Just specified you to receive the benefice. He was very troubled, Tom."

"Are we safe now?" I watched the spectral tree before us, immediately had my answer by the pressure of her hand closing on my arm. Her hushed words astonished me.

"Stop! They are near. I sense Colte and Dos. And Hecate, yes. Three." She continued to read the night. "Only three."

Three Clever Men. Anna was sensing them, already tracking their mind-lines.

I wished I had a ballistic weapon then and not just the light deck sticker charvolant crews usually carried. But such thoughts were short-lived.

There were two figures ahead of us on the Promenade; another emerged from the seagrass on our left, leapt nimbly to the stones, became still. Three Ab'Os communing, drawing aspect.

Twilight Beach seemed a thousand miles behind. The chiming of the tree was a mournful thing.

Anna released my arm and tensed.

"Do nothing!" she said, and went into trance. Just like that, her eyes were gone, rolled back. She stood with her feet apart, arms raised partway out from her body as if about to lift, hands turned down.

It was the Owl configuration. She was going after one of the strongest heroes, Imbaro the War Owl, stronger than Dos or Hecate, usually more than the equal of Colte. I could hear her initial chant, a husky breathing.

"Imbaro. Imbaro. Imbaro."

I watched the three dark shapes blocking our way, tensed for mind-war as Anna was and possibly for dealing with the National who accompanied her.

All three were silent. One wore a cloak that had fallen open to reveal a suit of lights underneath, the lozenges of mirror-glass catching starshine and moonlight and giving him an oily, quicksilver sheen, hypnotic to look upon. Seeing that, more than anything, told me what was about to happen, the signature of mind-war.

Beside me, Anna did not move. She kept her Owl shape, but was silent now too, translating.

A wash of dizziness hit me, astonished me in the same instant. How could I be feeling it? How? Nationals never suffered the effects of these combats. Some of us read the corroboree mind-dragons, true, some even felt the haldane fields as the faintest frissons, as the uncanny recognition I felt with Anna, but that was all. We didn't have the gift.

I reeled, startled by the wash of colour before me, pulses, vortices in a consuming blackness. I rubbed my eyes. The haldane field had to be enormously powerful to affect me like this.

I staggered to the balustrade and steadied myself, gripped the cool stone, desperately gripped it. Somewhere off to my right the belltree thrummed, waves crashed. Grass keened in the on-shore wind — marking the outer world I could not reach.

Inside, there was colour everywhere, pulsing bands of it, with elongated shadows, twisting reds, golds and purples, startling blues, surging black that streamed on those colours as highlights themselves. Black as colour. Shadow as light.

I was part of the trance-war — I was! — as incredible as it seemed. I *saw* shapes, had the conviction of shapes before me, Dos faltering, fading, losing force, could see Colte looming as a mighty cowled image alongside a serpentine Hecate, and Imbaro the Great Owl opposing — godforms from every place and time streaming from them, residues exploding into the false memory of template-recognition.

They were too beautiful to resist. I wanted them, wanted to reach out and pull them to me — must have tried, for I lost balance, felt cold stone, the pain of scraped skin, seized that dim urgent reality and made it my way through...

I was leaning against the Promenade wall, blinking, rubbing my eyes, trying to rid myself of the trance vision, hating, loving it, desperately needing to be free.

It took effort, effort to see Anna and the three dark figures, but it came at last, squeezed out of the startling play of colour, the spirals and detonations, helped by the sound of waves falling and the belltree and the rush of seagrass on the wind-swept dunes.

And there was one of the Clever Men, the one who had been Dos, drawing his kitana from across his shoulder and advancing on Anna.

I knew at once what it meant. Conventions of mind-war had been set aside. The withdrawal of Dos had been a deliberate thing. My involvement too probably, a means of keeping me out of the way.

These men were desperately intent on getting Anna.

I snatched my sticker from its sheath, rushed across to where the Clever Man stood and thrust the narrow blade between his ribs, at the same time pulling his head back and down. The kitana rattled on the stones; the Ab'O died.

It was as if the others knew. They broke trance almost at once, fought quickly to regain composure. When they saw their fallen comrade, they fled into the seagrass, both stumbling from the effort of concentrating and now being forced to act on the physical plane; clearly surprised, that Anna had been beating them at mind-fighting and that their treachery had been found out and prevented. There was a flash of mirror-light from the cloaked figure and they were gone.

Anna leant on my arm, panting and shaken.

"You — ought not to have interfered," she said. "I was managing."

"Not as I saw it."

I told her about the one who had broken trance to use his sword.

"It wasn't your fight. This will cause an Incident. You'll be targeted."

"I am already, Anna. I know very little about mind-war, but I do know that no-one engaging in it can pursue the fight when driven out of trance — or relinquishes aspect. This one went for his sword in front of me, and that means they didn't care if I knew. I was probably to be next."

"But your Colour..."

"They're desperate. An error of judgement on their part. They thought the mind-field had me."

Anna's eyes narrowed at that.

"You felt the field?"

"I saw the heroes."

Anna stared in momentary disbelief, then slowly nodded, accepting it.

"No wonder Arredeni specified you, Tom. Not just any National doing field work for Council. Not just any of the Seven. The Blue Captain, he said. Insisted on it. You're sighted."

"Some Nationals sense the energies. They wanted me involved and disoriented. They included me."

"That's one thing. The disorientation. But you say you saw them."

"Vague shapes, that's all. I identified them though, sensed which ones were which. I — knew them. You've got to tell me about them, Anna."

"Not now. This area's charged, and they'll return for the body. Tomorrow. Tomorrow when we're far from here."

We began walking then, back towards Twilight Beach, back to the Pier and the lights. Behind us the old belltree thrummed and sang and held its rusted arms out to the wind and the sea. The seagrass stirred in the dunes, adding its song to the ancient night.

"Tom?" Anna said when the place was far behind.

"Yes?"

"You saw the War Owl I became?"

"I'm — not sure now."

"No?"

"At first, yes. Then I read it as something else."

"What?"

"I have no idea."

"Try to remember. It's very important."

"I'll tell you if I do."

By noon the next day, *Rynosseros* was doing a steady 90 k's along the Great Arunta Road, running under twenty kites and a hot sun with a strong dry wind at our backs.

Scarbo had the helm, Rim tended the lines, Strengi was below at com. Shannon and Hammon were down on the commons doing repairs to our Cody man-lifter. Apart from Strengi, all of us wore djellabas and burnouses over our fatigues and fighting leathers and had our personal weapons close by, expecting attack.

I stood with Anna in the bows under a canopy, away from the others, watching the desert flash by and the red sand disappear under our wheels.

Anna seemed to be listening for something, interpreting the distances, reading the bright air and far-off haze at the horizon. Finally she came to a decision.

"We can talk about it now, Tom."

"Good."

I was watching the land as well, reading it in my own way as we crossed one of the outer Ab'O States, Here-We-Stand, on an official Road. Technically we were safe, Colour-protected. Officially. But I had seen the Ab'O use his sword, and Anna had told us to expect attack; it was impossible now to relax, to do other than see every far-off shimmer, every flash of quartz and errant willy-willy as hunter trace, deadly pursuit. Scan showed nothing; com channels remained clear, but there was nothing else for it. I knew that the others — Rim, Shannon, Strengi, old Ben, young Hammon — would be doing the same.

Anna must have heard me answer but still she did not speak; she seemed to be translating what the land told her, probably searching for mind-lines, no doubt considering the possibility of gain-monitors, though transit noise protected us there. It was other ships she was trying for too, but by the presence of Clever Men, instinctively mistrusting surveillance tech no less than I did.

"Nothing," she said at last. "Nothing else."

We had seen only two other charvolants since early morning, both tribal vessels, Madupan ships, brightly-painted hulls under thirty kites each. They had passed us at a distance of twenty metres, going the other way, so Shannon reported at the end of his dawn watch, and seemed to give us no special attention.

Anna gripped the rail, watching the horizon and the clutch of kites above and ahead of us, drawing us along.

"Anna?"

"Sorry, Tom. It's a matter of finding the words, and of knowing the risk you all face. But you're right. They already think you know, all of you, so you're targeted already, aren't you?"

"This isn't a tribal ship. We choose to be here."

Anna gave a rueful smile, but still hesitated. She did not face me.

"So," I said. "Dreamtime business."

"It is."

"Haldane lore."

"Yes."

But she said nothing more for the moment.

I tried another way. "Tell me about the haldanes. What are they?"

She shrugged. "Who truly knows?"

"That's heresy."

"Yes."

Again the silence, but I sensed what might be behind it — how like a hard, bright, impenetrable box that had no lock and could never be opened, its contents forever out of sight, this could only be approached, discussed, as the form, the container serving the thing contained, defining it as a door or a chair might show in some small way what gave them purpose.

"The Madhouse at Cape Bedlam is run by the Haldanian Order," I said, leading her into it the only way I could.

"Sign of the red wheel," she said, accepting my overture, talking out at the wide land, at the sky of vivid killing blue.

"I know that sign. It's where I was. That was Dreamtime business too. Tartalen told me that on the first morning — when they released me."

She nodded. It was as if the words freed her.

"The haldanes, Tom?" she asked, repeating my earlier question. "What are they?"

I felt a thrill of excitement. Was she actually going to say?

"Whose view? Yours? Nation's?"

"Consensus. Better yet, give me the range. Start with how Nationals prefer to see them."

"How you've made us see them. The other parts of our humanity. The lost parts. Power vectors on another plane available for our use — *intended* for our use. If we can reach them. At the other extreme, the ancient gods — mythogenesis: the mythic underpinnings of our race. Some shared unconscious your people are able to tap into. Near enough?"

Anna turned to me now.

"You accept that?"

"I can, yes."

"Even though you're shut off from it?"

"We accept there must be reasons. Your people have found the way through. The rest of us may. I'd say this benefice Arredeni wants to share with Nation is something important about haldane theory, and you have a conflict of interests."

Anna glanced out at a distant flash of quartz, at the canopy bellying above us, faced me again.

"He is prepared to see the Dreamtime differently, yes. He continues to question the traditional views of the Clever Men."

"He is famous for it."

"Notorious for it. At least he's brave enough to question."

"Yes. What I meant was that it must happen all the time. Honest scientific enquiry."

"It does. But only so far, only ever so far. This is different. Our tribe is a handful, Tom, nearly gone. Normally it would not matter. But Arredeni — for all his National ways — is still a Prince as well as a great scientist. The world listens to what he has to say."

Now the dark eyes did not leave me; now I was the one staring out at the red land, watching the Road disappear under our wheels, an endless red-gold ribbon spanning that desolation. I had forgotten to look for ships.

"Tom, in our continuing research into the haldane phenomenon, my father and I have come up with many theories, some very extreme. Generally the tribes have ignored us. Now, one line of enquiry is causing an incredible outcry."

"Tell me."

"What would you say if I told you that sometime in our past we were hit with a weapon, a mental weapon?"

"Your people?"

"All of us. Humanity. All our earliest societies."

"I'd be keen to see proof of it is what I'd say. But a weapon?"

"What Arredeni is postulating. A 'device' — to call it that — which possibly impaired genetic memory as well, so basic DNA templates were tampered with, changed, new ones laid down."

I faced her again. "Anna..."

"It could have happened, Tom. Part of the evidence is in the mind-wars my people fight. This weapon would have shut us off from something we were starting to know, from some natural direction we were taking. Left us with a — a religious bias instead."

She gave me time to absorb that. The silence of the desert was broken only by the sounds of our passing, the steady roar of the travel platform, the hiss of sand, the thrum of taut cables in the wind, the lift and fall of the bellying canopy.

"All right," I said, because too much was no worse right then than too little.

Anna looked reassured, as if this first hurdle had been the hardest. She did not know how vividly I had been involved in the mind-fight. I had *seen* haldane forms.

"By this theory, all our religions, our whole mythic bias, are nothing more than the residues of that weapon being turned on us. A clever way of shutting us off from the full mental capacity we had then or were developing. Through recorded history we've been slowly working our way out of the after-effects of this vast wounding."

"Recovering from shell-shock."

Anna nodded. "Like working fragments of shrapnel out of an injured body, yes. These fragments are our god-responses, our inclination to believe in deities...entities beyond ourselves, and be satisfied by them."

"So some large picture became lost to us, obscured by lots of fascinating small ones?"

"That's it," she said. "What we've always called gods. This weapon would have used our own best parts against us, to keep us from seeing that larger picture by giving us feelings of rapture and exaltation, yearnings for communion and divine approval. Perhaps there were other things we all lost as a result of such a wounding. Telepathy, psychokinesis, things like that. It would be a matter of rediscovering what we all once had."

"So in such a view," I said, "what the tribes see as a special and privileged link with ancient forces is no more than lucky individuals — Ab'O individuals, Clever Men — finding a way around the wounding? You've locked in on what we all once were?"

I saw the relief settle on Anna's lovely face, easing the eyes, relaxing the muscles in her jaw.

"It's a different way of looking at the Dreamtime, I know."

"And does Arredeni think that at last we might be recovering from the effects of this mythic weapon?"

"No. Not necessarily. Tom, we would not be meant to understand that this has happened to us. The wounding would be subtle. The more we recovered from it, the worse we'd be afflicted, if that makes sense. The more a society looked like shaking free of its gods and superstitions, the more social turmoil, stress, internal crisis, even external invasion there'd be. Arredeni suspects we would not be meant to recover. Individuals might, the shamans and great magicians, the prophets and healers, but not society at large unless helped.

"But at least we'd know we'd been hit, which would mean a new external element could be added, a catalytic element. That is what Arredeni wants to suggest — wants revealed to all the world. The possibility of such a phenomenon, and the self-perpetuating nature of the wounding. Humanity could not grow without such knowledge."

"If he's right."

"If he's right, yes."

Anna was the excited scientist now, so close to the facts that she forgot others were not. The words came rushing out.

"Allow that the theory is true, that those assassins at Twilight Beach were sent not to stop heresy but in response to this line of enquiry. Say that some Ab'Os — my father and I, other free-thinkers — have managed to shake free of the wounding, reaching through to the haldanes, locking onto them, but not as gods. Our people in general have done it because the Dreamtime is so fresh and vital, still so flexible and all-accommodating. Most religions lose their flexibility very quickly. Grant that our Clever Men found a functioning connection with the lost part of our humanity, but — allowing for this theory — saw the haldanes as gods, ancestors, ancient spirits, so that such a connection was dramatically tainted. Misunderstood."

I was losing it again.

"Why tainted?"

"Those locking on to those original energy vectors would naturally believe it unique to their own correct view of the universe, believe that *they* were the chosen ones. Our tribal societies are founded on that elitism. All along my father and I have wanted free and open discussion of the possibilities we've raised, to allow that we too may be refusing to see the full implications of our own privileged position. Arredeni and I have never been popular because of our liberal thinking, but this weapon theory has caused such a reaction that — automatically — it warrants further study. Only now do they call us heretics, you see? Only now."

"I can imagine. The Dreamtime is being debased. Anna, you and your father could be wrong."

"Of course we could. That's the point. But we feel we have discovered something more, something different. As Clever Men we think we may be confirming it within ourselves. And they have not ignored us, you see, simply let us peddle this theory along with the rest."

The Dreamtime was sacrosanct enough to justify such a fierce reaction, but I let it pass.

"How long have other Princes known of this...weapon?"

"A long time. Many of them have been following the research, discussing it in Convocation and at corroboree, trying to decide when Arredeni had gone too far. He is a Prince, after all. But now I am confirming his claims — another Clever Man, even if blood-related, and female at that, added sacrilege, who has so recently gained in power. A few tribes know I was sent to Twilight Beach to find you. They will know what that means."

We were silent at the rail then, Anna sorting her own thoughts, me lost in the shift of kites above and before us, trapped in the play of tribal signs: chevrons, suns, curving lines and totems in brilliant reds, yellows and blues, now a startling orange and purple, there, tricking with the blue of our huge Sode Star, a flash of green from a Chinese Hawk. The sky danced with the compelling ciphers of an undeclared mythology.

I found my questions again, tried to find ways to ask them, as if words could ever encompass this. I thought of the world's great religions, the uproar when these conjectures were made known.

"Does this impulse to see God have to be part of the wounding? Couldn't the god-impulse be our own; something worthy we've had misled rather than imposed?"

Anna shook her head but wasn't disagreeing.

"We can't be sure. And we may be the wrong ones to ask considering the psychogenetic tampering from our long-term exposure to the haldanes. But, again, it's not the point. My father and I — sense — that this impulse to see God, to feel spiritual exaltation, is something other: our thwarted ability to lock in on the rest of what we were."

"I envy you that link with the haldanes, Anna. Perhaps we all knew the face of God. Perhaps we refined the god-impulse to read the infinite, to find meaning; with knowledge of what it was anchored to and there for. Perhaps we were getting free of this god-need, having discovered who or what God was. A noosphere. Gaea. Our higher selves."

"Perhaps we did," she said.

"The haldanes, whatever they are."

Anna smiled. "Perhaps. I like your 'they'. At the very least 'they' are a power source. Volatile energy vectors which have changed us forever, and our land, our whole way of seeing things. And who knows, maybe that's why we descendants of the Kooris discovered this knowledge. Perhaps we will find that our Dreamtime was not just one of these woundings — one of these 'goddings' — but an imperfectly understood knowledge of our former state. Perhaps we *can* prove it. That would be marvellous."

There was the question that could not wait.

"So who fired the weapon, Anna? Since it's this natural link with the haldanes the great majority of us are cut off from, then perhaps it was they who thought it necessary to hold humanity back. Our own secret selves."

"There's your 'they' again! You keep making them conscious entities..."

"I saw shapes. I *saw* them!"

"It's difficult, I know. They're power vectors available for our use. Parts of us, if you like. We can't know the system while we're in the system. I said before that it would have been a weapon of mind, but perhaps it was a physical thing — technology. What was it? Who made it? Who fired it? All good questions. Arredeni has the — certainty — that it could have happened. He wants to open it up to general debate. Coming from an Ab'O Prince, a Clever Man who can access the vectors, it would be taken very seriously; control situations could be established. At the very least, the rest of humanity could be made to know they are part of the great mystery too. Which is not something many Princes want."

"A divine empiricism — I'm not surprised."

And again Anna smiled, for a moment like one of her own Koori ancestors, alien and detached not in the new way but in the old; not just the elegant daughter and colleague of a great Australian scientist, leader of a barely existing Ab'O State.

16

I was guilty of over-humanizing these things, as I once had with a robot, Lud, and belltrees and the dream machines in the Madhouse. The whole nature of the haldanes was a caution against that. But here I was persisting in reading the unknown by the known. My bias, my own handicap.

So the tribes made use of these vectors, imposed...no, sought and found personalities, identities, entities in them. Used them. Became them. Found their way through to a better, more dynamic use of some collective unconscious, of what it really meant to be human.

But on the creaking windy deck of a speeding charvolant, under a hot sun and a canopy of straining painted kites, the questions remained. Not if such a thing as Arredeni's god-gun could exist, but who would have fired it and why?

It was quiet for the next hour, just the steady cushioned jolting of *Rynosseros'* suspension, the muted gritty drone of the wheels on sand, the singing and soughing of the cables in a healthy tailwind — the roadsong all ships made.

I took the opportunity to brief the crew on what Anna had told me. Her enemies would assume I'd done so anyway, and it wasn't our way not to share mission talk.

Shortly after our midday meal, Shannon took up his guitar and soon had a song going which had us all laughing.

> "Oh, I've been hit by a god's bright gun,
>   I'm wounded through and through.
>   A Logos-bomb has made me numb,
>   I've forgotten what I knew.
>   Stigmata up and down my soul
>   And wounds that look divine,
>   Oh, I've been hit by a god's bright gun,
>   I've forgotten what was mine —
>   Oh, I've forgotten what was mine.
>
> "Oh, I've been cut by a god's sweet sword,
>   It's hurt me to my pith.
>   The closest shot at my target spot

Becomes the nearest myth.
Epiphanies are de rigueur,
Syncresis a delight.
Oh, I've been cut by a god's sweet sword
And I'm blinded by the light,
Oh, I'm blinded by the light."

So it went, with Rim and crusty old Scarbo adding verses.

But all this had the feeling of gallow's humour about it. By mid-afternoon, when Strengi called up from scan that two bogies were coming at us down Lateral 101 on what had to be an intercept course, we were actually relieved.

Our speed had been kept down so as not to attract undue attention from the tribal comsats; now Scarbo and Hammon put more kites in the sky and Shannon took us up to 100 k's.

The bogies read the speed change and added to their own canopies, but had to control speed ready for a turn into the Road. We were past them before they could move in to block and delay, but we saw them clearly enough.

Rushing at us down the wide trail of the 101 Lateral were two brightly-painted charvolants, Soti ships, displaying at least thirty kites apiece, a brave tribal showing. Even as Scarbo used scan to read deck and canopy array for ordnance capability, we could see their kitemasters busily winding most of those canopies in, dropping drogues from the big primary parafoils to slow them for the turn. As the colourful displays came down, death-lamps were revealed, fierce diamond djinn flashing at the end of their insulated cables.

Through scan we saw crewmen bringing more lamps and fighting kites to the lines, others manning deck-lenses, harpoons and hot-pots. Only their need for duplicity had saved us so far.

We kept our own kites where they were, using speed to buy time the best tactic now. Shannon helped Scarbo send up our racing-footmen, put three more lines with the twenty we already had, risking that, while Hammon brought out our own death-lamps and Rimmon issued snaphaunces and kitanas. Even Anna took them. Strengi was below at com and I had the helm. Heart-and-Hand was an hour away at most, but so much could happen in that time.

When Scarbo was satisfied there would be no line-fouling, he came to the poop.

"There'll be others, Tom. They aren't trying hard enough."

"Agreed. They'll pen us ahead. Anna, why the Soti?"

"They've been the ones following Arredeni's research most closely. Their Prince has had dealings with my father."

"So it may still be tribal rather than Pan-tribal. One Prince against another?"

"So far, yes. He probably wants to strike, is probably urging open war, but doesn't dare try it alone. Not until all the tribes rule."

Ben laughed. "Look what's behind! I'd call this open war. The question is, will they break Code for this?"

"Anna?" I asked her. "Lasers, ballistics, what?"

"No hi-tech. They know you have com. The satellites may be watching. They can't afford an incident. I think mercenaries, a staged pirate action, and I think they'll try the heroes again."

I almost asked why, then realized it was Anna they wanted, and her father eventually, through siege and attrition, possibly me for the trouble and insult I'd caused them. As for using the heroes, there was the prestige of it. They would want a victory at that level. A Dreamtime victory. Needed it after what had happened at Twilight Beach.

Anna was good at courting the haldanes. She had found Imbaro, could probably do so again. They wanted to beat Imbaro-in-Anna. Whatever else they tried, they would arrange it so they were sure of such a victory.

On the poop, Anna went into trance, easily, rolling back her eyes. It wasn't a deep trance, a searching really, tracking mind-lines to see if any of the charvis behind us had Clever Men aboard, if she had cause to fear attack at that level.

She came out of it seconds later.

"Nothing," she said, releasing a deep breath.

So it remained a contest of aeropleuristics, a race across the desert, a run down the wide red Road into See-Me-There and finally through the low far-off ranges that marked the border of Heart-and-Hand.

Rynosseros kept its lead easily, but the Soti ships had at least used the time to get the boxes and screens of their lamps and fighters aloft, well clear of the drab insulated battle canopies underneath. Through scan we saw them, both vessels plainly dressed for war.

No sooner had we taken the broad sweep from the Great Arunta Road into the 304 Lateral, a neat turn that swept us into Heart-and-Hand and had the border diligent pinging and chiming on its iron pole, than three more Soti ships appeared ahead, moving steadily towards us on the graded red sand.

Engagement was inevitable, unless we decided to run out on to the open desert with its uneven terrain, a desperate choice.

Logically, the Soti didn't have to stop us. They had only to wait until we were at Arredeni's tower and then make sure we never left. This whole action had to be a preferred option: to keep Anna from reaching her father, from re-enforcing him where — Prince's right — he could call for mind-war with comsat surveillance.

It was divide and conquer.

Nor did I have to ask if the new ships had Clever Men aboard. We ran at them, manoeuvring our kites for the direction change to keep maximum speed, hoping they would think we intended to ram our way through if necessary.

We could never be that desperate; the cost was too great. Better the desert first. But they might settle for such a tactic — reasoning that two charvolants to stop the one might be a small price to pay. I was hoping too that with so many ships to coordinate, they might underestimate us.

"Ready to dump!" I shouted.

Down on the commons, Strengi and Scarbo ran to the trip-lines. Hammon and Rim brought our black Javanese fighter to the mains, hooked it on, set the small helium lifts to clear it of the deck when needed, patched that function through to cable-boss and helm.

"Now!" I cried, judging distances, feeling the adrenalin rush, the thrill and anxiety of being committed.

Trip-lines were pulled. Drogues dropped from the bellies of seven of our largest kites, snapped out into long trailing cones. I applied brakes to all six wheels.

Rynosseros slowed at once. Our two pursuers were caught half-prepared. Had they been ready, they could have held their course and rammed, a quick and decisive solution.

But captains love their ships, their precious, hand-made, painted hulls with long pedigrees and hard-won reputations, and they cannot help themselves. Just as I would not give *Rynosseros* over to ramming, nor could the captains of the charvis behind us.

Those captains responded from instinct and emotion, not intellect. As we dropped back, they angled aside, not having time to consider alternatives, the contingency orders they had been given.

And as they ran by, one to each side, Scarbo freed our gleaming Javanese fighter, all wicked edges, chitin and beetle black. It angled out sharply at a thirty-degree lift towards the ship on our right, lacquered blades cutting the lines of at least eight kites, the whole canopy — our black fighter included — falling to the deck and the desert, snagging the remaining kites and fouling the front wheels. A perfect manoeuvre — child's play for Scarbo, one of the best kitesmen there is.

At the same time, Shannon, Hammon and Anna fired harpoons at the charvi on our left, one of the shafts a hot-pot. Two tyres went; the hot-pot burst against their forepeak and sent flaming oil down onto the commons.

We felt the brief flash of their lamps and a deck lens, but there was no time to keep a burn point. We lost a little paint on the hull, that was all. Their harpoons missed entirely, their gunners unable to adjust to our sudden loss of speed.

Both charvis raced at their oncoming fellows, one fouled and erratic, losing speed and veering dangerously to starboard, the other aflame, its crew in a panic. The dust-trail obscured much of what was occurring, but scan showed all five manoeuvring to avoid collision.

At such speeds it was difficult, and I could only wonder how they had orchestrated it originally. Two vessels ran together with a tremendous crash of timber and fibre-glass, a shattering of metal and ceramic. Two others broke Road and went out on to the ungraded desert, their captains shedding kites — angels, wind-thieves, even their parafoils, all they had — and braking as best they could. The third came on through the debacle, but lost half its kites through fouling with the settling lines of the two wrecked ships. A smaller, less ornate charvi than the rest, it had probably been intended as the ramming ship.

We broke Road ourselves, rushing onto the gibber, bucking and tossing, shedding kites to avoid fouling, but gaining precious speed as Scarbo sent up Red Man, our big parafoil, and Hammon helped Rim bring in the drogues.

It was a gamble. I'd seen the flat swathe of sand amid the uneven terrain — perhaps the intended ramming site chosen by the Soti strategists. Though we lost a tyre, most of our footmen and more paintwork from the hull, we got *Rynosseros* back on to 304 and completed the last part of our journey unhindered.

Now the Soti had no options.

Heart-and-Hand, the State, was a small principality, a mere seventy square miles of gibber desert and scrub, with two impressive ranges shouldering into it from the west and the 304 Lateral giving access across it for charvolants.

Heart-and-Hand, the capital, was a metal and rock-melt tower some fifty metres high set in this desolation, surrounded by outbuildings and testing stations, with a skirt of dusty imported trees and the big dish of the radio telescope that used to get the State so much National funding.

Arredeni had us on scan even before we broke free of the Soti trap, and his half-caste research assistants, Jeremy and Cole, were waiting at the low perimeter fence to bring us in. That fence would not stop hostiles for long, but when crossed without invitation it meant war. The tradition that charvolants kite down and be ushered through the elaborate totemic gateway was an old one, and though these were special circumstances, the custom was observed now.

We brought in our canopy, waited while Arredeni's aides shackled our travel platform to a team of four draft horses, then pulled us to our mooring in the yard.

The whole installation looked more National than tribal, which could not have helped intertribal relations any, such flagrant departures from tradition, and a lot of small signs showed that Arredeni expected attack. The doors at ground level were locked and bolted, the windows of the sheds all shuttered, the livestock already in the earthen bunkers. Weather shields were in place; the great solar vanes along the western perimeter were angled to act as low-level shields themselves.

While Jeremy and Cole took the horses to safety, Anna led us to our quarters in the tower. Though the Soti and their allies had to be gathering, we took time to shower and change into fresh fatigues before being served a fine meal in the dining room which occupied almost the entire sixth floor.

Arredeni Paxton Kemp met us there. He was impressive, a tall Ab'O quadroon — like his daughter one of the last authentic blood-members of the Qaentimae, as dark-skinned as Anna was, with a wide handsome face and a grizzle of grey hair down each side of his head.

The Qaentimae had long ago merged with the Soti culturally and for all practical purposes politically; a compromise allowed Arredeni because of his international reputation. The tower, the land it surveyed, this man's authority as legitimate ruler of at least this much, were allowed to him; all that remained of a tribe which had fought too many mind-wars, had gone once too often to settle disputes by fleet action on Lake Air. The Qaentimae no longer had ships larger than skiffs; possibly only that had saved them from complete extinction.

As he entered the dining room, Arredeni gave us his magnificent smile, an easy man caught in uneasy times. The smile, his elegant gestures during the introductions Anna made, could not hide what his full dark eyes were telling us: This will be the end of it. This is our final night. His first words after the greetings were directly on that point.

"Thank you for coming, all of you. Thank you for bringing Anna home. Captain, contrary to how it may seem, I did not know what I expected you to do. I left it for Anna to choose. First option: to extend the invitation to receive a benefice and so have you come here; second: to keep Anna safe, to see her safely out of Australia so our research into the haldane phenomenon could continue. Your decision, Tom."

I immediately faced Anna, who met my enquiring look with

equal directness.

"Ah," Arredeni said, "she did not tell you what my other request was. She chose for us both."

I went to speak, but Arredeni raised a hand.

"Please, Captain, I realize I have trapped Blue into a major involvement in tribal affairs. I did not mean to do this out of hand. I believed you would hear what Anna had to say and then decide what was best. So now you must decide again. You might still break their cordon, either now or at first light. We can cover you with lasers from the tower."

"Out of the question, Doctor."

He nodded, looked at each of us in turn, saw we understood how it was. Being here would ensure it became the major incident he needed. More than just comsat surveillance. One of the Coloured Captains involved. Tribes and Nation watching.

While he listened, calm and attentive, I told him about the ambush on the Promenade and the narrow escape from the Soti fleet he had partly witnessed on his screens. He in turn told us about the god-gun.

It was more or less what Anna had told me earlier — how some collective 'firing' may have shut most of humanity off from its higher mental powers, the Ab'Os and other less 'sophisticated' anthrotypes being less severely wounded by being non-intellectually closer to those powers, less prone to pinning things down empirically. The dynamic maiming would have started once a race began using reason to sort its experience of the universe.

I brought up my earlier question to Anna.

"But who would've fired the weapon, Doctor?"

Arredeni gave his first laugh. It was directed partly at himself, partly at the extreme subtlety of how a god-gun might have worked.

"For a long time — you will laugh at this, Tom, all of you — we felt the land itself could have fired the weapon in us. By using the word 'weapon' we pre-suppose a purpose, not just an effect. But there are planetary fields, as you know, the noosphere, magnetics, properties of gravity, cosmic disturbances, a host of other things. We granted it could have been pure chance, a by-product of this world being 'alive' for the first time, Gaea evolving, dealing with radiation, cosmic rays, solar activity. So we explored those. Wonderfully crackpot stuff. Since they were reacting to this particular theory so vehemently, we kept at it far beyond what we might have done if they'd ignored us."

"And now?"

Arredeni exchanged glances with Anna, Jeremy and Cole, even with Cilla the cook who was pouring tisn into gorgeous porcelain cups.

"We probably would have fired it ourselves. Anything from all of us participating in a lemming-leap of mind at a certain point in our evolution, almost a delaying action to slow humanity down, to a minority of more developed individuals, who can say? A powerful shaman or magician, a group of gifted elitists discovering how to hamstring the rest of the race.

"Maybe it was always there as an evolutionary option in case it was needed, like the 'death-switch' down there in the DNA telling an organism when to start dying. Maybe a 'god-switch' re-routed us out of too much mental evolution before we were ready for it, sent us into a more viable, more balanced physical existence. It could have meant survival for the race. But you see, Tom, here we are talking as if this amazing notion has been demonstrated as true; already we are doing more than the tribes will even begin to do. Why?, I want to know. Why are they taking such exception to this theory? It is more fascinating than the theory itself."

I went to ask it again. "Arredeni..."

"What are the haldanes?" Arredeni smiled, stretched his arms wide. "The very least we believe, Anna and I — it's where human stuff becomes cosmic stuff. Where we *become* our universe. That's all. We claim no more. We have certainties, convictions out of trance that it can be more — like the god-gun theory — feelings, things that are sensed, but that is all we offer here, all we can prove. As Anna and I say constantly, our fundamental maxim: we cannot know the system while we're in the system."

Anna interrupted. "And if a god-gun is what has alienated us from tribal sympathy, we need to learn if the National and International scientific community, the world at large, will resent us for it as well."

"We haven't," Scarbo said.

The Qaentimae Prince set down his cup. "No, Ben. You've accepted it now, but what about later? And what will Council decide? That only Ab'Os could come up with this — Dreamtimers touting nonsense? Whatever we offer about the Dreamtime should be considered. We have the haldanes to demonstrate our integrity. And mind-fighting. We are changing our physiotype, using mumbo-jumbo to affect genetic patterns. But our problems don't come from the Nationals and Internationals — not yet anyway — but from our own people. Could they be resenting us because of such a wounding? Could that be it?"

Scarbo seized on the point. "We're a State of Nation ship using approved Roads. Tom holds a Colour. They went against us."

"The wounding would be a spectacular thing for the individual, Ben, commanding enormous force. We are used to the haldanes being gods, not parts of us at all. You probably know that the Soti Prince, Stoutheart Tiberias Kra, is a trained astrophysicist. Yet Kra and the Soti Clever Men see my work as total heresy, trying to do harm, tampering with the profound spiritual truth of the Dreamtime. Kra used to be a dear friend — he saved the Qaentimae — but now he can't help what he feels. We are the worst possible enemy: the Speakers of the Lie. I'm surprised so few Princes are actively against me."

"But now there's Anna," I said.

"The very best of us at translating, yes. The media want to see her. International research groups request interviews. They want to know what gives her such strength at berking. You may not realize it, but the three who went against her at Twilight Beach would have been among the Soti's best.

"Anything we reveal is going to cause a sensation. It's one of those revelations you can't go back from. Like evolution, powered flight, quantum mechanics. You may not like it or agree with it; you may try to ignore it, but it will have changed everything. I wanted you here, Tom, because something that happened to you in the Madhouse caused you to become a sensitive." Everyone at the table was watching me. "You sense the hero-shapes. You make the perfect go-between."

I was aware of the eyes turned in my direction, of the fascination there in old Ben, Shannon and the others. Perhaps Anna's questions had been Arredeni's after all.

"What do you know?" I hated asking it, having the others watch, hated being so reasonable, so controlled.

"Only that."

"How?" I found I was straining to hear him through the fierce drumbeat of my heart.

"I spoke with Tartalen shortly after you were discharged, after you won *Rynosseros* and were given Blue. Word had come to me, a rumour, that you came out of the Madhouse a sensitive."

"What did Tartalen say?"

"Tom, he denied it. He would not speak of it further, I swear."

"The rumour..."

"Four times removed when it got to me. It was not possible to track it down further. I am still trying."

"Nothing about three images, three signs?"

"My word on it. Nothing. But I will do my best on your behalf. There are more pressing concerns now."

Are there?, I wanted to shout through the hammering drumbeat, through the acid wash of adrenalin and the closeted rage, then remembered the others, saw the looks of genuine concern, most of them as old as having *Rynosseros* and Blue, remembered what was soon to happen and how the world would react to the claims being made here. Other truths, my truths, had to wait. I forced myself back to it.

"So Kra and his allies will try to stop you here. Keep it very much a tribal matter."

Arredeni nodded, his eyes shining with a sharp understanding of my own emotion.

"Precisely. Hence my wish to proclaim my discovery a benefice to Nation and so to the world at large, and calling you in if you would come. You, Tom, because I'd read of your many exploits among the Princes, and myself divined — forgive the pun, please — that the rumours were correct, you were this special thing — a sensitive." He made his final admission. "You could follow the contest if it came to that, bear witness to the truth of it being possibly as we say. That if there is fighting..."

"Then we'll be fighting ourselves."

"As it's always been. The wounded, 'godded' ones against the few who see it as it is. The heretics and the outcasts. Only now we do have Anna. She can reach Mithras, Anbas and Challamang. Even Imbaro and Vanu at the same time, multiple bonding. Because she knows what they are. She's even glimpsed an immensely powerful vector along her mind-line that will match all the others, if only it will come to her at the right moment or let her reach it. She is my proof."

"Which is why he did not want me to come back," Anna said. "He forgets he is the only father I have."

"Anna..."

Arredeni got no further. The diligent on top of the tower sang its single warning hoot. The Soti and their allies were approaching.

We left the table and climbed to the battlements. Cole went off to log messages and key in for comsat surveillance; the Qaentimae no longer operated their own tribal satellite, but rented access with a Japano facility. Jeremy activated the hi-tech armaments and brought an assortment of hand-weapons to the roof.

Far out on the desert, we could see a fleet of charvolants moving slowly towards us in the last light of day, canopies like glorious many-coloured flowers, death-lamps and photonic parafoils glinting like dew on those gorgeous, sinister blooms.

"They'll be kiting down soon," Arredeni said, then gave in to a sudden outburst of anger, a Prince whose territory had been invaded. "Let them come! Let them try us!" And he said more words in dialect.

It was quiet on the battlements then, just the low thrumming of the diligent, the wind off the desert stirring the dusty trees in the yard, whistling about the parapets and getting in among the spines of the sensor array.

Finally Arredeni turned to Anna and his assistants.

"We have to rest, ready ourselves for tomorrow. Tom, you have the tower. Wake us if we're needed."

Anna came to me in my room a little after midnight, let herself in without knocking, roused me by placing a hand on my arm. I woke to find her sitting on the edge of my bed.

"Anna?"

"I couldn't leave him to face this alone."

"I know."

"He told the truth about Tartalen. He asked about you but was told nothing. They are very secretive about you there. My father read you as a sensitive some time ago, just as I did when we met at the Gaza. In berking terms there is a field horizon to you. Arredeni wasn't sure if the rumours were true. He was very excited when I told him that you read the shapes. It tells us that something *is* emerging in you. What it means in practical terms now is that you can witness mind-war and later confirm what occurred. Using tech verification so there can be no doubt."

"You read this field now?"

"I'm deliberately not trying to. I need to remain clear for tomorrow."

Moonlight came through the windows, washed the darkness of her skin. It reminded me of our night on the Promenade, of the first translation I had seen.

"Anna, the haldane you reached? Imbaro. Why that one?"

"The War Owl?" She hesitated, frowned. "All haldanes are available to us. I found Imbaro then. Others can."

"At the same time?"

"Not common, but yes. Some are more — *feel* more amenable than others. Like the one Arredeni told you I am questing for. Others can access it; it is generally available. All I know is that — like Imbaro — it is right for me."

"What will it be like?"

She smiled, imagining it. "As if I am completed somehow. It will be — right."

I watched the night through the windows.

"Will you try for it tomorrow?"

"If there's time. It has never come to me before."

She was silent for a moment.

"Tom, what are your body taboos?"

"What?"

"Not mating. Pleasure. Your body taboos?"

"Anna..."

"You like me?"

"Yes."

"Shall I stay?"

I smiled. "Distraction. Of course."

"More than that. Shall I stay?"

"Yes."

She slipped off her robe, revealed the curves of her hips and belly, her firm high breasts, and more — the whorls of her *ais* scars, her delicate body-map, so strange and beautiful, then joined me on the bed. We held one another, made slow love, falling into deep sleep afterwards, waking just after 0400 during Strengi's watch and going upstairs to join him on the battlements. He was playing his guitar, sending gentle notes at the tower diligent, making it answer him in low, languid murmurings.

The moon was near zenith, the desert washed with a cool light, showing us the tree-tops tossing in the wind, making shadows in the yard, dressing the ceremonial gate in armour of silver and pearl. We could see the ranges far off, and in the middle distance two dim lights.

"Ships," Anna said, as if we had met taking in the air. "Kra's people."

"Full fleet?" I asked, looking out over this great wind-swept expanse, smiling at how dreamlike it all seemed, the lovemaking, the yard washed in moonlight, the prospect of what lay ahead.

"Nothing near it. This cannot be elevated to the status of war. The satellites would know. Kurdaitcha would come."

Twenty minutes went by above that vast emptiness of sand and stars while we stood with Strengi playing his guitar at our backs, the wind sounding around the parapets and sensor poles.

"Should you rest?" I asked her finally.

"Not now. I couldn't sleep now. You go down. I'll stay, go through my summoning patterns."

"Anna?"

She turned to face me, dark eyes glittering.

"Did you read the plaque fixed to the helm of *Rynosseros*?"

"Yes. Important words."

"From Alexander the Great."

"He actually said them?"

"Who knows? But they're how we must live — as if we could die at any moment but at the same time live forever."

She laughed. "Tonight I'm immortal, Tom."

"I know," I said. "I feel that too." And I headed for the stairwell.

By mid-morning, Heart-and-Hand was under siege. Thirteen charvolants from three different Ab'O nations — Soti, Madupan, Chitalice — and three approved mercenary ships ringed the tower at a three hundred metre radius. I recognized the signs: the Arab, the African and the Tongan. Eighty tribesmen and at least thirty mercenaries, rogue Nationals, Niuginians, Islanders, Arabs, Indonesians, others, formed a perimeter for which the charvis made impromptu gun-towers.

The wind had dropped, but the ships had helium-filled parafoils lofted, supporting death-lamps and hot-pot fighters from their hooks and delivery assemblies. A man-lifter, another inflatable, supported a lookout at a hundred feet. The tiny figure — a deck-boy no older than Hammon — drifted back and forth in the thermals in long slow sweeps, watching our preparations, relaying information to those waiting below.

Apart from precautions taken to ensure we wouldn't run for it, no attempt had been made to destroy *Rynosseros*. She sat on her travel platform, her six tyres blown by death-lamps at first light, but otherwise untouched. The platform was fair game; they dared not touch the hull.

Now a battle was waiting to commence on one of three levels.

If it was to be Code, there were kites aloft on the ships, angled to the sun, their cells charged; the big lenses and accumulators on the tower. It would be a protracted, vicious affair — snaphaunces and kitanas and war boomerangs, a regular siege with scaling ladders, kite landings and aerial sorties, hot-pots and battering-rams. The tower was durable but badly undermanned; without outside assistance, it would fall.

If it was hi-tech, then someone would incur enormous debts for an easy victory. Certainly Arredeni would not be the one, not with his reputation both as scientist and moderate. Heart-and-Hand had two laser points, short-range, ugly-looking Bok units mounted on gimbals and pointed out at the two grandest of the charvolants just in case.

The charvis had a dozen such portables, half of them turned on the crown of the tower where we stood watching, the rest focused on the generator and accumulator facilities in the shielded outbuildings. Most of the tribesmen and many of the mercenaries had combat laser-tech and selected ballistics close by.

If it came to that, comp estimate gave us a four to eight minute siege before we were destroyed.

But the comsats orbited and watched and tallies would be kept. Tribal debts would grow. Explanations would be required, with the possibility of ship forfeitures and service penalties, things no tribe could easily afford. And there would still be time for us to put through a final account of what was happening. Arredeni's findings were already lodged; a final speed transmission would simply speak of what had occurred, give a Prince's parting words.

Once it was hi-tech, they could kill us but never stop us.

No, it would be the third kind of warfare, the one that would discredit the Qaentimae and put the seal of holy approval on what they were trying to achieve here.

The heroes.

Anna, Arredeni, Jeremy and Cole were getting ready, donning ceremonial dress, while down on the sand the Clever Men were drawing up. The air throbbed with the sound of bullroarers and didgeridoos. The perimeter belltrees and tower diligent caught the rhythms and gave them back in an eerie counterpoint of pinging and chiming.

There were seventeen Clever Men standing on the desert, waiting fifty metres from the tower — all Soti, since officially the Madupan and Chitalice were here as interested observers.

Heart-and-Hand had four.

Four and a half. Four and a sensitive — one who could read the shapes. When the four were ready, I went with them down onto the desert, walking beside Anna and her father out to where the line of Ab'Os waited. Scarbo, Shannon, Strengi, Hammon and Rim, and old Cilla too, waited behind on the tower, their weapons untended now that the choice of combats had been made.

Today there would be no treachery, no Ab'O breaking trance to use his sword. That much was certain.

I stood with Arredeni and his Clever Men, last of the Qaentimae, facing the Soti mind-fighters. They made an impressive sight. Fully half of them — like Arredeni beside me — wore their suits of lights, each transformed into a dazzling column by the hundreds of tiny mirrors sewn to the leather.

Beyond that proud line of seventeen was the waiting line of tribesmen and mercenaries, the silent ships under their barely-moving canopies. The drone of didgeridoos and bullroarers suddenly ceased; the belltree song dwindled and faded as well, though an occasional sad chiming from the dim-recall rods came to us through the heated air.

The Prince of the Soti, Stoutheart Tiberias Kra, a tall man, massively built, took three steps forward and addressed Arredeni.

"You have the Blue Captain with you."

"He is the National who accepts the officially-proclaimed benefice. The sensitive who saw Dos fail at Twilight Beach. The one you need to kill."

Kra nodded, pleased in spite of himself at how Arredeni was conducting this. No threats. No idle words or loose ends.

But there were the protocols. He wanted me to own my pedigree as Blue and thereby relinquish National rights for what now occurred.

"An outsider all the same, Arredeni."

I indicated the three State of Nation charvolants anchored with the rest. "So are the Tongan, the Arab and the African."

"Not State of Nation. Mercenary ships," Kra said, glad to be answered.

"I too am a mercenary," I told him. "My name is in the Great Passage Book, which is reason enough for me to be here. I have been paid with the gift of great knowledge to stay and watch injustice."

"Careful, Tom Rynosseros!" Kra said, very pleased now and

confident of the power building in him. "I am a demon you can fear!"

It was Anna, smiling, wearing her drab unadorned fighting leathers, who stepped forward and said in a voice that sent a thrill of power through the tiny Qaentimae line: "I am a hammer to demons!"

That was it.

Stoutheart Tiberias Kra rejoined his fellows, called out the ritual words.

"This body is mine, my place to stand up in, where I surface in this world, where I break through, my place to die from. I put this on the line. I abrogate the right to fight in this place. We go to be gods now."

And the battle began.

Without further preamble, the twenty-one Ab'Os went into trance, effortlessly, seventeen against four.

Now would be the test, the great test, down there, up there, in there, wherever it was, with the berking, questing spirits, with the haldanes waiting to receive them and be received.

The bodies of the fighters all tensed, as if seeking to thrust themselves into the ground, to gain power from it Antaeus-like. Kra and his allies were fighting to protect the 'godness' of their haldanes, things poorly understood but dynamically powered, the continuation of a reverence and respect for what had always been theirs. They were blinded by the very light that made it possible for them to almost see it all, the wisest, most gifted fools. Our fighters were at least armed with the added knowledge that they weren't communing with ancient gods, but were breaking through to the power base of our original humanity. What difference that would make no-one could say.

I was a passenger, an observer to this, and within minutes of translation I slid into a trance of my own, aided this time not by the enemy but by Anna herself, reaching back to bring me along. It was like being pulled back into oneself, a falling away from inside the eyes, into a world of coloured, elongated shadows set in the reflection infinity of clever mirrors so it was self, self, self, then not at all, everything but that. Distorted forms, shapes converging, rushing together, crowding, blurring only to resolve again.

The seventeen went for Arredeni at once. He had gained Challamang and was immensely powerful, a worthy opponent for any ten of them if he could keep it. But they were trying for a quick kill, discounting Anna and the others for the moment.

The reason for their choice soon became clear. Anna was taking an unusually long time to translate, questing for more than just any haldane to accommodate her, obviously searching down her mind-line for that mightiest haldane she had sensed before.

Jeremy and Cole, on the other hand, were trainees and not true Clever Men at all. Cole had difficulty keeping himself with Marduk, while Jeremy had locked on to a surging power mass that could only be called Enlil, trying to translate.

It was not going well.

Arredeni/Challamang was hard-pressed, faltering. Cole/Marduk was trying to assist, a mite on the backs of demons, an insect, a nuisance. Jeremy had cleared to Enlil and added its power to Arredeni's whenever he could, whenever he wasn't being savaged himself.

The scene was confused, turgid, uncertain. Too many vectors, too many conflicting images overlapping.

I tried to see Anna in that flux, consciously sought her, concentrating on her vital form, and it was as if the seeking led me to her centre.

For there she was. Suddenly, awesomely powerful, her most dynamic translation yet — something like a composite, with a great deal of overlapping herself.

There was — Imbaro! No mistaking the Great Owl, that flux of shapes and colours. But more. With parts of Ishtar and Ashbiani, vectors already commandeered, and — incredibly — much of Colte, a stunning, surging presence in that shadowland.

Kra had cleared to Gris, a rarely-won atavism equal to Challamang and Colte, but harder to hold for long, and as that irresistible form was beating Arredeni easily. Kra was very good.

It was Anna's appearance that kept him back from dealing the blow that could kill Arredeni on the physical plane. Her presence distracted him, brought puzzlement and doubt.

Jeremy and Cole, I discovered, had already abandoned

aspect, had withdrawn from trance and retreated back to the desert under the morning sun.

It was Anna and her father against them all — and now the tide of battle was turning. One by one the Clever Men fled from trance as Anna blanketed them, fed on them. Kra kept his Gris at Challamang's centre, hammering and devouring, spiriting him out. But the distraction, the pressure, were too much.

There was a surging rush from where Anna's composite — her Imbaro/Ishtar/Ashbiani/Colte — loomed, something like the white light of an exploding star — a star, yes! — and she was alone! *We* were alone.

They had all gone — Arredeni, Kra, all of them.

As Anna relaxed aspect, I let myself flow to her and with her, spiralled back to the desert and the day and came alive behind my eyes, stood up in myself.

Wavering, gaining my balance and astonished to find myself still standing, I took in everything at a glance: the figures on the sand before the tower, the collapsed shapes in their suits of leather and glass; took in the silence, the smells, the watching eyes of the satellites overhead through the clear blue shield of the sky.

Five of the Clever Men were dead — Kra among them. The other twelve lay unconscious, catatonic. They would emerge later, most if not all of them, though even now, down in the deep well of self, they knew what had happened.

Arredeni was in the same state, pried loose from Challamang, though limp and resting now, recovering. Jeremy and Cole were standing to one side, badly shaken.

In the other, outer world of charvolants and paid professionals, the Tongan and the African had already gone, sailing off with their mercenaries when the outcome had become clear. The Arab's charvi was pulling out from the ring of sand-ships even now, breaking away, off to an assignment elsewhere.

Some of my crewmates — I half-noticed Hammon and Rim and Strengi — came down to us, to provide numbers, a visual warning-off just in case.

But nothing would happen now, no further conflict. What the Soti and the other Ab'O Princes would do about the Qaentimae knowledge, no-one could say. But they — all of us — had been taught a startling lesson, that Anna was the best of the Clever Men, the most powerful mind-fighter there was.

I stood holding her as she eased herself out of trance, steadying her.

"You did it, didn't you?" I said.

She nodded, trembling but smiling, supremely fulfilled, her eyes flashing with the inexpressible emotion of it.

Jeremy and Cole came rushing over, stumbling with fatigue and eagerness.

"You reached Ashbiani!" Jeremy said. "I saw Ashbiani!"

"It was Colte!" Cole said. "But with Imbaro. I saw the War Owl."

"And some of Ishtar. There was some of that too!"

"Which one did you reach?" Cole asked.

"Which one was it?"

And all that I had sensed and witnessed came together in a moment of absolute certainty that, yes, perhaps we could be free, perhaps it could be done. By looking within, beyond the bright distractions. By glimpsing the fullness of our humanity.

Awed by it, shaken, I answered for her, said what I knew was true.

"You found your own haldane, didn't you? The one that is best for you, truest for you. Your other part. You found yourself."

Arredeni's daughter looked at me again and smiled, then turned that smile out at the land, at the sun and the kites that shifted and strained in the new wind.

"I reached Anna," she said, her smile a badge of supreme triumph, of joy and vindication. "I found Anna."

Going to the Angels

The way to space for the tribes of Australia is a door with three threshholds. In the high deserts you can see them paving the way, three bright doorsteps: the shuttle fields at Tinbilla and Throwing Stick and, by far the most famous, the field at Long Reach, two hours' journey in from the coast by tribal sand-ship.

There, in the clear cool evenings, with brilliant meteor swarms marking the sky, envious Nationals can watch the shuttles planing up to orbit, or the costly VTO link-ships making their fiery climb.

And each month, the quota of lucky Nationals and Internationals who have won places among the 'sky stones' — the gragens — march through the linkmesh gates and go through the doorway that exists as both idea and physical fact. Each year, the fortunate thousands take their places aboard the shuttles and join the far settlements, or go to the orbiting tribal demesnes, the celebrated estates known to all as the Angels.

There the National emigrés train and serve and live out their lives as menials, but with privilege, a measure of respect, with choices — though never the choice of returning, never that.

That is what is offered. Thereafter it is infrequent letter transcripts and even rarer relayed messages with the burden of time-delay and tribal censorship.

For the Nationals of Australia, for most of the non-Ab'O peoples of the world, the door that falls at Long Reach, Tinbilla and Throwing Stick is a one-way door.

Soby chose that door, as many do, and the editorial team of *Caravanserai* wanted me to stop him. Beth phoned to ask the favour; Sam knew I would find it difficult to refuse her — my dear friend, my special love, Beth.

"He's too young, Tom," she said, her lovely face filling the screen in my room at the Gaza. "He's seeing the romance of a gragen life. He thinks he'll write better songs, change things, be some exception and come back a hero. A working spaceman like the bravos out at Long Reach. A famous songsmith like Afervarro, but in space, representing Nation up there."

"He's twenty-years-old, Beth. He knows he can't come back. He's old enough to choose."

Beth shook her long dark hair. The face which had brought such surprise, such true joy, as it always did when I saw it again, looked tired and worried. "No. Not fairly. Soby's too impatient. He wants it all now. His cadetship with us is nearly over. He'll get to go on stories; Sam and I will make sure of that. His writing is good. He can apply for a gragen permit; they could give him a tour of the Angels."

"But Soby knows that."

"We've all told him. It's not enough. He's seen the promos — Nationals working in the garden domes, serving in the labs, walking on the promenades. He wants to go out to the stones. He wants to be a spaceman who sings, not a journo singer who's had a twenty-four-hour safe tour. He says he'd only come back hungry for more."

I didn't know what to say. I knew Soby from visits to see Beth at the *Caravanserai* offices here in Twilight Beach, and at their solstice parties. He was young, vital, talented. He made good songs — romantic, desperate, eager songs that touched the heart because they were made so full of what soon slipped from so many hearts: the easy total giving of the young and the new, what was so quickly put aside and hidden.

I had heard some of his songs. Among the Angels he would be a leveller, a good thing, a fine ambassador for Nation, for all humanity. There above the Earth in some gragen — some 'high stone place' — he would sing songs of common feeling.

And who could tell? Perhaps he would make a difference, change the feeling, make the future different, better. We needed a thousand Sobys, one on every ship that went, on every colony stone — every gragen there was.

Perhaps he knew exactly what he was trading to do it.

I saw Beth quietly watching my reverie, understanding my reflections, and knew how much she felt for her young friend. I wondered what to do.

"Parents? Family?" I asked.

"Already gone through. Two years now."

"Messages? What do they say?"

"What you'd expect," Beth answered. "Come home. But they're a long way out. Soby wouldn't see them for quite a while. Orientation and Skills Training takes at least a year."

"Friends?"

"Quite a few in our offices. He's very popular, as you know. Quite a few in Twilight Beach. But he's young enough to move free. Persuade him to wait! He admires you. You may not have picked that up from the parties but he really does. He asks about you a lot. He was at the Farrady talk you gave on the Coloured Captains."

"Soby was? That was pre-sold, booked out weeks in advance."

"He paid what the scalpers were asking. He wanted to hear you talk about the Seven — about the special philosophy of those holding Hero Colours from the tribes."

"Then he heard me say that winning the Colours was an accident — a faulty comp/belltree link-up. It couldn't happen again."

"But equally true: you *are* a hero to him, Tom."

"Then what good can I do? Everything I am will convince him to go. He'll quote me back to myself."

"You may be the only one who can pierce the dream..."

"Which is exactly what I mustn't do, don't you see?"

"...in case it's piercable! So he can choose later, apply later." I saw the yearning to protect in Beth's eyes. A lone spirit herself, she loved what Soby had in full measure. "Let him get his knocks down here. Keep his options for awhile."

"When does he go?"

"He's gone. He's already on his way to Long Reach."

I studied the calm lovely face, the dark brown eyes, saw the respect for Soby and me which had kept her from asking this help sooner. It was her last resort, left till the very last hour when she had already resolved not to do anything to interfere with this young man's dream.

"All right, Beth. I'll go to Long Reach. When is his flight?"

"This evening. At 1900."

Which left little time. *Rynosseros* was out on mission, so I took passage on *Mason Fire* with two hundred others — equally divided among those bound for the Angels and relatives and friends there to see the travellers off.

The big sand-ship lofted kites at 1315, sailed through the afternoon and moored at Long Reach at 1520. Some passengers went to the hotels in the National tourist concession at Hindel; others went straight out to the field to wait by the boundaries, eager to be gone, psyching themselves up for the absolute change in their lives that was to come, as if afraid of being tempted to stay behind if they dallied too long in the town.

Some did that, stayed, running back from the queues at the last minute, forfeiting their chance ever again. But there were always the last-minute volunteers to take their places, speculators who could pay the fare and hoped to jump ahead of their rostered departure dates. The ships always went up full — taking their thousands upon thousands every year, men, women, children, each one a seed, a clod of Earth as the popular sayings had it, the 'cloddies' going forth to carve the greater night into some semblance of home.

I believed I knew where Soby would be — Soby who dreamed of becoming a spaceman, the forbidden vocation for Nationals, for all non-Ab'Os. Not at the bars of Hindel, not lined up at the linkmesh fences at the spaceport.

Close to the field, on a dusty perimeter road, was a weathered inn called The Stranded Man, run by Jack Clancy. It was a special haven for me, a National concession like the town of Hindel itself, but of a curious and unique kind. Soby would be there.

Clancy — of all the Nationals I knew — had managed to surmount the racial differences between the evicted white Nationals and the Ab'O ascendants whose Dreamtime/haldane-augmented minds had given them space as it had the rule of Australia.

On afternoons when no flights were scheduled, the off-duty spacemen would saunter into his bar: quiet serious men, splendid-looking in their torch-jackets and bodyforms, heads shaved and gleaming, chests oiled and covered with birkin signs.

A former charvi captain himself, Clancy understood sailors' ways, all sailors' ways. He accepted the stern gazes and distracted, taciturn manner, allowed for reasons and needs. During the long off-duty hours, he would serve them their drinks and meals, charm them, bring them to smiles and laughter, bits of confidences given out because this old weather-beaten sailor never needed such things. It was as if Clancy simply wanted to probe those distracted looks and defeat them.

His two cats, Charlie and Max, the famous 'duelling cats' of The Stranded Man, assisted in this, weaving love-courses between booted legs, winning pats and smiles, winning invitations to tour the gragens (though that offer was never made, even jokingly, to Clancy).

When they softened, the Ab'Os showed the other side of their curious philosophical bent: that they loved life, all life; that they missed the red earth and their deserts. They petted the cats and looked beyond them into nothing; they sat peering into the lights and depths of their drinks and listened to the wind. After sunset, they kept away from the windows, not wanting to watch the night and the stars of that greater desert above them — their high stone place, the gragen — not wanting to see the Angels and powerful comsats orbiting there, not wanting to watch the brilliant meteor swarms that sometimes scattered fistfuls of light across the sky.

They seemed like men who were tired and wished to forget — but that was the common life of bars, after all, and Clancy worked with it to the betterment of everyone.

Some Nationals did find their way around to Clancy's — some of those who meant to step through the Door, though not many.

Usually it was journalists and media teams, sand-ship crews who wanted to share the same elusive kinship as Clancy did — to be with these fierce totemic sailors.

The low voices of the off-duty crews, the bright hard looks that never quite fixed, deterred many would-be visitors; the stories of such things discouraged most. The Stranded Man was that indeed: often empty of customers for fifteen hours out of any day.

Soby was there.

When I wandered in at 1600, I saw him sitting alone at a corner table below a display of Astani duelling masks, his bag and his guitar on the floor near him. He had a pen and paper before him, and there were two empty glasses near a half-filled third.

There were other National customers: a group of three sitting below the wheel of the heavy green glass chandelier, another two at the magazine stand Clancy kept scrupulously up to date by some mysterious means, the rest — a few solitaries scattered about the big taproom.

But no spacemen today: it was a full launch roster. Come nightfall, there would only be techs and mank crews out at Long Reach, and the relatives and disappointed line-jumpers trailing back to Hindel and all the space-hungry places of the world.

Soby saw me. His grey eyes widened in surprise and obvious pleasure, then set into a look of wary concern as he realized what Beth and Sam must have done, that there could be only one reason for my presence. He set down his pen, brushed back his long brown hair with one hand, and waited.

"May I buy a friend a final drink?" I said.

His guarded look softened. He nodded and I sat. Clancy wandered over, took an order for two light beers and returned to the bar.

"I came because of Beth, Soby, not because I believe I have anything more to say than goodbye and good fortune."

"Thanks," he said with evident relief, smiling now. It was a good smile, a winning smile, making his tanned face more conventionally handsome. "Thanks. They don't understand."

"They do. You know they do. It's just hard to lose someone

you care for."

"I'll be in touch. I'll send songs through, maybe approved stories. They make exceptions. I can be a correspondent."

"You know it doesn't work like that. You pay dearly for every word. There's censorship up there."

"I can make a difference, Tom."

"Yea, I'm for that. But you'll be busy paying for rations and environmentals for quite some time. The tribes control the means."

"It's not all like that," Soby said. "In the outer gragens, maybe, but not in the Angels. I've seen the promos, the tour broadcasts. There are good positions. I talked to the counsellor at Wins."

Clancy placed our beers on the table and left us.

"The promos make it look good," I agreed. "But not everyone can stay in the inner orbits. They have to move them out; they have to make the gragens work. Which one are you down for?"

"I'm going through Krombi. After that it's wherever there's a vacancy. They were impressed with my training."

"What did the Wins man say?"

"I told them I was a songwriter and singer like Afervarro, and a trained wordsmith. The counsellor said there were places in the recreation and information services. He gave me a 75% chance of a posting in the Angels within two years."

"That high?"

"That's what he said. He said once people have been in the orbits for a while, they grow stale. They want more, want to get out to the stones. We serve them, but we get to move around. It's not as bad as Nation makes out. It's low-feudal status, but offspring are born citizens. Earth-barred, yes, but they'll get to sculpt the planets, bring down biospheres..."

"They don't have that capability yet. They may never leave the home orbits..."

"No, Tom, they will. It's the only way. We'll work on the roads between the worlds."

"But always low-feudal."

Soby leant forward, excited now. "You've seen the skies above Long Reach. That's the universe out there. This is the only chance I get. You've never been up? Not even a safe tour?"

"I haven't, no." It annoyed me that Soby brought this up now. "Why?"

I hesitated, barely recognizing what I felt as a telling resentment, wanting to be sure my answer wasn't just the handy lie because of that.

"A little of it is fear," I said. "And there are things I need to discover here first. Within me."

Soby watched me, waiting, and his eyes were clear, the look he gave me composed, very adult.

"And there's pride," I admitted. "A lot of that. If I go through Long Reach on their terms, I acknowledge claims that cannot be allowed, on things no-one has a right to own."

"Such an old pride," Soby said. "So you, a great adventurer, a sensitive, deny yourself. One of the only seven Nationals to win a Colour from the tribes. You who at any time can use your status in the Great Passage Book to request a tour, who *can* come back, for heaven's sake, don't go!"

"Soby..." I was bristling with anger now, trying not to show it.

"You don't know what it will do, being there! It might answer your questions, unlock mysteries for you! Don't you see, Tom! Being off the Earth, seeing it as a world, can do that — more than simulations can. You'll fly. Fly! Not in an approved dirigible, but higher, faster. You'll see Australia from above as the comsats see it. Huxley said it: the doors of perception will be cleansed!"

"Soby, I'm fighting my best down here to swing that Door wide for all the world, for all of us. Not just for Tosi-Go and Mikel and the other sanctioned franchises. While I have *Rynosseros* and Blue, while I'm in the Book as one of their heroes, by whatever chance and error I have that amazing privilege, I have to earn the view you talk about. It's like..."

"Jacob and Esau, right?" Soby was warming to this, using defences he had prepared for answering others. "You think I'm selling my birthright for a mess of pottage..."

"For rations and environmentals," I said. "For low-feudal and working on the roads — digging in the sky-stones!"

"Same thing! But I'm better than that! I'm worth more than that."

"Yes. Yes, I know. But you really said it yourself when you

spoke of me. Make it so you have choices too. Ask for a special study tour as a National correspondent. Go up, come back, decide then. You can go later. Close the one-way Door then! Do it for you!"

He looked at me in silence, his eyes fixed and calm, and I knew that I had just now used the arguments Sam and the others must have used, that Beth had probably wanted to, and everyone who knew him and loved him and wanted him safe and in their lives.

"Sing me the song about the Apollo ships," I said.

"*The Aftertime*?"

"If it's okay."

Soby smiled, took out his guitar, played a few chords in preparation. Clancy's cats were sleeping on chairs below the chandelier; one of them opened an eye, flicked an ear at the new sounds, and slept on. In the quiet taproom, Soby sang his ballad of an age we would never see again.

> "Exactly what was over
> Wasn't very plain,
> As David caught the Greyhound
> And Allan took the train.
> A pendant made of meteor,
> Some moondust on a string,
> Not even the hero-maker saved us
> From that mighty coming down.
>
> "The corporation stardog
> With the Gemini on his desk,
> Is closer to the truth he is
> Than we can ever be.
> We're brittle from the raw abyss
> That no-one understands,
> From afternoons of rocket fire,
> High-road-down.
>
> "The sun in a razor,
> The moon inside a cube,

> The wind among the gantries
> Haunting and alone.
> Weekends spent in ancient hills
> Remembering the dawn,
> Not even the hero-maker saved us
> From that mighty coming down."

When he finished, I thanked him, saw him smile with quiet pride as he put his guitar away. Then we sat in silence together, watching the golden light through the bottle-lens windows, waiting out the final parts of our leavetaking.

At 1840, in growing dusk, we went to the field together, walking in a sad purple-grey gloaming along the road from Clancy's towards the fenced perimeter. It was the sort of road and haunted windy evening when you believed you could actually meet the likes of the Spirit Malingee high-stepping towards you, his huge eyes burning in his devil face, the sharp stone knives on his elbows flashing.

Behind us, the inn glowed with suffused light, like a carved filigree box filled with cashiered suns, though it seemed far off now, and would not save us from the likes of an angry Djuan spirit like Malingee hunting souls. It was that kind of evening.

In the distance we could see the twinkling lights of Hindel; ahead, the harsher, more functional lights of the hangars and launch towers — with the startling shapes of the aerospace rocketry: the great aeromankers and VTOs.

It was a lonely road, the spacemen's road, leading us to a private gate in the perimeter mesh where a lone Ab'O stood watch, his djellaba gathered close about him against the cool wind which was rising now and stirring the dust at our feet.

"Stop!" the tribesman said. "This is not the way in. You must go round."

"I am Blue Tyson," I told him, indicating the patches on my jacket. "We wish to use the spacemen's gate."

Soby said nothing, but I sensed what it meant for him just to be here at their gate in the fence.

The Ab'O reached for his comlink.

"My responsibility, tribesman," I said, and he paused. "It is not for me. My friend has a launch in twenty minutes. Let him go in by this special gate, please. A favour."

The Ab'O was a young man too, his dusky face lost in the gloom.

"Which launch?" he asked, and it was hard to know whether he knew the Hero Colour and the name or whether it was simple kindness. He did not ask for further proof. "There are three tonight."

"K-94," Soby said. "Plat 4. Flight 601-B."

"That's *Crosa*. Over there." He pointed to the closest tower. "They've already started sequence. You must hurry!" And he unlocked the gate.

Soby and I embraced, awkwardly, urgently, around his bag and guitar.

"Come up, Tom!" he said. "Come and see!"

And he ran through the gate out onto the field, towards the splayed arrow silhouette of the shuttle.

The wind had strengthened and become cooler, seeming to whisper down from the heavens. Desert night was about us now. The young Ab'O's djellaba snapped in the wind. Stars filled the vault overhead, chill and bright, beckoning as stars have always done since humans first watched birds and stars, and up was perceived as out. Meteors cut bright, fleeting arcs there — six, twenty, more than I could easily count, there and gone, a threadbare veil but a vivid one. Then another came, and another, a beautiful sight, wave on sparkling wave.

"Thank you, tribesman," I said. "I hope it will cause you no hardship."

"It was not your Colour," he said. "Others come this way. Others persuade their way in."

I smiled. Of course they did. And he kept the gate often enough to know, to make this small gift of brotherhood.

"National spacemen," I said. "Other good men like you."

The young man did not answer.

"Brothers," I said. "In time."

Still no answer. Just the wind soughing in the mesh, blowing the dust. Just the snapping of a djellaba.

I turned from the gate without another word, and was almost at The Stranded Man again when *Crosa* stood on fire, left its place in a long rolling thunder and slid up towards the stars.

I stood in the road and watched the red fantail rising, flanked by stars and meteor trails, until it was no longer visible, until the silence measured itself again as a weave of sounds that did not need humanity to be complete, that could take the absence of our kind.

Clancy's inn burned ahead, bright and empty — empty of spacemen, empty of conversations and chances for a time, with the wind rattling at its doors and casements, the dust blowing by as it did every night.

For me, so fitting. So, so fitting. The Stranded Man.

I stood in the roadway and considered Soby's words. Perhaps he was right. Perhaps my principles were not the real reason. Possibly it was pride and envy and rarified, well-processed rage; quite possibly seeing our world from the Angels would change something vital, help in my task with the other Coloured Captains of changing how the tribes saw us, help too in placing the images from out of my private night.

Yes, I decided, affected by the night wind and the stars and the meteor tides, by the warm precious light falling through the mullioned windows of Clancy's, by the lingering, elemental fear that Malingee might yet come high-stepping down that lonely road, eyes blazing, elbow knives gleaming in the night, a thrilling fancy.

Yes, change for me too. Something vital. A glimpse through the Door (I capitalized it again in my thoughts). Informed judgement. Passion dealt with. Rage. Secret need. Yes.

I would arrange a room, call Beth and have her come out to help make this a media event Nation could use, then walk back round to the young Ab'O at the gate. There were no spacemen tonight, but perhaps he would answer some questions. Perhaps without using my Colour at all, he would help me unlock the Door.

Though he wouldn't say it, perhaps he wanted that too.

Sein Ammas Cosiro at the Long Reach office gazed across his desk at Beth and me, paying more attention perhaps to her shoulder camera than to either of us.

"This will take time, Captain," the handsome, middle-aged port official said. He wore elegant grey robes, with his tribal sign — Chonsye — given as patches on his shoulders, and an insignia I didn't know: a vivid blue hook, a turquoise and faience amalgam set in silver, fixed just below his collar. "We will need confirmation and station co-operation, special Kurdaitcha sanctions..."

"Why, Mr Cosiro?" I said. "I want this to be impromptu. It is 1100. There is plenty of time. My friend, Soby Parovin, went up to Krombi last night. I would like to surprise him there. I am in the Book. There are entitlements you would know of." And gambling on something neither Beth nor I could be sure of in the time we'd had: "Other Captains listed in the Book have had no difficulties. Ab'O Captains. It is our right. Are you saying..."

"No. No, Captain," Cosiro said, eyeing the camera as if it were indeed another person in his office. "Not at all. There are merely protocols for this. Reasonable courtesies. Especially with busy station crews processing so many arrivals last night. You understand how it is."

"Officer Cosiro, I know that one flight is due for 1900 tonight, the *Dhal*. I also know it has less than a third payload. There is..."

"Pardon me, but who told you this?" He said the words with more acerbity than he may have intended. The telltale of the camera sobered him quickly.

"Spacemen talk," I said. "A pilot, I think, or a mank tech."

"There is altogether too much talk!"

"Are you being obstructive, Mr Cosiro?"

"Are you being reasonable, Captain Tyson? I am appealing to reason here. We should have Kurdaitcha sanction. Or Clever Men to..."

"Why? Tell me why!"

"Because..."

"Because you consider me National?"

"No! No, Captain! Please!" The camera telltale burned. "You are forcing words."

51

"Do you question my listing in the Great Passage Book?"

Oh how he yearned to say yes to that, as many Ab'Os did. I saw it in his eyes, saw the lie sent out into his gestures, into the set of his body.

"Not at all. But it is different."

There, he had said it. Damning himself.

"I mean by that," he added quickly, "that as realists we must allow that your status *is* unusual. You are National and with tribal honours."

Deeper and deeper.

"I am a Coloured Captain, Mr Cosiro. One of seven Nationals with that honour but the Book makes no discrimination. I ask to be on *Dhal* and mean to be. I would appreciate a call to Krombi where *Crosa* docked — a Chonsye station, I believe — arranging for this Coloured Captain to meet his young friend, Soby Parovin. A small thing. No special arrangements. Not even a safe tour. Just an opportunity to see my friend one more time. To look down at the Earth together. To share space. To finish a conversation."

Cosiro nodded. "Where will you be?"

"At The Stranded Man. Out on the perimeter road. You can reach me there."

"Very well," Cosiro said, standing, eager to be away from the camera Beth wore on her shoulder.

We moved to the door, the Ab'O ushering us ahead of him, wanting to be free of us.

"Oh yes, Mr Cosiro, one more thing. I trust there will be no technical difficulties, no last-minute flight cancellations. *Dhal* goes tonight. I know that *Pyrani* goes up tomorrow night, and *Crosa* again the night after. Put a call through to Krombi, inform your Chonsye administration there. Tell Parovin to expect me on *Dhal*."

The closed hatred in Cosiro's eyes was chilling to see. It seemed to hover over Beth and me as we walked away from the field, back through the hot afternoon towards Clancy's.

"I don't think I've seen such naked contempt for Nationals before," Beth said. "I knew it existed..."

"Not often like that, Beth. Thankfully. It's the gragen mentality. Cosiro is part of an extremist minority."

We did not speak then. The linkmesh fence beside the dusty road shimmered. The launch towers out on the field — some, far off, with dirigibles tethered to their totemic crowns — were roiling spectres, indistinct, dreamlike, hints of tech. The Stranded Man was a dark mass on the desert ahead, its condensation tower making it look like some desolate roadside church, the old windmill in the yard behind lifting like a black flower defeated by too much sunlight.

There was little else to do but wait. Inside, away from the heat, we sat at the table Soby had used, contemplating the Astani masks and watching the handful of National customers who came in, stayed awhile for whatever reasons, and finally went their way. The 'duelling cats' slept in the shadows beneath the green glass chandelier; they cocked an eye at each newcomer and returned to their slumbers.

Beth reviewed the footage from our meeting with Cosiro. She wrote copy and phoned some through to Sam at *Caravanserai*. Then, not wanting to talk over the material yet again, but unable to discuss anything else that existed between us because of *Dhal* waiting out there in the noon shimmer and Krombi swinging by overhead, we drowsed, we read the day-old news-sheets and week-old magazines, and stayed alone with our thoughts, but together too. Waiting for sunset, waiting for Cosiro's call confirming passage, living minutes with a slowness known only in waiting rooms and during childhood.

At 1400, two Ab'Os entered from the street, two tall robed men wearing dark glasses, with the distinctive signs painted on their faces.

Kurdaitcha at The Stranded Man.

Clancy stirred at once, but not too quickly. It was an uncommon thing this, but not unknown. He moved to the bar, quietly bid them good day. Charlie and Max opened sleepy eyes, went back to their dreams.

The Ab'Os murmured something in the habitually low tones of their kind, words that were always heard no matter how softly they were delivered. Clancy replied, though the avengi had already seen us. They came to stand before our table.

"Captain Tyson, Ms Leossa-Tojian, may we join you?" one of

them said. He had a pale mauve triangle on each cheek.

"Of course, gentlemen," I said, not surprised that they were here either, but feeling a tension grip my body. "I am most honoured. Please record this, Beth."

"Please, no," the Ab'O with the mauve triangles said, raising his hand, and Beth paused in activating her camera.

"Excuse me, avengi," — I made myself meet those hard eyes — "but *Caravanserai* operates by National and International charter. With tribal sanctions. You agree?"

They did not bother to answer the question.

"I am Chybere," the mauve-marked Kurdaitcha said. "This is Amly. If that camera is on, we cannot be direct. We must withhold things you might care to hear."

"I prefer this to be official, Chybere. Beth, please record this."

Beth touched the tab; the telltale shone red.

The Ab'Os gazed impassively, accepting the decision, necessarily caught here at The Stranded Man no less than I was.

"Cosiro told us of your intention," Chybere said. "Let me ask, why this urgency? What do you accomplish by being so unreasonable? Rushing beyond procedures and convenience?"

"I am in the Book, Chybere. Not just a Nation man. Within reason I can do what I wish. I would like to see one of the Angels, now, tonight, to perform a special meditation, to share a new thing with a young friend while it is still new for both of us. Even were it just impulse, it would be my right. As I dearly wish it, there can be no refusal."

"We are sorry but your visit may have to be — postponed — for a time."

"Refused, you mean? No, that will not be. Other tribal Captains listed in the Book have been allowed. If you discriminate between listed Captains, attempt to bar me, I will ask for immediate Convocation and see how the holy colleges deal with that. All Princes, all tribes. As a Coloured Captain that is also my right."

Chybere spoke for the camera now as well as to me. "We have not — barred you, Captain. We have not, as you say, discriminated. But there are practicalities. Fair considerations. Such a request..."

"I have announced my intention, gentlemen. Your official reaction is being recorded."

Chybere glanced at Beth's camera again; Amly took in the handful of Nationals covertly watching, muttered something in dialect, a low sharp Kurdaitcha code impossible to interpret, making no apology for it.

They were considering outright refusal, I knew, or worse, accustomed to commanding absolute obedience, to showing the patient and reasonable gentleness of all inquisitors, but caught now by the need to be delicate and correct, to adapt to this novelty situation and turn it their way. The arrogance and ruthlessness were held back, came out in a smile from Chybere such as Torquemada or the Witchfinder Matthew Hopkins might have given.

Had Beth's camera not been running, he might have hinted at consequences, reprisals, moves against friends and Nation, things I did not want to hear. I did not know how vindictive these holy warriors were, to what extent they truly believed in the Colour right, regardless of who held it.

Chybere's voice was poisonously calm when he spoke again.

"Part of the difficulty is that Krombi underwent orbit adjustment following *Dhal's* arrival last night. It will not be set up for another twenty-four hours."

"Yet *Dhal* is scheduled for Krombi tonight."

"A tribal payload, Captain, not for the emigrant docking areas. You understand me?"

I nodded, but it was at something else which occurred to me about these Kurdaitcha. The ancient clan of ritual avengers was drawn from all tribes, but individuals might retain tribal loyalties.

"Tell me, Chybere. Krombi is a Chonsye holding, I realize now. May I ask which tribe you and Amly were originally from?"

It had to be an infuriating question, catching them like this. Their eyes glittered like beads of obsidian.

"We are not permitted to say," Chybere answered.

He had been right about Beth's camera: natural, true conversation could not exist, just smooth formality, the right things said. I was trapped no less than these avengi were in a secret world of contingencies, expedience and cynicism. All of us deceivers.

Though technically, publicly, the law held; my claim was valid. Only I could withdraw it. And that was the unasked question here. That is what these Kurdaitcha, these former Chonsye, waited for now.

"Thank you for coming," I said. "I mean to make no further trouble. I will call Nation, tell them what I intend. All I require is a seat on *Dhal*, a room with a window when I reach Krombi, and a few hours with my friend, Soby Parovin."

The Kurdaitcha rose without further comment, turned away from the table and left the inn. The cats stirred; above their heads the green glass chandelier turned slowly like a galaxy carved from emerald. Clancy went to stand in the open doorway and watched them go.

"They vanish in the heat like anyone else," he said, then came over to our table.

"Sorry, Jack," I said. "Will they make trouble?"

"Nah. Their psychologists give me a clear. They come here themselves. The spacemen need me." The old sailor took a folded paper from the pocket of his apron and handed it to me. "The boy left this." And he began clearing a nearby table.

I read what the paper said, placed it so Beth could see it while I read it again.

Another Day at The Stranded Man

Sometimes we need a broken road
To see the road more clearly,
I was on a broken road
And I was blind.
Reaching out for something new,
Tell me, were you reaching too?
Drinking our wine
So close to the borderline
We could feel the emptiness from here.

Another day at The Stranded Man
Has come over me,

Another calm in the hurricane
And I'm beginning to see
From bridges I've burned down
Another waiting for me.
Drinking my wine
So close to the borderline,
I can feel the emptiness from here.

Another day at The Stranded Man
Has come to its end,
Another glimpse at the patient stars
So we can pretend.
There's a bridge to be burned now
There's a fire to be free,
Biding its time
So close to the borderline,
We can touch the endlessness from here.

For you, Tom.

Soby.

"He didn't finish it," Clancy said. "He meant to."

"Jack, are you saying Soby had been here before yesterday?"

The big man nodded. "That's right. Just like you do now and then, so you can feel it. Checking on the spacemen. He'd watch the pilots, listen to the test runs, talk about the Captains, you..."

"Jack..."

"You're doing the right thing, Tom," Clancy said, and carried the empty glasses back to the bar.

Beth gave a sad smile. "I knew he was fond of you. He'd say things. I'm glad you're going."

Oh Beth, I thought, how loving you are, how ready to let things be as they have to be, in their own time, in their own way, never forced, never too soon.

I reached out and squeezed her hand, met those startling eyes, then pocketed Soby's letter. "I'll take it up to him. He can finish it while I wait."

We laughed. The galaxy turned, the green of fields and jungles and Aztec gods. The cats lifted their heads, pondered the strange ways of humans, and the afternoon sun fell down the sky towards the Door that was swinging open at Long Reach.

At 1830, I walked with Beth to the spacemen's gate but found it locked and untended, no-one on duty. Wind whistled and thrummed in the linkmesh fence, raised eddies of dust along the lonely road.

I felt a sadness at what it might mean. Perhaps the Kurdaitcha — in league with Cosiro — had acted already, had found small immediate things that mattered, like punishing a young gatekeeper. Perhaps they would poison Clancy's cats, make little tragedies of that kind.

But when we had walked around the field to the main gate, there were no avengi waiting to trade or warn, just two gatekeepers who checked and signed their manifest and handed me an ident tab.

This evening there were no crowds of emigrés lined up and waiting. *Dhal* carried an official payload — station officers returning from ground duty and leave, vital supplies.

"Tower 3," one Ab'O said, and pointed. "There."

I kissed Beth. For a moment we clung to each other with an urgency that words could never hope to explain, then I picked up my small bag and entered the field, walking towards *Dhal* where it slanted into the sky. I thought I could see the figure of Beth moving beyond the fence towards Clancy's, but it was too dark now to tell. Knowing Beth, she would not look back — her destination was the lonely inn beside the spacemen's road.

I boarded the aeromanker, took the seat indicated by the young half-caste steward. She smiled with practised courtesy as she helped me fit my harness.

"You've done sims before?" she asked.

"A hundred hours at least. High Frontier. Starfall. Some others."

"You'll be fine," she said. "The hard thing will be processing it as real this time." She gave her professional smile again and moved away.

My forty or so fellow passengers were not as generous.

When they glanced my way, their eyes were hard like those of Amly and Chybere, each glance a challenge, a calculated defiance, though made gentle with practice.

I made myself look around them, through them, studying the soft tones of the passenger salon, reacting to what the steward had said, trying to make it real, more than just the POV simulations.

The shuttle's interior was decorated in earthen tones, with fibre-ceramic panelling and totemic skeuomorphs. Even here, functional tech did not escape the psychic essentials. True to the tribal philosophies, there were things for the soul and the mind, function at all levels of what a person was, not simply the physical. Nothing casual here: ergonomic and psychonomic, every shape and form powered the ultimate reality of this ship.

I would not see the spacemen, of course. They would enter by another port, had probably done so already. I wondered if they were men I had seen at Clancy's — it was more than likely. Ship crews rotated, did the high-low circuit. Very likely.

As the digital crept towards 1900, I sat wondering how many of my fellow passengers — twenty-eight men, twelve women — were Kurdaitcha or special Chonsye agents assigned to this flight. Not for the first time, I considered the possibility of an accident going up to orbit: just what price would they pay to be free of one of the Coloured Captains, one of the seven chosen by a faulty belltree playing at God, placing names in the Great Passage Book, obliging the tribes to such a burden of honour?

Perhaps this payload was made up of last-minute volunteers, Ab'Os prepared to give their lives to chip away at the ignominy, to prevent *this* man exercising *this* right, willing to die for tribal favours to friends and family. While I waited at Clancy's with Beth, who knew what plans had been made?

Tonight my death — by Kurdaitcha or Chonsye (or a mixture of both if my suspicions about Amly and Chybere had been correct). A month, a year later, one of the other Captains: Afervarro or Lucas or Glaive, on and on down the list until the Seven were gone and the weight of the shame was diminished, eliminated at last.

It would look obvious, of course it would, once the process

was started. But, then again, modern Australia was a dangerous land and memories were often short, especially given careful media biasing by the tribes. My call to Council had involved a briefing of the six remaining Captains, plus passing on an account of what I now did to Arredeni and Anna at Heart-and-Hand. Beth had called *Caravanserai* with copy for a major feature. Perhaps there was too much attention for them to risk payback.

Dhal had been alive in small ways: air-conditioning, electrical systems, soft hull noises. Now it sprang alive in earnest, urgently, the engines switched in, building for lift. Like the sims, but real. *Real*.

There was the ten-chime. *Dhal* moved forward, moved quickly, alarmingly, as if flung from a giant's hand. I was pressed back into the seat; the aeromanker angled up and lost Long Reach, threw it behind.

And none of it was real — all part of a virtual reality conditioning, senses dulled by hours in the High Frontier sim on Breaklight Pier. But I tried. Desperately tried.

I remembered *Crosa* the night before, calculated the vanishment we made, the dislocation of proportion and reality for Beth and Clancy should they be watching far, far, impossibly far below. I had the bewilderment that fitted theirs, a suspension of all the usual causal expectations as big became small, up became out, heaviness slipped away, and unminded dragon roar became uncanny silence.

My time sense was gone, I discovered. It seemed moments, mere seconds, and I was glancing out the ports at the curve of the world, blue, white, radiant with someone else's day. It was another sim shot, another VR insert, or like one of those antique astronautics photographs, brilliantly back-lit by a sunrise corona at the terminator.

But I fought the disappointment, worked to let the reality press in too. I'd been in a dirigible many times, had read about the old aircraft and early space planes. I made myself see truth, forced it about my over-conditioned senses, used smaller, nearer things like the weightlessness being defied by my harness, the shift of my organs and body-tides, subtle, so subtle, sought and found a language to encompass it. Believed I did.

My fellow passengers had done this before. Some read or dozed, but most watched the view as well, pointing out sights, making quiet comments. These weren't the comsat orbits; many of them were identifying nearby Angels which shone as points of light, beacon stars in this preternatural midnight day.

That was reassuring. I detected no undue tension in how they sat, saw no last-minute knowing glances for a shared mutual fate.

Finally a voice spoke from com, words in dialect. I heard the name Krombi and searched the starfield for the Chonsye station, saw it suddenly as *Dhal* heeled over for docking, a great sculpted aerolith turning about its long axis, showing us first its glistening clubbed end, the plantings inside the ribbed and domed surface works, then — as we toured its length — the tapering stem, the production facs and labs, a series of ugly vent tubes, EVA access ports, the shuttle docks.

Again, real. Not sim, not documentary footage.

Krombi looked both fragile and sturdy, a great inverted stalactite hanging from the ceiling of the night, geosynched above Australia. Its bright, jewel-encrusted end pointed towards the Earth, its jagged service tail faced out into the deeps where it had been found and dragged forth, carried home like some lost sceptre to where its carved, bejewelled brother gragens swung through the same dark, sentinel stones left here on the doorstep of forever.

Dhal turned in towards the throat of the docking tube, heading for the sealing fac which waited like a surgeon, grapples, locks and umbilici poised and ready.

Again, superb irony, all more real than I dreamed — and less. The reality barrier barely remained intact. Soby had talked of true space in the taproom of Clancy's, had conceived and shared a madman's visionary portion of it that had been more real than this slide to station could ever be. Something defined by opposites. The more remote, the more vivid. Nationals compensated for the loss of space by desensitizing on the wonderful simulations, no longer able to relate. Perhaps all this would not become finally real until I was standing on the windy deck of *Rynosseros* again, sailing the red deserts. Perhaps then it would happen, overload falling away, simple truth remaining.

I laughed aloud at the paradox, the ultimately terrifying yet unassimilable sensory trap, and the Ab'Os near me frowned and muttered. I was a drunk on a fairground ride, that was all. Soon the ride would end and I would step out onto the Pier in bright sunshine, go back to the deserts and my ship.

Oh Soby, were you young enough, unsullied enough, to keep it pure? Did you avoid the sims, needing to keep this real, the edges sure and sharp?

Dhal crept into dock like a slow-motion swimmer, received the grapples and service tubes, became one more piece of Krombi's glistening crust.

Then, when we had gravity again, when I was free of my harness and leaving *Dhal*, the place became truly, meaningfully strange. As we moved into the flight lounge, the estrangement began — with the walls of thick meteoric iron and rock-melt, shiny black streaked with green and violet, the array of tonson poles of space metal and gragen-grown timbers, a grove of fantastic totems with crests spun into filigree or shimmering with bright wires inside metal throats so that they sang in the wind from the pressured hearts of docking ships.

Things for the soul, I kept telling myself. Parts of a functional reality, everything working to feed the psyche and ease the spirit. These weren't like those antique NASA sims of O'Neill colonies; this was another way, as different as *Soyuz* from *Apollo*, as Egyptian Ptah to Baiame.

The returning Ab'Os knew where they were going in this strange metal garden. The tonson totems communicated something vital: welcoming them to their other home, their high stone place, directing them to concealed exits. The small group quickly dispersed, vanished through coded space-iron access-ways almost faster than I could see, like beads of mercury scattered on a polished floor. By the time I understood what was happening — a routine withdrawal to known destinations — I found myself alone in an iron glade in the tinkling, shimmering ship-wind from our aeromanker.

It was disturbing, even vaguely alarming, standing there on the gently curving floor as the wind died away and the totems became still once more.

No Kurdaitcha came, no Clever Men or Unseen Spears. A single port opened beyond the stark cluster of gragen trees. A single Ab'O, tall, patrician-like, my own age, stepped onto the deck on the other side of the grove and headed towards me. The tonson poles reacted to his bodywind, started stirring and murmuring again.

I saw that he wore patterned bodyforms, ochre like the old stones of Earth, covered with a hatching of darker brown lines. He had the blood-red infinity sign on his forehead, a tattoo and not a painted mutable. On each cheek he had a turquoise chevron. He wore the double swords.

A space captain, and captain of the *Dhal*, I was certain. He had inherited the problem I represented, showing just how unwelcome I was at this Angel.

I swore to myself. Damn them for involving him like this! Damn them!

"I am Dwar Ingers," the spaceman said.

"Captain Ingers, I regret this inconvenience..."

"You have the Colour," he said with absolute solemnity, with total acceptance.

This was truly a tribal man, one who challenged no rulings, questioned no Book. The subtleties and questions he had were for a different medium than this.

I needed to confirm the expectations he might have, needed to do so in this alien place where I had no allies but Soby, no other friend.

Captain Ingers was determined to do his duty. "I have been asked..."

"Captain, attend the Colour!" I interrupted with the ritual line because I needed the help he could give. "I have no honour sword for this visit. Lend me your second."

He frowned, dark brows turning down, a pointing of infinity towards the bright blue chevrons. He took out his second sword and passed it to me, holding it horizontal in both hands.

I took it, put it through my belt. "I am greatly honoured, Dwar Ingers. You were speaking."

The fine face was composed at once. "They instructed me to

bring you unfortunate news. This stone had stationing manoeuvres last night. Your friend, Parovin, went out to the Gragens of Io. He wanted true space, and all positions on Krombi and the other Angels were taken. There was a ship going, the *Pearl*. It was a chance and he took it. That is what I have been told to tell you. Station administration is sorry. The Towradji sends his regrets..."

"But did not come himself."

"No. He asked me to tell you."

And he watched my reaction, as if expecting me to demand that we commandeer a ship and follow *Pearl*.

"Soby Parovin was on *Crosa*," I said. "Please take me to what Nationals do remain from that flight."

"Station authorities must be consulted for that," Ingers said. "I must call the Towradji who presides here..."

"No, Captain Ingers. They forfeited that right when they left you to meet with me. The Towradji should have come himself to honour the Colour. You gave me your second sword. You will take me immediately to the nearest comp and give me clearance into station records. So I can be sure. Please. For the Colour."

I sensed that Dwar Ingers was pleased with my adherence to protocol, as if he had been warned that we made light of the Book honours and now found it otherwise. He turned and led the way to the door he had used before, touched it so it opened, and we stepped through into a short corridor, and from that into a large staging chamber fitted with pods and painted EVA suits. It was plainly an off-limits area. There was a small comp station in one wall. Ingers went to it and touched first the ident plate, then the keys.

"They will know almost at once."

"This is a Security area. Why did you bring me here?"

"The nearest, you said."

"But..." And then I understood the significance of what he had done, and of his earlier words: *They instructed me...That is what I have been told to tell you.*

"They will know almost at once," Ingers repeated, telling me something more by his few words, by his tight delivery of them.

"They've locked you into service, Dwar," I said, first-naming him, Captain to Captain, daring more than might be fitting for an honour companion, but sensing the intention behind what he had said and done.

"Records," the Ab'O said, hand on the plate, then stood aside. I keyed in:

Information. National emigré. Soby Parovin.

There was a lapse of four seconds, then the display appeared, amber on black.

JT10BA4   Soby Parovin. *Crosa* 86.
Long Reach 601-B.

Despatched. Malasi-2. 2300-7-77AS554.
Storage A-2.

An alarm sounded somewhere beyond our chamber, and another somewhere beyond that. Dwar Ingers glanced at the door on the far side of the EVA room, then back to the screen.

I keyed another request, not wanting to use voice.

Enhancement: Malasi-2.

I expected to see a gragen ident for some lonely satellite in the Jovian mantle. What I saw chilled me, struck me like a harsh black tide, made me see not words on a screen but a window into overwhelming pain and despair. Stunned, speechless, I felt only rage, a fierce rage locked in numbing disbelief. It was too much to deal with. The tonson poles, the Spirit Malingee on the dark windy road, the flight to station, all that had been more real.

There were new alarms, the sounds of people running, shouts in other chambers and corridors near ours.

"Look!" I cried to Ingers, pointing at the display. "Look!"

But saw he knew.

"I do not need to look," he said with winter locked hard in his words, a frown of identical despair crushing the infinity on his brow into a burning wire.

"You knew!"

The infinity blazed. This was a man trapped by oaths, tribal loyalties, a man who had used the chance I provided.

I drew Ingers' second sword. "*Dhal* has fuel?"

"I can bring you home," he said, honour-bound but more than that, wanting this, choosing, driven by more than the honour of spacemen, led now by simple human decency.

Draw for Blue, Captain, I almost said, but knew I had to use the right words. And it had to be his continuing decision, his choice.

"Should I return your sword, Captain? I may need it but I will return it if you say."

He drew his first sword, and seemed easier having done so, as if the decision had freed him, was something made possible only by the set forms. He also produced a small laser baton, a very deadly thing in this sealed environment, certainly a forbidden thing except under the most extreme circumstances.

The door at the far end of the EVA chamber slid back. Five Kurdaitcha entered, saw our swords and drew theirs. Their eyes widened at the sight of Ingers' baton. One of the newcomers came forward. He had the sigil of a commander on his station fatigues and near it a blue hook like Cosiro had worn.

"Captain Ingers," he said. "Step aside, please, or you will be placed under station arrest."

The spaceman did not move. "You gave me a duty I did not want, Mora. You know me, but you insisted! Deal with this, you said. I am doing so. Your instructions have been superseded by a claim of Colour, a sword-duty to the Book which you know supersedes all other oaths. All others, you understand me?"

I would have spoken but left him to state what was probably more directly true here, the local currency which made the purchase.

The five Kurdaitcha — Chonsye Kurdaitcha, to make the important distinction — stared at us across the metal floor. The screen still showed the hateful knowledge Records had so innocently yielded up.

Mora was in charge, that much was clear, not the Towradji of this stone. Mora's actions would be reckoned here; it was his responsibility forever, passed on to family and tribe. Before he could order my death, *our* deaths — would Ingers serve so far? — I turned back to comp.

"Dwar, if Mora or any of his companions move against Blue, you will take the Colour," I said, and placed my palm on the touch-plate Ingers had used to bring up function. "Voice," I said. "Acknowledge ident: Blue Captain GPB/T-298. Tom Tyson."

The avengi stirred.

"Accepted," comp said, using voice function now, a calm neutral voice unruffled by what was happening. "Waiting."

"General broadcast," I said. "To Tell Records and Nation."

Mora took a step forward. "Captain!"

"The Blue Captain will be home on *Dhal* within the hour. All National emigration to the gragens is suspended indefinitely, pending an investigation of Krombi..."

"I warn you!"

"...Djuringa priority: Blue!"

"Listen!"

"Immediate transfer..."

"Don't!"

"Execute!"

"We can blanket that!" Mora cried, but his face told me otherwise, that it was too late — here where the communications net for the planet lay spread out below us. The calculated slight of appointing Ingers to be my contact with station had gone this far amiss.

"Count your losses!" I said, and could barely speak the words, hold back the aching weight of emotion. "Save this and earn your tribe's gratitude. I'm sure the Chonsye people — do not know what their holy sons have done here."

A Kurdaitcha was furtively reaching into his robe; Ingers shifted his baton and the warrior stopped at once. I made myself continue.

"The world is waiting for an incident of this scale, for a Coloured Captain to die." My voice was shaking badly now, but I did not let myself think beyond the need to get free of Krombi, to get down the gravity well and carry the news. "S-Soby Parovin?" I made myself say it. "He is dead?"

Mora hesitated only a moment. "Yes."

"Show me the body."

"It is too late," he said. The Kurdaitcha swords remained steady, reminding us that Mora was weighing the worth of a single shot at the pressure wall, an environment accident on Krombi. "The malasi was added last night. Quick and painless. The bodies have been sealed in their ejection pods for disposal."

Disposal. Such a word, such an easy word.

I stared at the man, feeling such an emptiness inside that should the wall go, if it came to that and Ingers would fire, the cold of space could never match it.

"The world will learn of this."

"No," Mora said. "You will not do that. You will say nothing. Word has gone out. The Chonsye comsat has — let us say — been temporarily seconded by Kurdaitcha here at Krombi. It is above Long Reach, has lasers focused on The Stranded Man, on your friends there. Your ship, *Rynosseros*, is near Mider. We were prepared for the need to coerce, not over this, I admit, but we have taken the precautions. And if this is to be the way of it, then all seven Captains will go. Do you understand? Though I doubt that will be necessary: they will not believe you."

"Coming from me they would."

"No, Captain Tom. It is too big a thing. You know it is."

"Great Passage Book! Djuringa!"

"Still too big," Mora said. "But it will not come to that. We will stop you here."

Which was likely. Swords remained raised as calculations were made moment to moment. Only Ingers' baton had stopped them, and Ingers was Chonsye, a tribesman, while it was plain that Mora had full executive authority over the Towradji of this station. No doubt he was considering a space accident, a terrible misfortune, weighing the cost of pre-emptive deaths against trade reprisals and tribal, National and global censure. But such things could not begin to matter in the face of what filled my thoughts.

"The ancient Assyrians moved entire peoples from their homelands into harsh desert so survival took all their energy. It was shrewd and effective. The Amerind tribes suffered the same fate: re-location, estrangement, neutralization. But you chose the Nazi way. Active genocide!"

"No!" Mora said, watching the silent Ab'O beside me, one of those who had been sworn to secrecy, Kurdaitcha directive, who had brought so many emigrés up to die, whose craft and skill had been turned to such an end. "Not genocide! Not atrocity at all. You know nothing of Nepelle, ruler of the heavens. It's an equation, an atonement. A transformation. A Baiame ritual, part of a creation myth. We give life gifts to the Earth, dead stones which are the seeds, the children of the stars. Nothing is destroyed."

He may have believed what he said, but I doubted it, saw it instead as a strategy, an appeal to the beliefs and simple honesty of Dwar Ingers.

Ingers' voice was flat and hard, filled with bitter irony when he spoke. "Always the handy myth. Baiame giving his seed."

"Enough, Dwar!"

"Just a few sworn captains."

"Sworn, yes! So keep your silence! Captain Tom, your friend is dead, accept it! Emigration will stop for awhile. There will be investigations, questions, but who will believe? Profiles exist in comp for all the emigrés through Krombi, personality prints for message simulations. Anyone you name, your Soby Parovin, can be made to contradict you. Holoforms from far places. If necessary, our labs can work up an andromorph along his somatotype — we can send him home to refute your claims in person..."

"Mora, you miss the point. All emigration is ended. The other tribes will be asking you why. Your own Prince will ask."

"You do not understand, Captain. You can be made to contradict you, don't you see? We can simulate *you*."

"Then, Mora, I am prepared to die here, to ask Captain Ingers to take us all. Following my transmission, that would provide some sort of evidence at least."

"Difficult, agreed, but the project will survive it. Harming Krombi will simply corroborate the story of an accident taking your life. We might even discredit you, mention sabotage."

"No!" I said, furious that Mora could use a word like 'project', could turn the subject so easily from Soby and — how many? The numbers eluded me. How many through Krombi in a year: twenty thousand? Fifty?

"No," Dwar Ingers said, standing beside me, echoing me. "Kill this man and the Coloured Captains will know. Harm them and the spacemen will know. *All* the tribes. You will not survive this." And he put aside his sword, reached up, and turned down his collar, revealed his bridge comlink. "This has been transmitted to others of my order."

I felt a rush of gratitude for the spaceman. His loyalty to Blue, to the Book, to simple humanity, was startling, almost embarrassing in its fullness. He was simply a man who believed.

Mora had gone beyond fury, beyond any display of rage or threat. "What do we do?"

"What you do, Mora, is endorse my next directive!" I said.

"You are not serious!"

I turned to comp, placed my hand on the plate once more.

"Blue Tyson," I said. "Djuringa priority. Access 601-B. Soby Parovin file. Store print at permanent, to be revoked only by my command. Give continuing broadcast status, priority variation and enhancement on songs. Sealed by order. Execute."

"Authorization required, Krombi station," comp said.

"Continue recording. Mora?"

"Impossible!" Mora cried.

"You do it! You build your andromorph and give it Soby's print. You do that. But for now you raise his profile to active in a sealed leader file. You give it AI assist and let it go random in the system. Those songs go wide, clean and forever, you understand? You send them to God or I tell it all. Or you get our deaths, damn you, and the spacemen knowing."

"And you will not tell? You swear to that, Captain Tyson?"

"Provided emigration ends, I do. Not just through Krombi. All emigration. Use your Kurdaitcha status. Make them ask what has gone wrong. You swear and I will, before this Captain of Space. This man and — yes! — the young tribesman who guarded the spaceman's gate at Long Reach yesterday. Only while they live in true honour and as true spacemen. They are my witnesses for Blue in this, Mora, the keepers of my bond, do you hear me? This is my price and my warning. Swear to it all and endorse!"

"Agreed," Mora said. Again the lack of hesitation told me how much power he had, how much of this was his own enterprise.

"Swear to it then!"

"I swear," Mora said. He walked over and placed his palm on the plate. "Endorsed. Zer Mora Dhunmajira."

"Initiated," comp said in its calm, unaffected voice.

I turned to the spaceman beside me. "Dwar, please take me home."

On the flight back down the well, sitting alone in the empty salon (for not even Blue could get me onto Dwar's flight deck: the rulings of his brotherhood), I asked to have broadcast patched through to my chair, just in case.

Mora had kept the first part of his promise. Soby was already there.

> "...came in early
> For the shuttle bound for Krombi,
> With his little bits of all the hopes there are.
> Read the wanted ads and classifieds
> For the high sky stones near Ceres,
> And waited for his moment at the bar.

> "Standing in the lobby
> Was a lady fit for fever,
> With Astani on her mother's side at least.
> And she read him like a gypsy
> And she told him like a demon,
> Called him clod of earth
> And image of the beast.

> "And he's going,
> Going to the Angels,
> Going up to join the people in the skies.
> And he's going,
> Going to the Angels,
> Going to sing them crazy right between the eyes."

Which was as much as I could stand before turning it off. By then we were deep in the well. Earth was 'down' again, and the engines' roar was a more insistent song, urgent and blessedly distracting, great dragons of the night.

I watched Long Reach resolve below me, growing from a dish of earth-golds set with blue-white edges, to deep night, blurred now, gently, so I barely knew, by the memory of Soby Parovin.

The news of emigration ending had had the expected response. As *Dhal* settled on the runway, more than a late-night mank crew was waiting. The lights of Hindel were tellingly ablaze. By the field gates, a crowd of National and International officers, media crews and sightseers had gathered already, among them many angry, would-be emigrés.

Ingers unlocked the spaceman's gate in the linkmesh fence. We clasped hands and I made to return his second sword.

"No," he said. "I am your witness, Blue Tyson. Keep it for me."

"For your honour, Dwar."

"For yours, Blue Captain."

And we parted.

I met Beth on the road back to Clancy's. She waited in the chill night wind, her robe gathered close about her against the cold and the blowing dust. She opened it to take me within, and we stood in the road together in our warmth and shared emotion.

"What, Tom? What happened?"

"The Door has to be closed for awhile. That's all. Just for awhile. I can't say more, Beth. Accept that, please. I can't."

"I do. I do, Tom. What about Soby?"

"He's fine. He's happy. You'll be hearing his songs soon. The Towradji himself has taken an interest."

And we walked back to The Stranded Man.

The newsboard outside the door told it already, the early editions of *The Beach Gazette* and *The National* shouting the terrible accusations:

ANGELS OFF LIMITS!
BLUE CAPTAIN CLOSES SPACE DOOR
NATION COUNCIL FURIOUS
What World Leaders are Saying

Seeing the headlines, Beth turned to me again.

"What, Tom? Please."

"I can't tell you. I've sworn."

And I saw she was weeping, for Soby, for me, for something she sensed — the deep distress held in check, something of what was filling me. We stood in the dark road, Beth clinging to me, our tears merging as we held each other.

"Come inside," she said, needing more help now than she felt she could give, sensing the loss, the unnamed something, needing the magic of Clancy and his cats, the warm lights.

"I have to stay out here awhile."

"It's a lovely night," she said, misunderstanding, or pretending to, looking up. "We don't need that."

"We don't."

"Come in, Tom."

"No, Beth." I thought of the spacemen who might be there — who would always be there now in my memories — facing away from the windows, looking into their drinks and listening to the wind, serious forgetting men. "You go in. Wait for me. There'll be meteors soon. I want to watch them fall."

"He'll do well, Tom. He'll make us proud."

"Yes," I said. "He will."

And still she didn't leave. She stood watching me watch the night sky, so clear, so deep, so high.

"He'll burn brightly up there, won't he?" she said, the tears rolling down her cheeks.

She knew. Beth knew.

"He'll shine!" I said, and took her hand to keep her at my side.

Together we stood in the cold wind blowing down from the stars and waited for Soby to come home.

Vanities

The first thing I did when I reached the Tattamorano/Crater Lake concession, after checking in at the Pier Hotel, was to go down to Full Moon Pier and watch them fishing for vanities.

It gave me time to think about Hal, to decide whether or not the young Ab'O would have taken his own life like that. The lake and the Piers, Full Moon especially, invited such silent contemplation. There were sixty or more men and women lined up at the rails, their buckets and pressure flasks beside them, their lines running down into the shifting gas just far enough, flickering with the mirrors that they use to lure the creatures. These fisherfolk, too, were quiet, or spoke in low murmurs. Their various stances told me it had been a slow morning, that no catches had been made yet.

You can always tell when someone has been fortunate. The anglers stand differently, and hold their lines with just that much more expectation. The vanities travel in groups; one success usually means others. The first catch pays for the week's fishing licence and accommodation; the rest are profit.

I moved among the waiting figures, now and then intruding on someone's private domain at the rail so I received hostile glances. When they saw my sailor's fatigues, my Nation and Colour patches, their hard looks softened somewhat; one or two even smiled. I was not a rival fisherman after all, just a sand-ship sailor here beside this famous Australian lake, enjoying the hot early morning sun and the wide views of the desert that hemmed in the small resort town.

"No luck?" I said to an old man. He was standing in one precious corner of the Pier, his place marked out by canisters and rods and a bucket of the small square baiting mirrors.

"Nah!" he answered, and spat into the gas. It seethed and roiled about the timbers of the Pier, thick yellow eddies that hid the bottom and dulled the light reflected from the squares of glass. "They're out in the middle somewhere. Or over there." He nodded in the direction of the nearest sacred beach: the Quni precinct. "Probably an Ab'O funeral. Them and their mirror suits. Probably won't be a catch for days now; an' me takin' months to save for a licence!"

I looked along the low curving shoreline of the lake to where the gas lapped and twisted in a restless meniscus as it met the sand. But on the three flag-poles at the sacred beach there were no flags raised to show an Ab'O had gone into the gas (not that Hal's death would be 'flagged'). The poles stood empty; the beach deserted. The door of the large stone reliquary was shut and locked.

But I stood there watching the lake just the same, though this time the quiet of Full Moon did nothing to ease my mind. Mita's letter had specified a time and place — the lobby of the Pier Hotel — but there had been no sign of the Ab'O girl, let alone her twin brother, Hal.

Obviously a lot had happened in the week it had taken her letter to reach me at the coast, and for me to make the three-day journey into the desert. That worried me. There could be no doubting that I would come. It was more than Mita's claim on my friendship with her late uncle; it was that one line, following the news that a tribal crime had made Hal decide to take his life: "He has already bought a Wagiri suit from Anthony Wessex".

Anthony Wessex. Not quite my friend and almost a ghoul. And a black marketeer, dealing in tribal relics. Suits of lights.

Mita had known that news would bring me to Crater Lake.

A cry went up half-way down the Pier. A woman had made a catch and was now winding it in.

I watched, fascinated as always, as the prize appeared — the strange starfish-shaped creature closed like a fist around the mirror square, concealing it completely. As it came out of the gas, the dying vanity was already beginning to petrify in the air, becoming a hard vitrophyric lump glinting briefly in the light as the change took place.

Amid shouts and congratulations from her neighbours, the woman cut the violet-green siliceous ball from her line and placed it in her storage canister. It was a fair-sized creature and a perfect enclosure; none of the mirror showed. She would get a good price for it from any gallery assayer.

I left the Pier and went down the stone steps onto the sand. I moved around the lake, past the empty flag-poles and the locked reliquary, stopping to peer through the dusty panes of amber glass in the door to see the dim shapes of the vanitied Ab'Os standing in the gloom. There was a Niuginian caretaker who came out of his little shack further up the shore to see who was trespassing, but he just waved me on when he saw the patches on my jacket. Not a word was said between us.

I was on my way back to the hotel to see if Mita or Hal had appeared when I noticed the Crater Lake Gallery, still closed at this early hour. I inspected the eight vanities Anthony Wessex had on show in the windows. All were minor specimens and overpriced, none as splendid as that caught by the woman on the Pier. My premonition that Tony was involved in something more than a possible suicide was stronger than ever.

No-one was waiting for me back at the hotel, so I sat in one of the big leather chairs in the lobby and watched the people coming in off the street. After forty minutes of skimming magazines and looking up whenever the doors opened, a young Indonesian girl in a red dress entered. It was Bess, Mita's friend. She saw me and hurried over.

"Captain Tyson!" Tears were already forming in her large brown eyes.

"Where are they, Bess?"

She shook her head. "Hal is gone, I fear. Yesterday. Mita is hiding. I am very worried. I looked for you earlier."

"I was down on Full Moon," I said. "I wanted to see the Quni reliquary."

"Hal could be there, yes?"

"I don't know. The place is locked up. I can't tell. There's a Quni immersion tomorrow. If Hal has gone into the gas, we may know then. But, Bess, I've got to see Mita. It's important that I talk to her."

Tears rolled down Bess's cheeks. "She's hiding. I don't know where. She won't show herself now."

"Why not? What was Hal's crime? What made him do it?"

Bess did not answer, and I realized that the twins had not told her. I suspected it was fornication or adultery, or possibly incest, which could explain Mita's caution, and that Hal had suicided rather than endure being sung to death for it. His punishment — well, perhaps he had chosen wisely. As an outcast, he died in shame, hunted and killed from within by Ab'O mind-fighters. By entering the lake, smothered by the gas and the vanities, he became a priceless Stone Man, a curious and public insult to his tribe, hated but revered; an artefact worth a fortune on the world markets — if ever it reached them.

If Hal had suicided, *if* he were in the reliquary, would the Quni Clever Men admit to it? It was unlikely. But at least we might learn if there had been an anonymous transformation recently; all the Stone Men were named and dated. And a recent annealing would show.

For, according to Mita's letter, Hal had found himself a suit of lights.

I sent Bess to look for Mita, and went down to the Crater Lake Gallery.

Crater lake is a vast funerary precinct, a necropolis on all but the one small section of strand abutting the National resort town of Crater Lake, with its fashionable hotels and villas, its shopping plazas, galleries and two long Piers.

Dotted along the gentle beaches all around the lake are the tribal reliquaries, over a hundred and twenty of them; each building a large sandstone block with narrow sky-lights and a single amber-paned door; each one fronted by its three flag-poles, its small funerary jetty reaching out into the gas on spindly legs, and usually a shanty with a caretaker like the old Niuginian I had seen.

When an Ab'O Clever Man dies, if he deserves the honour, he is fitted out in his suit of leather sewn with tiny mirrors, carried out on to the jetty, and lowered into the gas just far enough for the hot desert sun to set him flashing. The vanities come, sooner or later; the corpse is brought forth as a Stone Man and placed in the tribal reliquary.

That Hal had gone into the gas as a taboobreaker and an outcast was an insult of a very special kind. The Stone Men were sacred, each one the sign of a blessed spirit. This was sacrilege *and* heresy.

It has happened before. Forsaken lovers, dying elders, even Nationals wanting something of the glory reserved for the Clever Men, have plunged from one of the Piers. Sometimes, when the gas is clearer, you can see their corpses on the bottom, sad forsaken shapes transformed by nothing but death itself. Rarely do they become Stone Men, though a few have fitted mirrors to their garments in imitation of the gorgeous mirror suits worn by the tribal mystics.

But Hal had gone further, departing from the strict training of his people. How he had heard of Anthony Wessex's black market operations, his buying up the unvanitied mirror suits of the extinct Wagiri, was a mystery. I had heard the tales but had preferred not to believe them. After all, Tony, my not-quite-friend, was reckless, but his life was in Crater Lake. He could not afford to be caught out and censured by the tribes.

Tony was serving a couple of Niuginian tourists when I entered, looking as urbane as ever in his maroon Maiquin fatigues, white shirt and soft black boots, his steel-grey hair cropped close to his head, making his fine features more handsome than ever. His face lit up when he saw me and he signed that he would be with me in a moment.

I went and studied a large framed wall-map of the Tattamorano concession, and wondered how much he would tell me. He knew Hal and Mita; he would probably know why Hal had gone into the gas, and why his sister was in hiding. He might even talk black-market with me, though I doubted he would say much. I was a State of Nation officer after all.

I let my gaze wander about the vitrine displays, then located the door to his Special Room, as Tony called it. In that inner sanctum, I had once seen six prime vanities on sale at ridiculous prices, reserved for the special buyers of curiosa who came to Crater Lake — the ones who wanted something extra.

Though everything about Tony Wessex bespoke charm and elegance, he was fascinated by teratology. The six balls of vitrophyre aggregate had looked innocent enough, but each was one of his 'grotesques'. One, the size of a melon, was said to contain a human hand. Tony had sewn and fitted the mirror glove himself. Another held a foetus. What the rest had closeted at their centres, Tony wouldn't say. It was the vitreous ball itself that mattered, he argued; he had simply added mystery to the mysterious.

I moved on to one of the display cases and stared down at the vanity on the turquoise velvet display mat. I thought of the small square of mirror buried at its heart, and how it had reflected the creature's tiny death. I could still make out the hairline fissures where the petals of its arms had closed like a flower about that final image of itself. Every night in Crater Lake, moths were drawn by lantern flames to such moments of fatal rapture, and we barely noticed.

But after my morning at the Piers, after looking in at the Ab'O dead at the reliquary, it wasn't hard to let this small closed stone flower do more than the moths could: to suggest the abstractions of love and desire, of power, beauty and need, the patterns of ego and shadow that consumed us all. The hard part was admitting to the quests as quests, giving them their correct importance in our dealings with others, recognizing them for what they were — as in moths around a flame, or vanities spinning in to a final act of self-worship, or people fishing on a pier. The hardest part was knowing what they meant from person to person. Like Hal's suicide. Not the fact that he had done it, but why it had no longer mattered to him that he had. And why as a heretic Stone Man, compounding the crime?

The first 'why' was Hal and Mita's secret. The second was Tony's.

The Niuginians left the Gallery; Tony came over and shook

my hand.

"Tom! Beloved! Welcome, welcome! How's *Rynosseros*? How's the crew?"

"Hello, Tony. Where are Hal and Mita? They wrote to me."

"Ah, a discerning buyer. Straight to the point. Let's close shop and take in the air. We can haggle at the lake."

Five minutes later we were walking out on Full Moon. The atmosphere had changed. There had been two more catches and an air of excitement prevailed; it had become a good morning. Some of these people would be able to renew their licences for another week.

Tony pointed out a rather statuesque woman in beige sand-robes and imported Clové sunglasses. She had two valets with her, nervous-looking young men in light desert suits and caps, but only the woman had a line dangling down into the gas, with a baiting mirror twinkling and flashing as it caught the sun.

"That's Cara Bressenden," Tony said. "The Offshore Ten heiress from Broome. She's spent six weekends here trying to make a catch herself."

"Crater Lake has a way of making people dedicated, Tony. Look at you."

"Oh, but she's a special case, Tom." He looked about him, became conspiratorial. "Her baiting mirror is one-sided. It's backed with a photograph of herself. She's looking for a receptacle. But shh! Not a word, eh?"

I smiled. "I'm convinced no-one knows who's going to be immortalized, Tony."

"True," he said. "Look at poor Machiavelli."

"Or Van Gogh."

"Look at Hal."

"Why do you say that?" We had reached the end and were re-tracing our steps back into town.

"He came into the Gallery four days ago. Wanted to know about the gas and the vanities. Signed a few documents."

"What sort of documents, Tony?"

"Permission notes. Releases. I let him have a suit of lights. I've picked up a few."

"Tony!"

"Well, he was going to kill himself anyway, Tom. He was being sung to death. The Quni Clever Men were coming for him."

"Where's Hal now?"

Tony Wessex looked defensive. "Where do you think? Down at the Quni reliquary."

"The Stone Men belong to the tribes."

"Not this one, Tom. They may have retrieved the body but I own it. I'm filing claim."

"For heaven's sake! This will cause an Incident. Crater Lake belongs to the Princes..."

"Except for the part here."

"So?"

Tony Wessex laughed. "Hal didn't go into the gas from the Quni pier. That was part of our deal for the suit. He went off Full Moon."

"What!"

"The Quni dragged for him that night, took him into their reliquary, then claimed he went off their pier."

"But you can prove he went from here."

"Right. I recorded the whole thing. Copies have gone to Twilight Beach and Adelaide. Hal gets his revenge. I get my Stone Man. The Quni are reprimanded and embarrassed."

"What happens to Hal's mummy?"

Tony gave his brilliant smile. "I may sell it back to one of the tribes for tribal favours. At a very high price."

"More of your Specials."

"It may go to one of the coastal museums. Or I'll sell it back to the Quni. For permission to build my own pier on their land. Think of it, Tom! Wessex Pier. I'll influence the world market, get rights to enter the lake in a pressure suit. I'll take my mirrors out into the centre."

I stared at Tony in wonder, unable to believe that he intended even a part of what he said.

"Tony, they'll kill you for this. You'll go into the gas yourself. Without mirrors." Then the truth occurred to me. "But you want an Incident. You want the Accord broken."

"You don't live here, Tom. The tribes don't use a fraction of what they own. They're locked up in rules and rituals, all those protocols. I'm talking about *our* ancient rights. We built this land."

I watched Tony's eyes. This was my tenth trip to this sacred domain in the inner desert. What did I know about land rights and legal entitlements? Or Anthony Wessex, for that matter? My teratophile was more of a mystery than he had ever been in our fond but occasional acquaintance.

For all I knew, this commitment to advancing the National cause — as wrong as it sounded coming from Tony's well-groomed, unsullied form — may have been the face of the real man, a large part of his reason for staying in Crater Lake and subsidising so many of the resort facilities. Or it may have been the indulgence of a man out of touch with reality. I smiled wryly at my svelte entrepreneur, my man with a mission.

"Help me in this, Tom," he said, as we reached the door of the Gallery again. "Help me do what Council won't. Use Blue to make this as big as we can get it."

"It's not the way, Tony."

"Not the way!" he cried. "It's never the way! When will you Captains do something? When will you, Tom?"

"Tony..."

"So, you've championed tangentals, closed down emigration though you won't say why. But what else? Mostly it's the diplomacy circuit for the lot of you: receiving benefices, representing Council in the tribal centres. But what have you really done for Nation?"

"The circumstances which make us special also limit us. You know that."

He shook his head, looked off down the street towards the Piers while he calmed himself. Finally he smiled, placed a well-manicured hand on the door jamb. "Forgiven?"

"Am I?"

"Always."

"Where's Mita, Tony?"

He shrugged. "I really don't know. You can look in the Special Room if you like."

"Or in where you store those Wagiri suits?"

The bonhomie flickered behind the eyes but held. Once again he had probably reminded himself that he liked me.

"Less to aid my ghoulishness, Tom, than to provide a weapon against the Clever Men. This land does not belong to the tribes. If I hear from Mita I'll send her to you. See you at the ceremony tomorrow."

The next morning, I walked down to the Quni beach. I went through the lines of tourists held back by the trespass warnings and by two Ab'O youths. These young men carried ritual woomeras but were spearless, though they wore the kitanas favoured by most of the tribes. They gave me cold looks but let me pass; I had assisted the Quni several times, and was known to them by the mark-signs I wore.

There was a flag on the furthest pole now — yellow to mark the beginning of the transformation. The door of the reliquary was open, and a bonfire, tended by a handful of boys, had been lit at the far end of the Quni section of beach.

I was just in time. The end of the funerary pier was a dazzle of light from a hundred Clever Men in their suits of lights, men gathered from the many tribes who revered the Stone Man transformation and had a reliquary at Crater Lake, or shared such a precinct with blood-related tribes.

I shaded my eyes against the dazzle and moved closer. All along the Quni strand stood the tribal menfolk with their sheathed kitanas over their backs and holding war boomerangs and spears. A didgeridoo was droning on in the morning silence, played by a man sitting by the open door of the reliquary. Apart from among the tourists, there was not a woman to be seen. As much as Ab'O society had changed over the years, it was still vigorously patriarchal in the matter of burial honours.

At the end of the jetty, the sling holding the dead Clever Man, Buyundar, was being lowered into the gas for the first stage of the annealing. Later in the day he would be turned in the sling, and again, and then again, until the 'enclosing' of the body was complete.

Sometimes it happened quickly, the vanities swarming to clutch at the lozenges of reflecting glass sewn to the leather. Often it took days for the annealing to be done, before the body could be lifted out for the vitrification itself.

I watched the immersion, then walked by the reliquary door, pretending to be interested in the didgeridoo player. By moving my eyes slightly, I could see down the long stone hall. There were at least sixty Stone Men in the Quni vault, vaguely human shapes standing in the gloom, arranged in order of succession. Hal would not be in those rows.

I moved around the man droning down his ancient instrument and studied the other side of the crypt.

There was Hal, the only figure unlabelled, and one still showing the violet-green, high vitreous gloss of a recent annealing.

The Quni had been careful. No wonder they had been quick to drag for Hal's body. Apart from their natural sensitivity to public knowledge of sacrilege, there was the added incentive that this was the first violation.

I immediately thought of Tony Wessex and shook my head. Then I had the sense to realize I'd been staring into the hall, and turned away in time to see three young warriors hurrying up the beach towards me. They carried the ornate woomeras of the Unseen Spears, and wore the sersifans of the tribal bodyguard. Their leader wore a leather fighting suit, unadorned as yet — an apprentice Clever Man.

As they came within talking distance, his gaze flicked over my fatigues and identified the State of Nation patches and mark-signs that allowed my presence. He assessed me coolly for a moment, then beckoned me away, raising his woomera as if to menace me with the invisible spear it was meant to carry.

I nodded acknowledgement and walked back along the beach.

When Tony met me around noon, the second flag had still not gone up. The body hung in its sling just below the surface of the gas, twinkling amid the eddies.

No vanities had come. All along the funerary beach, the Quni tribesmen waited in the hot sun. Even the fisherfolk on Full Moon and New Moon watched, their lines virtually untended. Only the lone didgeridoo player broke the silence, making the urgent monotone that one forgot to notice until the rhythm stopped for a few minutes. After 'first flag', they rotated players often, in the belief that a blessed player could summon the vanities.

Tony came up to me and smiled when he saw the other two flag-poles empty.

"Buyundar's not doing too well."

"It's been a long morning," I agreed, then added: "Hal is in there. No sign of his sister yet?"

"Not at the Gallery, Tom. I'd say she won't appear till after the Convocation. That fornication charge is probably not just a planned marriage breach. I think it was incest, a very serious crime with the Quni bloodlines diluting so quickly. It explains the agitation."

"Do you know the story of Pandora, Tony? Or do you prefer the myth of Jason and the Dragon's Teeth?"

Tony laughed, but before he could answer, a great shout went up from the beach, echoed by the eager fisherfolk on the Piers.

The red flag was rising on its pole; the annealing had begun. Buyunder was on his way.

That evening I had dinner with Bess and Tony on the terrace at Reginaldo's. It was a warm night and the lake was very still. The town Piers were two long fingers of light thrusting out into the darkness. The tribal precincts were part of that blackness too, with only an occasional ghost-light glimmering atop its post here and there to warn off evil spirits. Down on the Quni beach, the bonfire continued to burn, and the didgeridoo made its earnest drone as it had all day.

We sat under the paper lanterns, with one of Tony's linkboys on watch at the end of the terrace. Neither Bess nor Tony had been able to learn of Mita's whereabouts, which made me feel more than ever that Tony had her sequestered somewhere. I didn't raise the point; if that were the case then she was safe. With Tony's connections in the town, he would do a far better job of protecting her than I could. I only wished he would ease Bess's mind on the matter.

One subject I did raise when the Indonesian girl had gone was the existence of the Wagiri suits, but Tony put me off, saying he had given his word to protect his sources.

"What does it matter, Tom?" he said. "I could have had a suit made myself and given it to Hal. No-one's going to break open a Stone Man to see if he's wearing a legitimate tribal suit."

"They might, Tony. You're already driving them to extremes."

"I doubt it. The vanities are meant to be drawn by a worthy spirit, not by the mirrors. But tomorrow we'll see. I've lodged my claim for Hal, evidence and all..."

"What!"

"The Quni Prince has called a Convocation — with National observers. I'd like you to be one, Tom. You're impartial. Help me make a case for National law over tribal law. Let's re-define the Accord!"

"What if neither side backs down?"

"You said it yourself. I'll raise up an army of heretic Stone Men. My mute impassive Dragon's Teeth. I'll make the tribes so nervous about their anonymous mummies that the immersions will be cheapened, de-sanctified. Crater Lake will be tainted. I love the irony of it. The heretic outcast Wagiri coming back to help other outcasts claim their own. Finding vindication."

I smiled at his madness, at both the sophistication and the naivety of it. "They'll kill you first."

"Oh no, Tom. No. I'll have fifty paid soldiers here by morning. A carefully chosen bodyguard: Niuginians, Africans, Islanders — all with tribal kin of their own. The Ab'Os harm one of them and there'll be blood-feuds in Crater Lake for years. There'll be no end to it. Imagine: night raids on reliquaries, piers burnt, immersions spoilt. I'll have Crater Lake. We'll get it back."

"Not this way, Tony. Not like this."

"Yes, Tom. The only way that matters."

We parted then, Tony heading off to his villa, escorted by four armed linkboys. I sat watching the moths peppering the terrace lanterns with their deaths, then went to my room. I fell asleep with the lone didgeridoo calling to the waiting vanities in the lake, thinking of Hal and the Wagiri suits and the rebel Stone Men.

By late morning, Buyundar's progress into the spirit world was temporarily forgotten in the face of Convocation. There were at least four hundred Quni on the beach, plus large contingents from many other tribes. Tourists crowded the Crater Lake Piers and lined the promenade walls, three or four deep. National media teams recorded proceedings from the terraces of the closer hotels and palazzos; their reporters roamed the beach area as close as they dared, feeling nervous despite their mark-signs.

The sound of didgeridoos, rhythm sticks and bullroarers gave an imminence to the scene, an insistent fretful edge. Clever Men flashed in the hot sunlight, making an angry crackling dazzle that forced the camera crews to use filters. A hundred Unseen Spears guarded the door to the Quni reliquary — a token warning-off since Hal's mummy would be brought out, displayed, and — if it could happen (there was no knowing either way) — turned over to the National officers representing the Crater Lake authorities, who in turn represented Anthony Wessex, culprit, provocateur, Pandora or Narcissus or Loki in all this. Better yet, Tony Wessex the Trickster, the Joker, the most clever of Clever Men.

I felt there would be violence, that it could not be otherwise. I guessed many felt it, yet pretended the laws would be observed. But you cannot force a people to debase themselves with signed documents. The Quni Prince would not permit it, certainly his Clever Men could not.

But everyone *was* pretending, and that was strangest of all. The camera crews were there as if covering a routine Convocation; the tourists, dangling their lines into the gas or lining the stone walls and shading their eyes from the harsh play of light, were enjoying a unique diversion, nothing more. Many of them needed commentators and tour guides to tell them how important this was. It was bizarre to see.

Even Tony, standing with his solicitors and friends on Full Moon, was acting as if nothing could happen. I noticed the twitch of a smile at the corners of his mouth; he was enjoying his private joke too openly, I thought, or some other level of it. I appreciated then what a dangerous man he was.

The dronings stopped. Six tribesmen were carrying Hal's mummy from the reliquary, taking the heavy dark shape over to Tony's representatives. Everything was going to plan.

But suddenly there was a disturbance to my right, near the trespass signs and the steps leading down to the Quni beach. An Ab'O in street fatigues was rushing out to the assembled Clever

Men and the group handling the Stone Man.

It was Hal.

Cries went up, angry shouts. I jumped down onto the beach and rushed after him. I could hear Hal shouting at the Clever Men, while the Unseen Spears moved in from the reliquary doorway, woomeras raised.

Finally I was close enough to hear his words. He was pointing to the Stone Man on the bier, demanding that it be broken open — an unprecedented act, despite the talk about grave-robbers and reliquaries being defiled that were the ever-present rumours in Crater Lake. There was confusion, an uneasy hostile muttering from the massed tribesmen.

For a man working towards his own death, Hal's timing was perfect. He knew he would be dead at any moment, but that in the confusion he still had an advantage measured in seconds. He snatched a short iron club from his pocket and brought it down sharply on the head of the Stone Man, repeated the action four times.

The annealing cracked and fell away, revealing the face of his sister, Mita. There had been sacrilege, public humiliation, and now travesty: a suicide pact, a woman! A debasement of all Clever Men, all tribes.

Things happened quickly then. The Unseen Spears had their throwing sticks already raised; as a single man they flung their arms forward. The mind-spears killed Hal on the spot, faster than being sung, faster than any other mind-death I had seen, probably faster than a bullet or sword-thrust. He collapsed on the sand, almost on top of his sister in a last demonstration of their crime. Their other crime.

Tony's mercenaries received a signal and took a step forward to claim the body of the false Stone Man, but a thousand kitanas sang from their scabbards and the hired fighters stopped. Obviously Tony had briefed his men on this, for they did not press the claim. They turned and trudged back up the beach, followed by the news teams and the National observers.

The damage had been done. Tony would pursue his claim through the courts and would win. On paper. He might even get his pier, though knowing the tribes I doubted it. When I found him on Full Moon, he was smiling, safe among his group of friends and his legal people.

Cara Bressenden had made her catch on this momentous morning as well, a multiple enclosure, and was just then showing Tony the many-vanitied lump she was holding with both hands, announcing to all who would listen that her picture was enclosed in it.

"Prove it!" Tony said, then laughed too loudly, enjoying the poor woman's dilemma.

When the heiress had stalked off in a fury, he saw me and indicated the milling Ab'Os still in Convocation on the beach; the flashing Clever Men arguing in loud voices. "Well, Tom?"

"Nothing was learned here today, Tony. Not a damn thing! And you *are* a ghoul. You don't care what you use."

"This is important, Tom."

"Is it? Is it really? What the tribes and Nation hold between them is the illusion — the trappings — of something. A viable coexistence. A modus vivendi. All you have done is pierce that; drawn attention to how thin and how necessary — how inevitable — that illusion is. It'll take time to undo the harm, for them to search their laws and traditions to excuse the sacrilege, a handy myth, whatever, so they can live with themselves. We may lose Crater Lake for a while, or the Piers at least. It may take years, Tony, but things will settle again. Because we want them to."

And I turned and left Full Moon.

It took far less time than that. Tony's army of Stone Men never did appear to challenge the Accord.

When, two months later, I learned of Tony's death, I was not surprised. His corpse had been found in the Special Room of his gallery, the actual cause of death unknown. But his heart had been cut out afterwards, and when the package came in the mail and was brought to me in my room at the Gaza, I did not need to open it.

I only wondered how many of the creatures it had taken.

A Dragon
Between His Fingers

When he was 10, Shannon inherited a flawed Toby dough-beast from his uncle and raised a quarter-jack upon it.

The Toby was an old animal, its sides stained yellow from the baths, and feeble with age, but Shannon had tried and succeeded. For almost a minute, peering between the third and smallest fingers of his right hand, he had seen a quarter-jack, a dragon called a sirrush.

"It was the Dragon of Babylon," he told his father afterwards, who told Ben Scarbo, who later, years later, an hour out of Massi-Kallinga, told me because of the cargo we were carrying. After what had happened at Heart-and-Hand, discovering the extent of my gift as a sensitive, it was simply one more amazing thing to learn.

I went to where Shannon was tending the helm and, judging my time, carefully mentioned what Scarbo had told me.

"I never did it again," Shannon said, and seemed glad for the chance to discuss it. No doubt our cargo was on his mind.

"But once is enough, eh?"

"You never forget it, Tom. You never can. I saw my dragon. It made me seek out Dan."

Shannon told me how he and Dan had spent the following summer with the Toby, trying to raise dragons upon it, quarter-jacks and half-jacks, without success — two young boys working their hardest to develop the gift of dragon-sight. The dough-beast died soon afterwards, its DNA coded short-term.

Later, as a young man, Shannon had captained a sand-ship named *Sirrush* in memory of his dragon, a light, very fast 60-foot courier vessel which he lost to Timmsmen pirates on the desert outside Wani two years before he joined *Rynosseros*.

I knew of that *Sirrush* and how the relentless Timmsmen had driven her into the sand and taken her, but Scarbo's news of him raising aspect on the Toby as a boy had come as a surprise. However random and undeveloped it might be, Shannon had the gift. He was sighted.

My own reasons aside, it was just as well that I knew. We were ferrying three dough-beasts from the Massi-Kallinga vats out to You-Guess-What. They stood in long wooden pens on the deck, their four-legged, grey potato bodies motionless, little more than passive, omnivorous life-support mechanisms for their marvellous, overdeveloped hind-brains, with sufficient autonomic functions to ensure life but not even let them feed themselves properly. Without tribal jackmen aboard, young Hammon had the job of shovelling gruel into those slack maws twice a day. In return, the creatures gave some of us dragons — or, rather, could do so now that we were lucky enough to be this close to them.

Shannon had seen a sirrush, and in the time we had sailed together, we had never come close enough to a Toby for Shannon to betray his secret. Most sighted people discussed the gift if they had it, just as I had recently acknowledged my own sensitivity to the haldanes. But Shannon had lost a ship, a young man's first freehold vessel, a small charvi but his alone. The past intruded too much.

Now I knew about that past and was glad. Envious too. More curious than ever because mentalism was involved, something akin to what gave me my small part of the heroes.

Shannon had seen his sirrush. Scarbo had once seen a manticore, a billong and two of the higher bunyips. Stare as I might through one bifurcation of fingers after another, hand by hand, I saw only the blunt hippopotamus lumps of grey flesh mindlessly staring out at the desert as we ran along the Great Arunta Road. I had always accepted that I didn't have the gift, but knew as well that I would always need to prove that I didn't, that

I would keep trying, especially now that I had seen hero shapes, vital parts of the same universe of mind.

The cargo troubled Shannon. He kept to the poop, alert for raiders even when it wasn't his watch. Timms and his band of highwaymen would do anything to secure newly-made dough-beasts to sell back to the Ab'Os for their corroborees. They would even take on an armed and escorted ship like *Rynosseros* and a fighting crew to get such a prize. Full-jack dough-beasts took years to produce, and these three were primes, just the thing to touch our reptilian memories and bring forth Quetzalcoatl, the Plumed Serpent of the Aztecs, or Kukulcan of the Mayans, or Tiamat, the Chiaos and Lungs, or the great Rainbow Serpent itself.

We all felt Timms would try, or one of his highwayman colleagues, The Eagle Cleland Buchanan or the notorious Captain Ha-Ha. That is why we ran in a W battle formation with escorts — two 80-foot tribal sand-ships ahead, *Dancing Man* and *Attapa*, and two 90-foot National vessels behind, *Bellona* under Grey Ridley, and Radkin's *Ozymandis*. The hot late-morning sky was bright with our kites straining out ahead on taut cables, a dry blistering tailwind keeping up hopes for a three-hour journey.

I finished helping Scarbo trim a lazy parafoil, then returned to the poop, partly to check the instruments but also to see how Shannon was faring.

"You could have laid over, Rob," I said, mentioning it again.

Shannon's eyes were focused on the desert ahead. There was strong emotion in them, possibly anger, relief as well, I hoped.

"I'm okay, Tom. Really. It gives me a chance to practise. Three primes. I'm bound to see something." And he smiled.

"Good. Teach me how."

"In a way, you're lucky you don't see them. You've heard Ben. Once you do, you've always got a hand stuck in front of your face when a Toby's around. You keep hoping. Ben knew about it; I don't know how long I could've kept it from the rest of you. Not with this." He nodded to where the pens were.

"I envy you all the same."

"No, it's a mixed blessing, seeing the dragons. You love them because you know them somehow, like the recognition you felt around Anna Kemp. They're atavisms. What I saw as a boy was that beautiful, that familiar. Dan felt the same. It was like a drug — you had to keep doing it. Real but not real. We've left that behind."

"Well, after Heart-and-Hand it's like wetting your finger and trying to make a wine-glass sing. I have to keep trying too now. I'd like to see a sirrush." Because it brought me close to something crucial, I didn't need to add.

"Do what I used to do. Go down to the pens and stand up close. That's how Dan saw his first quarter-jack, saw his full-jack basilisk."

"The one that almost killed him? Ben mentioned that too."

"It was after our Toby died. My uncle took us to the vats. Dan tried to raise aspect while our backs were turned. He said he saw a basilisk. He cried it out to us before his mind said to die. My uncle told me that was how the basilisk template worked. Death-look. Dan was lucky. He was hospitalized for months. But it changed him; he was never the same."

"I'll go find a sirrush," I said.

Shannon smiled. "Call me if you do."

I saw nothing, of course. Just the blunt heads, the low thick bodies. And crouching there on the deck before the pens, I had the usual mix of doubts and acceptance, felt more urgency and fascination now after what had happened at Arredeni's tower and with Anna at Twilight Beach, but still had an underlying sense that it couldn't be as compelling as Shannon described.

The rationale wasn't hard to accept at all. It was easy to concede that our evolution from reptiles into mammals had left us with powerful reptilian memories, that as a race humanity had always had a predilection for dragons. They were a fundamental part of its race consciousness.

It was nothing as simple as remembering Tyrannosaurus Rex. That deep psychic stratum was filtered through the subconscious, through symbols and imagination, through analogs, cultural correlatives, mammalian taint and projection. It was diluted, distorted, but it was there — amplified and focused out of the mammalian bodyfield by the dough-beasts, given as a coherent signal back from their hypertrophied hind-brains, perceived by the receiving human mind through the ridiculously-simple, Kirlian intensifying hand-lattice.

At last, the human race could see its dragons, its reptile beginnings, its unhuman forbears. The deepest, most primordial archetypes had forms at last, recognizable, familiar forms. When the tampering from other conditioning strata was complete, there was a bestiary to encompass our wildest dreams, to explain our deepest fears — so the sighted ones assured the rest of us. A heraldry for the Ab'O Princes and the world at large, though all the exported Tobys were neuters and had short-term genetic codings. Thus the Ab'Os kept the monopoly, sold dragons to the world.

But like the wine-glass singing, like my encounter with the haldanes, however tenuous, what I knew and what I felt were at odds. I kept seeing the Tobys as dream amplifiers, as overrated man-made image transmitters and nothing more, as something of a hoax. Though it didn't look like it, there was probably reptile DNA in their genetic make-up, hence the bias towards dragonism. A lot of National scientists believed that, though they had never had Shannon's luck — a geneticist uncle, accepted by the tribal makens, who had once brought home a flawed dough-beast instead of destroying it outright.

"No luck?"

I looked up to see Shannon standing over me. He had been relieved at the helm by Strengi.

"Not a scale, Rob. You?"

"Not a scale."

We walked together back to the quarterdeck and shared the watch with Strengi, making ship-talk and watching the desert and the escort fleet spread out across the Road around us.

It was doubly hard for Shannon. Not only were the dough-beasts there, in plain sight or back under the tarpaulins draped over the cages to keep off the sun, but we were watching for Timms, the one who had taken *Sirrush*. Shannon had often told us of his fateful meeting with the brigand, of how Timms, in his air-cooled, augmented, bronze and leather talos suit, eyes burning through the eye-slit of his great helmet, had boarded

Sirrush and announced that he would spare the crew, even though they had defied him and tried to flee.

I would have defied him too.

I imagined losing my own ship to him, having her taken from me to be used as a pirate vessel or a blockade runner in the wars between the Princes. My thoughts went back to the ship-lotteries at Cyrimiri, to the day I had won *Rynosseros* and first saw the hull being lifted out of the storage cradle by the moving gantry, then carried to the chandler's yard where I had an old battered travel platform rented from Captain Albert and a dozen cast-off kites borrowed from Red Lucas. I remembered her being lowered to the housing and locked to the table, getting wheels again, legs for the desert Roads. It led me back to Rob's loss in a way that kept me silent, that made me watch for Timms and hope — for reasons other than the safety of our cargo — that he wouldn't come. But that he would as well.

It was an added difficulty having the Emmened mission commander aboard *Rynosseros* for this first part of the journey, here to ensure that the beasts reached his people safely.

Sos Wain Chrisos stood at the bow, a short, self-confident Ab'O in dark fighting leathers who seemed completely unaware that his strength of will translated as arrogance. I had avoided him since our disagreement over mission strategies at Massi-Kallinga, but now I went forward to make my peace with the man.

"Ah, Captain Tom! Please!" he said, and seemed conciliatory enough. "We are making good time."

"We are indeed, Chrisos," I said, joining him at the rail.

"You still fear this highwayman?"

"Timms is clever. These Tobys are worth the Emmened fleet at least."

"You know my views, Captain. We must not honour these brigands too much."

I went to answer but decided against it. If the stories were true, Chrisos held his position by luck rather than skill. In a recent engagement on the Air, in the midst of smokescreen warfare, his vessel had managed to ram the flagship of the enemy Prince, so ending the combat in his Prince's favour; more recently he had routed a Timmsmen 40-footer near Sollellen. He was no doubt feeling invincible. I changed the subject.

"Has Timms been much of a burden to your people?"

"Not since The Eagle Buchanan was taken by Kurdaitcha outside Cresa."

The news surprised me.

"They took Buchanan?" I thought of the ancient Dreamtime stories, of Ab'O assassins moving silently in their Kurdaitcha shoes of emu feathers. The world had not changed that much.

"We got them all," Chrisos said, as if he'd had a part in it. "Their jackmen came to us, but no Tobys. All the brigands have jackmen these days."

I watched the desert, my eyes half-shut against the glare.

"I saw you by the cages," Chrisos said after a while, still trying to ease things between us. "Do you see the dragons?"

"No. Shannon and Scarbo do. Not me."

"I am sorry. I knew you were a sensitive in other ways. They are beautiful beyond words. Our makens have discovered the secret mainsprings of our past."

There was no arguing with that, but still I felt something worrying, something unwholesome in how the Ab'Os — and sighted Nationals too — made use of that knowledge, took the chances they did.

"You can't go backwards, Chrisos," I said, and hated how envious and petty I sounded, as non-sighted people always did, aware too of my hypocrisy.

The Ab'O smiled. "But it is not backwards. The dragons are still there for us. For whatever reasons, they are there to be brought out and used."

I could think of nothing more to say, aware that I was still sorting my experiences, that by accepting the haldanes I too had gone backwards. And Chrisos was right. Despite the risks, in spite of the danger posed by some of the manifestations, the dragons brought harmony, healed the mind, eased something in the human spirit. Too many people said that they did.

The Ab'O makens had given new meaning to all our pieces of dragon lore: to St George fighting his own powerfully projected dragon dream in the North African desert; to Sigurd, Beowulf and Herakles defeating theirs; others ranged against the nagas and wyverns of the mind, the ladons, salamanders, chimeras and amphisbaenas.

A dough-beast could accommodate many different dragon vectors at the same time, quarter-jacks and half-jacks, depending on how many individuals were seeking. But with full-jack resolution, the manifestation was so strong, so concentrated, that all who sought aspect saw the same dragon — and risked the same consequences of that powerful summoning. A skilled jackman working with a prime could even determine which dragon he sought, imposing a template on the Toby that other sighted ones shared and few could override.

Such a delightful irony — the dragon fighters themselves *causing* the dragons, often the innate amplifiers, triggering dragon memory, sharing it at a mass level, subduing it again with mass hallucination. Or being the foil for some local shaman who could control his people by calling up a genetic echo of Allosaurus, an imperfectly-conceived Ankylosaur, or a blundering, harmless Steg. The effect was the same; the legends grew. Set into its rituals, the wild talent meant a viable and potent power-base. So what if the creatures were distorted beyond all sense of herpetological truth — the gryphons, tengus and manticores — imagination and inventive nightmare intruding on the memory to sway the form?

The power was always there. Dragons meant power. The display of them healed, lulled, resolved something in the mammal breast which evolution had not quite taken from it.

Yes, it was strange what the mammal mind did to that race memory, what it had added to the original. I had less cause to fear some dim, impossibly remote, infinitessimally tenuous connection with Tyrannosaurus Rex than the twisted, mind-enhanced residues being raised through the nearly mindless Tobys. Shannon's sirrush, summoned and shaped by the mammal mind, might kill a sighted person with dragon-shock, while its ancient dinosaur ancestors might have been scavengers and egg-stealers, coelurosaurs like Struthiomimus and Compsognathus, possibly more afraid of someone like Chrisos than he would ever need be of them.

I pretended to watch for Timms, then remembered from stories

I'd heard that he too was powerfully dragon-sighted. I made an excuse to Chrisos and returned to the helm.

Like the other great pirates who survived the continual Ab'O hunts, Timms knew how to use tribal law against the likes of Chrisos — knew exactly when to strike.

We lost the National vessels at the border of You-Guess-What because of the ruling that only a handful of approved State of Nation charvis could cross tribal land. The moment we went to turn off the Great Arunta Road on to Lateral 83, *Bellona* and *Ozymandis* veered off, began to alter their course for the coast. It was madness, but Chrisos would not hear of suspending tribal law even for this.

As a tactical manoeuvre, now that we were three instead of five, we stopped long enough to move the Tobys into the storage bay of *Dancing Man*, and left the empty pens, swathed under their tarpaulins, on the deck of *Rynosseros*. It took ten minutes longer than we rehearsed, but Chrisos felt it added to our chances. When that was done, he announced the next part of his plan.

"Now we separate. They cannot cover three elements."

"Chrisos, no! This..."

"Captain Tom, our Emmened comsat will track *Rynosseros*. You will be covered by laser all the way. Timms will read that. It will confirm suspicions that the Tobys are still with you."

"Timms has insulated hulls."

"Would he dare risk random strikes before and aft? I doubt it. Your ship will be safe."

"We can travel as three and be covered the same way, Chrisos. Why take the risk?"

But I knew the reason. There was a high-captain vacancy among the Emmened. Chrisos wanted to bring the Tobys in alone.

"Your sat will track *Rynosseros*?" I asked him, needing to be sure.

"The program is already set. Arman and Bria will go with you and do the confirmations."

"Then I'll come with you." I surprised myself saying it.

"Captain..."

"My assignment too, Chrisos. I'm accountable to Council on

this."

"Very well. Let us proceed."

Shannon came with me aboard *Dancing Man*, wanting to stay with the Tobys too, to practise dragons, he said. He didn't ask my reasons; he had been with me at Heart-and-Hand, had witnessed mind-war, its external part, had heard Anna talk afterwards. Dragonism belonged to the same universe of mind. He knew I was hoping it might reveal something, anything, about my Madhouse images, my new-found role as sensitive.

At Chrisos' signal, the three ships broke formation, *Attapa* heading off into the southwest on a little-used tribal Road, *Rynosseros* continuing on the Lateral to the tribal capital, and *Dancing Man* steering a course into the northwestern desert.

I felt the whole manoeuvre was obvious, preferring battle formation to decoys, but Sos Wain Chrisos had the responsibility now. He ran *Dancing Man* at top speed, fully kited and powered as well, while Shannon and I hid below with the Ab'O fighting crew and the Tobys.

It was in the rocking, musty gloom of the storage bay that Shannon saw his next dragon.

There was very little to do waiting there, so he was making the lattice as a way of passing time, going from one beast to the next, working down his hands as he crouched on the deck.

The Ab'O warriors didn't like it. Tribal law meant that they could not seek aspect or share it unless they had permission. But Shannon was a privileged guest. The tribesmen averted their gazes, muttering now and then and keeping watch through the four sand-scoured ports.

"Tom!" Shannon said, and I knew at once what was happening. He was peering between the middle finger and ring finger of his right hand at the dough-beast on the end, a Toby with a dark blemish on one shoulder. The creature stood very still, its dim eyes glazed, its wide toothless mouth fixed in a stupid, cartoon grin.

Shannon continued staring, so I knew there was no dragon-shock involved, no basilisk-stare, sandrake-sting or fire-vector to fear. Before I knew what I was doing, I found myself working through my hands too, first the left, then the right, with no luck. I saw one Ab'O moving his fingers at his side, fighting the impulse to try as well.

"What is it?" I asked.

"I think — it's manticore! Or billong! No! Tiamat! A tiamat!"

The Ab'Os muttered enviously. Most of them could access the dragons, wanted more than anything to do so whenever aspect was raised. But they dared not. Sos Wain Chrisos had a Clever Man aboard, constantly alert for such things as haldanes and mind-fields. Transgressors would be caught and punished.

"Oh!" Shannon cried, awed by the beauty of what he was seeing.

His rapture was short-lived. Shouts came from above; the ship's bell rang out over the roar of the wheels.

"Timmsmen! Timmsmen!" came the cry.

I steadied Shannon as he emerged from trance, helped him stand, then followed the tribesmen up on deck where I used my pocket glass to scan the raiders.

Four ships were coming at us, low fast ships, lighter than *Dancing Man*, insulated hulls running under drab battle-kites. The one in the lead was Timms' flagship, *Sorcerer*, with Timms himself standing in the bow, a powerful bronze figure with his helmet tipped back and a fierce gravure fear-face underneath hiding his real features. That was the sight which had made so many captains surrender their ships.

But Shannon had recognized the vessel second in formation, the one flying the Armoured Head pennon that was Timms' sign.

"It's *Sirrush!*" he cried in astonishment. "Tom, they've got *Sirrush* there! The one flying the Iron Ned! I knew they'd keep her."

"Easy, Rob," I said.

"But she's intact! They didn't destroy her!"

Two warriors looked round to see what the outcry was, then returned their attention to the approaching raiders. Chrisos already had death-lamps aloft and lenses fitted, trying to catch the sun. His kitesmen were bringing hot-pots, fighting kites and harpoons to the deck, preparing land-anchors and hedgehogs.

We ran to help, though I knew this had to be a nightmare for Shannon — preparing to make war on his own vessel. As it turned out he need not have worried. Timms had prepared this too well.

Before we could use our weapons, three harpoons struck the hull, their cables fastened to land-anchors thrown from the decks of the Timmsmen ships. When the first anchor grabbed, the momentum of *Dancing Man* tore the harpoon's barbed head out of the stern assembly. The vessel slowed noticeably. As it gathered speed again, the other hooks took hold. With a mighty wrench which threw us to the deck, *Dancing Man* jerked about savagely on its pedestal. Drive lines snapped; emergency overrides in the central pin slowly locked the wheels. The vessel careened wildly, nearly toppled, righted itself by the barest good fortune. At the same time, spring-shot boomerangs spun into the kite-lines, severing some, fouling the rest and dragging the canopy to the desert.

And that was it. The raider ships rolled up to us and stopped. A call to surrender came through a loud-hailer, but Sos Wain Chrisos and his men were obliged to fight. They did so bravely and uselessly, falling man by man first to snaphaunce fire, deck-lenses and spears, finally swordplay.

Shannon and I had no such obligation. We kept our hands away from our weapons and handed over our blades willingly when the raiders swarmed aboard. We were led back to *Sorcerer*, where Shannon had his second meeting with Timms and I had my first.

The desert highwaymen were consciously romantic figures who often worked carefully at their images, using media consultants, psychologists, getting advice from the network people in the coastal cities, secretly supported by foreign sponsors.

Timms was very successful at this. I had heard of captains who wound down their kites at the first glimpse of his Iron Ned, preferring to lose cargoes and possibly their ships rather than oppose him.

I understood why this was, having seen him standing in the bow of *Sorcerer*, looking across at us. The man on the quarterdeck was of medium build, though the talos battle-suit made him look taller and more massive — the gleaming bronze plates sewn to leather, the joints, clasps and armatures concealed under smooth couters, pauldrons and poleyns. So cunningly was the armour made that he did indeed resemble a man of bronze, an idealized Ned figure, though now both parts of his double mask were tipped back. The fearsome bronze morion with the Ned eye-slit was open as before, but now the heavily-circuited gravure fear-face underneath was split as well, revealing suntanned cheeks and forehead, a strong jaw and craggy brows over deep-set blue eyes.

Shannon cried out when he saw that rugged face.

"Dan! You! My God! You took my ship! You!"

The highwaymen around us raised their weapons. Timms' heavy brows sank into a frown, but one of humorous concern, not anger.

"Your ship, Rob?"

"Mine, damn you, yes! Mine!" Shannon was trembling with rage, from sheer astonishment.

"I repaired her, Rob. She's a fine vessel. I'm glad to have her."

"For God's sake, Dan! It's me! You took her from me!"

"Rasselou, take Captain Shannon down to the commons and confine him. He has had a nasty shock."

"Why, Dan? Why? You knew it was me that day! You knew!"

"Which is why you are alive now, Rob. Take him!"

The guards led Shannon away.

"Tom Rynosseros!" Timms said then, turning to me. "I am honoured to meet you, sir! And most surprised to find you on this ship. Rob doesn't understand destiny. He was meant to bring *Sirrush* to me."

"You live dangerously, Timms."

"I bow to expedience as we all do. I earn a living. I like being a dealer in dragons."

"It looks good for your legend, I suppose."

"Careful, Captain." Some of the humour left his face. "My men already call me The Basilisk." And he laughed.

I suddenly understood what the fear-face was meant to represent.

"You murdered those men..."

"No!" The humour vanished altogether. "They knew my code. Chrisos chose to fight. He had that choice."

"You knew the Emmened plan."

"What plan?" Timms laughed. The tanned face softened again. "But yes. I have agents."

"Then..."

"*Rynosseros* is safe, yes. She got through. We knew Chrisos had the Tobys."

I felt deep relief, thought again of how it had to be for Shannon.

"What happens to us?"

"I have no quarrel with you. I create no vendettas with Nation. You were right to surrender. Co-operate now and you go free, of course."

"When?"

"We go to rendezvous with Bunna, spokesman and head Clever Man for the Emmened. We transact business. When that is done, you go with Bunna and the Tobys back to *Rynosseros*, then return to the coast."

"What about *Sirrush*?"

"What about *Sirrush*, Captain? Talk sense! You expect me to give her up? Rob would not like the changes I have made to her."

"I want..."

"I don't care what you want!" Timms cried. "Enough! We go. Rasselou, confine Captain Tyson on the deck with his friend."

And with that he sealed the fearsome gravure face, brought down the great Ned helmet of the talos and became the gleaming legend of himself.

I was taken down to the commons and locked into leg-stocks next to Shannon. He had recovered from his initial surprise but did not take his eyes from the figure on the quarterdeck.

"Tom, I've always believed we have to value our continuities, the things we carry with us. Friends, family, confidences, things like that. Dan was my best friend. I loved him, probably more in my recollections of him down the years than I ever did at the time. We were close, Tom, both sighted. We shared a great adventure, had the old Toby to work with. How many people get a chance like that?"

"Very few, Rob."

"I'm too naive, aren't I? Too trusting?"

"I'm the last one to ask."

"But he took *my* ship! Innocent men's lives! He was never like that."

"Perhaps the basilisk-shock changed him. Too much dragonism might..."

"But my ship, Tom! Don't you see? It's like me taking *Rynosseros* from you. I couldn't do it. He knew it was me then. He kept his helmet closed."

The Timmsmen fleet sailed north until we reached the border of You-Guess-What and were no longer on tribal land. We approached a vast dry lake, an empty glaring strand that stretched almost to the horizon and shimmered in the afternoon sun. Timms sent up a lookout on a Cody man-lifter, who signalled back that a solitary Emmened charvi was waiting at the lake's centre.

Satisfied, Timms left his lookout in the sky and took his four raider-ships down onto the lake, having them stop 500 metres from the Emmened vessel, close to a low rise of sand with a crown of broken stones at the crest. It seemed to be the only natural feature marking this desolation.

The Tobys were led out onto the rise so the Ab'Os could see them and tethered under makeshift awnings, then fed and watered by a junior jackman, a young Niuginian from Timms' crew. The beasts blinked stupidly in the heat and looked none the worse for all that had happened.

A wooden Toby pen was brought from the hold of *Sorcerer*, carried to the rise and placed near the dough-beasts. Shannon and I were locked in it. We stood in the shade of the tarpaulin and watched the transactions.

The silence on the lake was nearly absolute, broken only by the snuffling of a Toby or a quiet word from one jackman to another.

Ten minutes went by, then shimmering indistinct shapes moved out from the Emmened ship. Some came ahead of the rest, heat-distorted figures, spectral and bonelike, with two others like columns of light moving behind them across the intervening ground. They resolved into four djellaba-shrouded Ab'Os, tribal jackmen, and two Clever Men in their ceremonial suits of mirrored leather. A second group were warriors carrying spears, boomerangs and nulla-nullas, a ritual guard which stopped midway and squatted on the sand.

The two Clever Men came to within several metres of Timms and stopped, two pillars of dazzling light.

It was almost like a carefully rehearsed ritual dance, a pavane. The four Ab'O jackmen came forward, their faces visible now, painted for corroboree with the lines that represented stylized hand-lattice. Timms stood his ground at the foot of the rise, a shining golden figure carrying a heavy Bok laser. His helmet was closed; we could hear the suit's cooling unit working away. Highwaymen were drawn up about him, while his own jackmen, all Niuginians, were close by the tethered Tobys, already carefully controlling which dragons could be coded from their dull minds, thereby preventing Bunna's jackmen from raising aspect first.

When the Ab'O jackmen were close enough and did lock in, their fingers splayed out stiffly in front of their eyes, they saw full-jack basilisk, sandrake and a fiery billong. They screamed and broke trance, one near death from basilisk-glance, two others in fire-shock from the billong's breath. Only one survived mentally unharmed, and he was badly shaken.

The Clever Men knew then that they were helpless. Timms had skilled jackmen, and their own mental powers were effective only against other Ab'O mystics and those rare Nationals — myself included now — who could in some way access the haldanes. These renegade jackmen were not susceptible to mind-fighting, and the ritual guard was outnumbered and less well-armed.

The bargaining would go ahead as arranged.

Timms approached the Ab'O party, a forbidding sight in his bronze talos armour.

"You want the Tobys?" he said. "You want these primes?"

One Clever Man stepped forward, a tall old Ab'O named Bunna, his calm dark face framed with tufts of grey hair above the dazzle. He didn't answer the highwayman but glanced over at the Tobys tethered on the rise, the beasts he was buying twice over.

"Well, Bunna?" Timms said, the hot sun gleaming off his bright talos shoulders.

"Kurdaitcha will come for you, Timms," the Ab'O said. "No chance now."

"Forget your Kurdaitcha, Bunna. We've got dragons and weapons. We've got hi-tech and good fast ships."

"You go too far. The tribes will work together to get you."

Timms laughed. "I doubt it. We're part of a system, you and I. When you lose, someone else gains. It won't happen."

"The time is coming. Our Kurdaitcha assassins don their feathered shoes. You will not hear; you will not know."

"Do you want the Tobys or not?"

Bunna nodded once. He knew when to count his losses. He knew, too, that Timms would work the northern and western deserts after this — that he had fast, non-metal, insulated ships, hard to read from tribal satellites. Though that was nothing to guide Timms' actions. He was on a hundred death-lists already.

"Good," Timms said. "You can give oaths for your Prince and tribe?"

Again Bunna nodded.

"Then we can begin. We shall do it beast by beast, for oaths, money, and other special considerations. *Sirrush* will then ferry them out to your ship."

So the bargaining began — first, pledges against vendetta in exchange for one dough-beast. The voices carried across the salt to where Shannon and I sat at the cage-front observing it all.

It was a strange scene in the glare and terrible heat, quite dreamlike. A man of gleaming bronze spoke with two creatures of dazzling quicksilver, while other white-shrouded figures lay about them in dragon-shock, with a clot of darker shapes out on the lake — the Ab'O guard — and beyond them the solitary Emmened ship, barely visible, shimmering in the heat like spun glass.

In the foreground, adjacent to our cage, the softly-snuffling Tobys stood under their awnings, quietly stirring now and then, with Timms' jackmen close by. These men had relaxed aspect now that Bunna's jackmen were wounded, and had moved down the rise a short way to be nearer their chief. To the side, the four raider ships waited, their parafoils idle in the overheated air, a single spider-line leading to the Cody man-lifter stirring in the thermals high overhead, its tiny rider alert for Emmened vendetta ships.

Shannon and I sat at the front of our cage, grateful for the tarpaulin, trying to hear each word.

With each beast bought, Timms signalled a jackman who ran back up the slope, freed a Toby from tether, and led it across to the open storage bay of *Sirrush*. It was a slow curious process, one of Timms' own rituals.

Finally, only one beast stood under the awning, the one with the dark shoulder mark. The business was almost over.

Then I noticed that Shannon was making the lattice, lifting a hand slowly in front of his eyes. The remaining Toby felt the mind-field and looked at us, entranced. It snuffled, then stood very still.

"I'm getting it!" Shannon said, very quietly.

I said nothing, torn between urging him on and telling him it would do no good.

The Toby stood motionless, its blank expression even more comical now that a human mind was directing thoughts at it.

Timms' jackmen were good. Whether augmented with implants or just highly attuned to any signs of dragonism, they sensed the Toby being used. The two still on the rise with us turned about, dropped into the crouch, their hands up before them making the lattice. The others came running back from *Sirrush* to join their comrades.

I saw their eyes widen, their looks of astonishment. Next to me, Shannon sat huddled, staring at the Toby between the first and second fingers of his left hand, beads of perspiration glistening on his brow.

"Quarter-jack!" he said.

"Which one?" I asked, daring to interrupt, fearing dragon-shock and what it might do to him, my own hands spread uselessly in front of my face.

Shannon didn't answer. He concentrated on the Toby, working at aspect.

The jackmen down the slope didn't know whether to keep their ground or flee. One looked quickly about him, at the Tobys being loaded on to *Sirrush*, but it was already too late to use them and they were too far away for any coherent result.

"Half-jack!" Shannon cried. "God! It's half-jack! It is!"

He had more than a flawed, worn-out animal to use now. The Toby with the blemish was a prime, the best the vats could produce. Even I could feel the coiling darkness of a mind-field, a chilling, terrifying wash of occlusion and dragon-sense, but without the images, without the deadly stigmata. What were they seeing?

"Which?" I cried. "Sirrush?"

"My God!" Shannon cried in turn. "My God! Full-jack!"

The jackmen fell dead where they stood. The rest of the Timmsmen heard their death-cries and went for their weapons. Timms left the Ab'Os and began to raise a hand-lattice, driven as all poor sighted human mammals were to see our dragon forbears, despite the cost.

But the highwayman stopped himself. He knew it would be beautiful beyond description and that it would probably kill him. A few of the others tried though: one Timmsman screamed and fell, another collapsed without a sound, a third curled up into a foetal position at his leader's feet.

"Kurdaitcha!" he managed to say, then began groaning softly.

Held by their disciplines, the Clever Men kept themselves steady. Their fingers did not even twitch.

Timms showed indecision now. He was no doubt recalling Bunna's words earlier. The compulsion to look had to be greater than ever, pouring over him from the Toby, urging him to share the vision it carried.

"Which one?" he cried, raising his Bok laser. "Tell and I'll spare you!"

But Shannon did not tell him, though our lives were in the balance.

"I'll destroy your ship! I'll burn *Sirrush*!"

Shannon stared at the Toby, not turning away for an instant.

Perhaps he could not; perhaps he chose between dragons; perhaps he knew exactly what he was doing.

"Tell me!" Timms screamed, and fired his Bok laser at *Sirrush*. The hull flared, burst open, burned on its travel platform. Crewmen and one of the Tobys died in a gout of flame.

"Tell me!"

"Full-jack!" I cried, blind to dragons, trusting what it meant to the sighted ones. "You hear that, Timms? How many full-jacks have you seen?"

Timms could not hold back any longer. He had to look, had to know. He brought a hand up in front of his eye-slit.

And he screamed as the others had, and he died, his eyes hidden from me by the great helmet, but no doubt as full of terror and wonderment as those of his jackmen. For a moment his armoured suit held him erect, then he collapsed heavily onto the sand, the cooling unit still working away.

Shannon fell to the sand as well, sobbing, trembling with exhaustion. Then he looked up and saw the smouldering ruin of his old ship. Tears ran down his cheeks.

"He killed *Sirrush*. He took her from me again."

"We can't go backwards, Rob. You have *Rynosseros* now. Good mammal name that. Better."

Shannon looked at me blankly for a second, then laughed through his tears.

The warriors were running in from the lake. Beyond them, out of the haze, came the hidden Emmened fleet, summoned from the lake's far side by com or sat transmission. Bunna came up the slope to us.

"Which one, jackman?" he asked. "Which one?"

"Quetzalcoatl," Shannon told him. "The Plumed Serpent."

"The Rainbow Serpent!" Bunna said.

"No," Shannon replied. "Quetzalcoatl. Aztec."

"Same thing. It's what we told him."

"It is?" I said, as he opened the cage for us.

"Yes," Bunna replied. "Feathered assassin. Kurdaitcha!"

Djinn of Anjoulis

djinn: (Moslem legend) A supernatural being that can take human or animal form.

gin: (Australian derogatory slang) An aboriginal woman.

Compared to the great souks in the Byzantine Quarter of Twilight Beach, the humble bazaar of the one-time Ghantown, Anjoulis, was like a fall from paradise, a little piece of the world gone wrong.

I stood at the edge of the wide dusty square, looking across at the solitary sheet-iron tower of the makeshift mosque and, laid out before that, the gathering of local merchants in their neat rows.

The morning sun was still low; the hour couldn't be much past 0800, but the day's heat was already there. The blue was leaching out of the sky, turning it into a pale phantom of itself, and a fitful morning wind sent sudden spirals of dust dancing across the open ground where the vendors displayed their meagre stacks of produce and other modest wares.

I roamed the aisles, ignoring the restless flurries, accepting that this was what you did when a sheared drive pin and damaged travel platform left you temporarily stranded in such a place. You took what Fate handed you; it was the only reality after all.

At least it had been Anjoulis and not Daralgo or Khomri right at the desert's edge. Anjoulis might only be an outpost town of forty or so mostly ramshackle buildings, but as two camel routes met here, and one reasonably well-used Road brought the occasional charvolant, it had both a com station and a combination chandlery-shipyard.

The merchants waited on their mats, embroidered rugs and low carved stools, some peering out from under parasols and faded awnings, and appraised what few customers there already were. Later in the day, a coincidence almost as momentous as a guide pin shearing off and stranding *Rynosseros*, the weekly passenger charvi, *Perenty*, would arrive with its handful of tourists and Nationals. This early turn-out was for them.

I entered the third aisle, moving away from the row of chatter-poles marking out the market's otherwise empty western edge. The wind set them clacking, making the small pieces of lacquered wood and bone dance and rattle on their cords. On one side a mosque, on the other that incomprehensible array, with a few shacks and stuccoed mud-brick buildings to give the square a claim to such a name.

Yes, Anjoulis did seem like a certain fall from grace just then, with a destination to reach and a mission to complete, no time for this but time snatched away by circumstance regardless.

I was halfway across the square when the sun lifted clear of the iron tower and stole the last of the shade. The vendors sat like stones in the dancing wind.

Shading my eyes from the glare, I moved on, stopping before a local kitemaker, with half an idea of buying a decorated town-kite for a souvenir. The bearded vendor in his dark-green robe launched into a half-hearted spiel, but *Perenty* had not yet arrived and his ship-worthy stock was way overpriced.

I moved on, paused again several metres later when I found a lamp-seller sitting shrouded and alone on her rug at the end of the aisle, a little apart from the others, with twenty or so down-graded metic lamps arranged about her like kiteless sand-ships.

Aladdin lamps, I immediately thought. Arabian Nights. Scheherazade telling her famous tales to the Sultan Schariar, finally winning his heart. Those small footed vessels did indeed look like tiny charvolants, bereft of travel platforms as *Rynosseros* was for a time.

The woman noted my interest and drew back the front of her hood, showing me a surprisingly young and unexpectedly dark face, an unlikely face, not the usual classic lines of haldane Ab'O but the ancient Koori lines, the fuller lips, wider nose, the distinctive full cheekbones and low forehead, the black deepset eyes. Too strange and heavy-featured to be beautiful, but a compelling face.

I stared a few seconds too long.

"Revenant," she explained, lips drawing back to show startling white teeth, dramatic contrast to the blackness of the skin. "Grown from trace DNA. Old remains. Buy a metic lamp, Captain?"

Her voice had the lilt of a dialect that had been worked carefully to a neutral marketplace patois. It was a deep rich contralto, calm and educated, the pronunciation exact. The eyes held me to each word.

"A lamp? Perhaps later. My ship is damaged and I'm waiting for com to open."

I turned away, bypassed the remaining aisles and headed straight for the two-storey building with the town's radio dish, though all the way I kept thinking of the startling sight in the square.

A revenant — and revealing herself that way.

It took more than four hours to make the call to Angel Bay, to locate Siras and patiently explain how there would be at least a day lost. Four long maddening hours for a six-minute call: to get my turn with the harried operator, to wait while she aligned the dish and found a satellite to take us. So much for progress.

At 1240, irritable and tired, I headed back to the shipyard at the other end of the town.

It had become a hot wild day in Anjoulis. The sky was streaked with long lines of cirrus, many with their tails kicked into distinctive wisps. The hot gusty wind that blew out of the west had the makings of our demon wind, the larrikin, the wind no-one can hold. There were doors banging, sheets of iron and fibreglass lifting on rooftops, the constant rattling song of the chatter-poles bordering the square. On the roof of the com centre, the dish and its guy-lines made a steady keening sound.

The vendors still kept to their lines in the dust, making a strange ideogram in the blustery afternoon.

I entered one aisle, then another, passed the kiteseller, found myself standing before the revenant woman again, her robed form surrounded by the tiny fleet of lamps.

The strong voice came to me through the gusts. "Sit, Captain. Please. Sit."

The honorific was general courtesy in the souks, though she may have interpreted the insignia on my fatigues correctly. Any ship arrival was an event; perhaps she even knew the patches.

I remained standing a moment longer, then settled myself on the spot indicated by one dark outstretched hand.

The assortment of old brass and iron prophecy lamps were laid out between us, inescapably portentous with their fortune-telling genies waiting within, locked away in the elaborate circuit mats.

Many were plain and battered, with dented lips and turned handles; some were mysteriously patterned with scrollwork and runic ciphers; a few still bore pedigree decals or brand-names in low-relief. Almost all shone dully in the sunlight; one or two kept a dead metal finish unmoved by the sun, as lustreless as the skin of the young woman herself; two gleamed with highlights on their intricately annealed surfaces.

More than surveying a collection of a child's toy ships, or even a scene out of Omar Khayyam, it was like beholding a field of carefully arranged Tarot-forms rendered in one more dimension than usual.

"You came on the damaged ship," she said when I was settled. "*Rynosseros*."

"Yes."

"Your crew?"

"At the shipyard. Doing repairs. They'll probably be by soon. One of them may take a lamp."

"Please. You choose, Captain."

"I don't want a metic lamp."

"You came here."

"I told you, I was using com. I thought I might take a town-kite as a souvenir."

"None took your fancy?"

"Too expensive."

"You sat when I asked. It will cost you nothing to say. Which would you choose?"

I shook my head, fascinated by the intense blackness of her face. I made myself study the various forms laid out before me. I had accepted the enforced stopover; now I did consider going with what that event had brought. If not a kite, why not a lamp? They had been fashionable once — the cognoscenti attended by their personal djinn. The fashion was twenty, thirty years gone. The lamps — even downgraded ones, worn and inconstant as these had to be — were plentiful enough.

But this was here. A lamp would be a memento of Anjoulis. Of this vivid, wild day, of the vendors and spiralling dust. Of this meeting.

I pointed to a plain one, narrow and elegant, a dusty pewter colour, liking its simple lines.

"That one," I said. "What's the resolution like?"

"Let us see." The young woman rose to her feet, and I saw that she had been cradling another lamp in her lap — verdigris-stained like something wrested from the sea, but with golden highlights from constant handling, touch-polished by the oils of her dark hands. "Bring it with you."

Clever, I might have said, getting me to carry my choice, but I was distracted by the lamp she carried against her side like a child.

"Where?" I said. "The sunlight..."

"Over there." She pointed to the iron tower at the eastern edge of the square.

"The mosque? Sacrilege surely."

"A tourist tower, Captain. Nothing more. A replica from the Ghantowns those ancient cameleers built. Used now for a meeting place. Come."

We left her belongings untended and crossed to the doorway, climbed the low steps and entered the dark mud-brick and sheet-iron interior.

119

It was a large space, hot and quiet but for the sudden flurries of dust hissing on the iron. We moved back into the gloom and she gestured for me to try the lamp I carried.

I set it down on the paving and touched the curved sides as I'd seen it done. At once the holoform began to surge up, and I moved clear.

Some metic jinniforms were wraiths, the frailest phantoms, tantalizing in their borealis elusiveness. Others were more dramatic — more in keeping with the ancient pre-Mohammedan Arab desert demons on which they were based. This was a roiling demon djinn, an impressive male resolution in reds and deep orange lifting upward at the end of a well-detailed cloudform, as if a brooding thunderhead had been tamed and sculpted during a particularly lurid sunset.

The jinniform rose, fierce-browed, heavily cornuted, with arms folded, extending a full eight feet above the lamp. It surveyed the Koori woman and myself.

"Arlas Bey! Arlas Bey!" it said, the lamp made it say. "You have called me..." But that was all. The demon dwindled at once, climbed down itself like a video reversal, the image swallowed, snatched back into the control aperture.

"Don't worry, Captain," the woman said, and laid a dark finger along the lamp she carried. "This one is for you."

"Look..."

"It is true. Those lamps outside are downgraded like that one there. This one is complete."

Which was something I had never seen — an intact metic lamp: a genie projection with its full run of counselling, datastore and predictive functions. More than just a novelty, not merely a quaint find or a relic.

"All right. Show me."

But when she had placed the lamp on the floor, she gestured to show it was again my task. I laid my hands on the touch-polished sides and pressed.

A hiss of sand on the walls startled me, sent me scrambling back. But there was no jinniform blossoming up from the spout, making its carefully nurtured phantom amid the dust motes. Not then. Not until my companion stepped over to it and touched it herself, leaning down to caress the lid, not the sides, with one black hand.

Then there was a rush of sudden, almost blinding light, veil photonics in an explosion of colour, so quick, settling quickly too, falling away. Residual photons faded; nothing remained but the lamp and the two of us.

No. There was something more, something momentarily occluded by the dwindling of that first startling discharge.

"Oh my!" I cried, unable to stop myself. "That is beautiful!"

The young Koori woman stood before me, transformed, picked out in ghost light, sheathed in it, her features overlaid and changed so that the eyes of her, then the smile, shone through a light veil, were the only constants, a startling superimposition, a dark centre for the shimmering overlay.

"I did not know they did this."

I had seen countless cosmetic and theatrical photonics, enantiomorphs and simulacra, but this was different, and probably much simpler tech — a jinniform customized about the body of its owner.

"This lamp was specially made. A man wanted to have a different kind of djinn."

I was crouching on the paving, gazing up at the shimmering form, part of that frozen moment, not knowing whether to stand or sit, finally settling down cross-legged, cueing her by that.

"This man — a Prince as you call them now, but a *kirda* in the old tongues, a ruler, initiated a secret program. He had a revenant made from ancient remains, raised her through childhood and adolescence, called her Anye. He wanted that specifically: a young full-blood Koori woman. He searched long and carefully for that. At the same time, he had a metic lamp made, found someone to do it, the other part of his plan. A magic house from which only she could draw this mantle of light you see, and came before him, the old in the new, resolved into the one, to counsel, to link up the years, to receive his attentions. A man who possibly wanted nothing more than to breed with his race's past, to bring back something, just a taste of the truest bloodlines.

"It might seem a coldly practical tale, Captain. Were it not for the lamp — whose eccentric, even obsessive role in this, you will agree, gives the whole thing a certain glamour — it would be one more attempt by my descendants to strengthen their ancient ties, to claim a more direct and untainted kinship. Heritage business.

"The lamp? It may have been from simple xenophobia, a flamboyant way of dealing with an aversion to an antique physiotype — I allow myself no illusions there. It may have been a finer thing, a setting for giving the experience a richer, more numinous caste, such as may have truly motivated this man. He never did say why. In our meetings, he used the lamp as often as not, yet always when I was counselling him, always when we made love. We made love dressed in light. In this mantle keyed only to my touch. Naturally it was never enough, not for him, certainly not for me after those early years. I realized I had been forced into this but not wanted for myself. It wasn't long before I felt I might never be truly a person to him — always something less or more."

Anye paused, stood quietly in her robe of light. And that mantle appeared to be ebbing slightly now; the nimbus seemed less radiant in the darkness of the false mosque.

I might have doubted what she told me but for the distinctive Koori features I saw more clearly now through her thinning houri's veil, and that patient long-suffering air her voice had about it, worn as close as her twinkling jinni coat of many colours.

"Captain..."

"Tom."

"Tom, I believed I was his, rightfully his, for such a long time — that I owed him the life he had caused. But in the royal household it was easy to maintain such fictions. I was a person out of time, raised up as something like a priestess, treated that way, the private oracle of a very powerful man. I sometimes think I was a work of art for him as well, part of some private celebration, a solitary mystery. He asked my advice on things far beyond my knowledge. At first I actually believed I was that for him, a djinn. But in time I learned the other truth as well, that I was both an item of status and a source of antique pedigree."

"You feel you had proof?" I said.

She turned to glance down the length of the dark interior and out the open door, finally nodded, but abstractedly, plainly thinking about what I'd asked.

"A perfect land for this, Tom. Full of shapechanger legends, full of meanings. The Rainbow Serpent's eggs become stones, the Lizard Ancestor turns into a hill, the Emu Man becomes a gorge. All those Dreaming Ancestors becoming the land, the ranges, the waterholes, the animals." Her gaze never left the doorway. "The deserts of the world all open into each other. They are the constants."

She may have left the silence for me to fill; it truly seemed she was crafting every part of what now happened.

"How did you come to Anjoulis?" I said.

She faced me again.

"A child's trust and gratitude, her pleasure too, became duty and confusion. My one concern became making sure he raised no other Anyes from the trace remains. He was long-lived, as many Princes are. I envisaged a line of revenants, years of them drawn from my original remains, a slavery for all my selves — more than just the potential of a breeding plan or a harem of clones from my living tissue. When one person seeks to control the reality perception and choices of another, it is slavery, isn't it? It is."

"What did you do?"

"After eight more years of feigned interest in his schemes? Of earning trust in the tribal life-house? One day I destroyed the samples and trace originals, spoilt the extant projects..."

"Stole the lamp?"

"That too, yes. In my deprived state I actually thought it to be mine, even believed the ancient Koori had such things. Came eventually to this place."

"And now?" Though I knew the answer.

"His State is far from here, but he has to search. My form gives me away. At least in the markets of road-towns I can pass for a nomad. But he has to find me. I cannot hope he will let me be. I have given him a quest; this is what he understands. And if I escape him in death, he'll raise me up again, keep any issue more strictly controlled. Enslavement."

"No children?"

"Thankfully, no. A great disappointment, I'm sure. A fitting irony. Perhaps it was the process. I can only be mother to my selves. That is what concerns me now." She paused, gave a sigh and an apologetic smile. "I'm sorry. Scheherazade told better stories than this."

It was as if the reality of Anjoulis came rushing back: the hiss of red sand against the walls, the dust motes dancing in the light from the doorway onto the square, the sound of vendors calling to one another — possibly to customers, I could not tell. For all I knew, *Perenty* may have arrived; the tourist reality might well be in action, one more falsehood in all this.

Visit fascinating market towns!

Buy souvenirs from genuine desert folk!

How did the brochures go?

I noticed that the metic shimmer had completely gone from Anye's form now. She was Koori again, unadorned, her physiotype distinctive and exotic. A displaced soul unable to re-capture a past that could not be gone but was. Forced to represent and support realities one of her own descendants had been raised from and now condemned her to, yet without the natural mind-set to make it truly her own. Apparently without that anyway.

If one did not reckon on atavisms and archetypes, on inherited secret knowledge of songlines and Dreamings and Djuringa lore, then Anye *was* free of this, of course. Such things would probably have been handed to her wholesale, if at all, a package of antique metaphysics as re-constructed as she herself was. Not felt, not known at the crucial level of being — but told to her: what her people had once believed, the way a child is told about haldanes or powered flight or the atom.

Or perhaps it did link up somehow, infinitely durable, carrying across the ages. Like an animal orienting itself to a migration pattern, perhaps she did have some affinity, some inbred sense of knowing.

She regarded me calmly, so young-looking yet so imbued with age — the impress of so much time understood without having been lived. Again, it was as if she wanted the silence, the slowing it gave, as if she knew it would do her work for her.

For that was the truth. I had met other revenants, other Ab'Os re-kindled from ancient Koori stuff, but had never truly understood, not until now, here in Anjoulis, with this figure from the windy square, this itinerant genie found cradling her own lamp, trying to find purpose in what she had to be yet no longer was.

"You are trusting me?"

"I am a creature of fortune, Tom. *I* was the one he found. *I* was raised up. *I* played counsellor, gave prophecies, helped shape policy most likely. This lamp is my birthright; it has defined my whole existence as this version of Anye, to call my progenitor self that too, whoever she was. How do you think it seemed when the village boys came shouting that a ship was coming in — the legendary *Rynosseros*, your ship, because of an accident, simple chance? I have lived my whole life with such chance. I tested you by it. I would not have sent someone to fetch you had you not come. But you did. Alone. You came to the square yourself. Destiny provided a champion."

"Anye..."

"I know now that today is the day he will come too, my Prince and his Kutungurlu, or his Clever Men or Unseen Spears. Perhaps Kurdaitcha. But I see the purpose of it. Of course it will be today. And I cannot let him have me."

"You don't know that..."

"But I do. It's clear now. On today's ship. It crosses his land. He will come."

"*Perenty?*"

"Why not? Or one of his own ships. But all chance. He found my remains himself; that search was part of it, the special design. He may not come alone; he may bring his handful, but he will come, and he will make it part of some ritual of acquisition, some symbolic act. A courtship quest. That's the level he wants it at. Something emblematic."

"Anye, you can't be certain..."

She thrust out a hand, palm turned stiffly downward; she would not debate it further.

But I could not leave it be. "We can take you on my ship. It will be ready soon."

"No. I have broken law. They could sing me, trace my mind-line. He wants to retrieve me his way. Alive or dead he can have me again."

"Can I challenge?"

It was as if she did not understand what I was offering, had not meant that when she had said 'champion'. Her eyes narrowed under her severe brow, steady lights in the deeper darkness. She paused before answering.

"You would do that? A Prince, Tom?" She shook her head. "But no. You have no rights here. His men would shoot you down. Burn your ship. Just be here when he comes. Having my story known will be enough."

I wanted to say again that she couldn't know, that the coincidence was too great. Only the intensity stopped me, the force of her belief in her way of seeing.

"When is *Perenty* due?"

"At last call there was a delay. Now it leaves Daralgo at 1600. It will be here at sunset."

"My crew can..."

"No!" Again the downturned palm, hard out, clearly an oracle's habit. "Send a message with one of the village children. Your friends must stay away. Just you. Please."

All fitting her idea of how it had to be, her way of crafting the reality.

"I'll go myself." But I hesitated, wanting reassurance that she would still be there when I returned. Anye anticipated that.

"I will gather my things and wait here."

I left the darkness of the mosque and crossed the windy square, heading north along the main street to the moorings and shipyard. I kept my pace steady, not wanting to seem in a hurry, and not once did I look back to see if she had followed me out of the mosque.

Rynosseros stood outside the yard gates, angled towards the Road as if eager to be away, strong-wind parafoils hard in, tethered low in case we did set out. Old Scarbo watched me crossing the yard, conspicuously cocking an eye at the striated sky, ever the kitemaster, reading sailing possibilities for what was quickly becoming a difficult afternoon.

"Larrikin!" he called, naming the wind, telling me that, yes, we could have miles between us and Anjoulis but hard sailing all the way.

I climbed to the quarterdeck.

"Town business, Ben," I said. "If we go, it'll be after *Perenty's* in."

Scarbo nodded, granting reasons.

"If she comes at all. Help?"

"No. Thanks."

"Good. In that case, I'll be at the tavern. You know what these towns are like. The local beer is designed for the usual two things: to make you want to leave or to keep you here permanently. Tell me we're going tomorrow."

"Tomorrow. Siras can wait a bit longer."

"He can. Let's get these kites stowed."

Twenty minutes later, wearing my djellaba as much to conceal my double swords as to provide protection from the rising wind, I returned to the square. The green-robed kiteseller, forseeing a day of low profits, called out a new price, but I waved him away, giving a gesture very much like Anye's downturned palm, aware of what an odd champion I had become.

I entered the mosque, sighed with relief to find Anye sitting in the gloom, her merchandise packed away, only her own lamp visible, still resting on the paving where she had placed it, as if it might indeed determine her existence.

"That's a larrikin out there," I told her. "Bad sailing wind. *Perenty* may not come."

"He will be here, Tom. You will stay?"

I read the desperation there. She needed reassurance as well. "I'll stay."

She nodded, gave a thin grateful smile. I noticed beads of perspiration on her forehead. Stress? Illness? I could not tell and nor would she when I asked about it.

"We wait now," was all she said, and sat facing the open doorway, watching while the day wore on, unravelling about us like an ancient and bloody flag.

At 1610, a boy came running from the com station, shouting that

Perenty was held over at Daralgo and would not be in until morning.

The merchants began gathering up their things, muttering to each other and eyeing the sky, as if finally allowed to blame the day for their misfortune. In minutes they had dispersed, most of them; the ideogram was broken, the square empty of all but a few laggards and die-hards who lingered, almost as if determined to resist this most irresistible of winds.

The sun hung low in the sky, bloody through the haze, itself like some angry red djinn suspended above the land. The chatter-poles rattled madly, sharp silhouettes at the sunset edge. Above us the tower creaked and moaned in the wind.

"Not today," I said, feeling deep relief, release from the burden of a part in this unwanted equation of destiny. I studied the antique face, worried by the beads of sweat glistening there.

Anye didn't answer. She watched the square, gazed out beyond the line of poles as if finding a message in the sun.

"He will be here," she said. "From the west."

I saw nothing but empty desert, spiralling dust.

"What will you do? What is your answer if he will not listen?"

"I have two. One is a poison — a necrogen. The nomad chemist assured me it would taint my DNA beyond useful recall. I took that while you were gone."

"What!"

"It is probably not life-threatening, Tom. Simply a genie of death in my own blood, a genetic spoiler."

I didn't know what to say. The bravery, the foolishness, the desperate wrongheaded courage of this woman! The sheen on her brow said it all, the signs of fever.

She turned to face me. "Tom, promise me you will take the lamp. He must not have even this part of me. Promise."

"Anye..."

"Promise me!"

"Yes. But your other answer?"

She looked out at the desert again. "Is fire."

I followed her gaze, trying to find her meaning out there.

"Tell me."

"An old piece of military ordnance. I have acquired a combat hot-pot I can detonate if necessary."

"Where? When?"

"Here, Tom. If he will not leave me be. A false mosque for a fake djinn." The fever sheen, the intent gaze, only added to the desperation of her bitter words.

"Let me speak to him first."

"Please. I want you to. But he will not have me again without my consent. Tell him that."

Without her consent? Did I imagine it — some subtle change in what she was telling me?

"If he comes..."

"When he comes!"

"Anye, just for a moment look at this as I am able to. You said it yourself. You were raised to the lamp. It defines your whole perception. It can't be otherwise. Simple coincidence must not make you..."

"You're here, Tom."

"Yes. But this is your only life. I'm going to find a doctor."

"My second time." Her eyes were fixed on the desert, her bitterness directed at the day out there.

"No. *You* have not been here before. Allow that he might never find you."

"My mind-line will give him..."

"May give! May not! Alien to his quite possibly. Allow for that. You may have ruined the whole illusion, you may have changed him."

"No!"

But I had to keep at it, had to try. "He has sensibilities, you said. He may not want to harm you — might never have meant to. He was a man used to power, to having his way. Grant that your going may have changed him. I'm getting a doctor."

"Look there!"

I did so immediately, saw dark silhouettes beyond the chatter-poles, tall black shapes mounted on camels, three, four, possibly more in the dust and uncertain heat-shimmer.

Coincidence again, I wanted to shout. Cameleers driven in by the wind. But her smile of acceptance made me trust for the moment that some deeper truth prevailed, the wisdom of genies.

"Wait here!" I told her, gathering my sand-robes about me, determined to do what I could. "Do nothing till I return. Promise me."

She might have nodded, I wasn't sure. I stepped out into the square, crossed to where the poles rattled like mad things, went through that perimeter towards the incoming shapes, stopped when the four riders dismounted and moved towards me.

"Anjoulis?" one called.

"Aye," I shouted back. "Are any of you after metic lamps?"

"Lamps?" another said, and laughed. No doubt he took me for a particularly eager merchant.

"Beer more likely," said the third, heading towards the perimeter with his friends.

The final rider, leading his restive beast, held back.

"Why do you ask?" Was there an added force to his question?

"I know where there's a special lamp."

"Good for you. We don't need souvenirs." And he too moved on.

Feeling incredible relief, I turned back towards the mosque. But as I did so, it burst open in front of me, exploded like a second sun, a ball of fire scattering fragments of its sudden violence on the unruly day.

I ran through the line of chatter-poles, stood staring at the blazing ruin, at the black cloud of smoke boiling up, a final djinn, quickly torn open, snatched away by the wind.

"Anye!"

There were townspeople standing in the square watching, the last of the vendors, a few children. Others came running to see what had happened.

"She didn't wait," I said to no-one.

But near me, the kiteseller answered. "No."

I turned and saw the bearded man in the green robe, tears coursing down his dirt-stained cheeks. He was holding Anye's lamp.

"Tell me."

"She came to the door of the mosque, called me over, made me promise to give this to the captain of *Rynosseros*."

When he did not hand it to me, when I saw the tears, I knew.

"You, Lord?"

"Yes."

"She was trapped inside her nature. You trapped her."

"Yes. But me too."

"I see that. Did she know?"

"I cannot say. I gave myself a new face."

A few moments passed, the smoke flattening, drawn out and dying upon the wind.

"Why?" he asked, as a child might.

"She was a friend to herself — to all her selves. She saw the truth her way. I believe that lamp is mine."

"Can I..?" he began, but stopped.

"It's broken," I told him. "Doesn't work anymore."

He held it close as Anye had, then finally surrendered it. I made myself take it from him.

"She misunderstood, Captain. I did love her."

"I know."

"I did."

"I know."

And I turned away, headed for the shipyards, holding the small fragment of genie-light that would never shine again.

My souvenir of Anjoulis. Mine.

Scheherazade told better stories than this.

A Song
to Keep Them Dancing

There were heat castles over Wani when Barratin ordered the fleet in, great toppling thunderheads which crackled with heat lightning at the horizon, dwarfing the four menage charvolants and sending long trains of shadow sweeping across the land.

It was dangerous weather for charvis, what seasoned sand-ship captains call a 'wired' sky. Barratin's decision was a good one. The four Exotic ships sent up fuming rooster-tails of sand, their kites bucking and plunging in the tricky thermals, and they ran for a mooring at Twilight Beach.

By chance, Barratin's flagship, *Gyges*, pulled in close by Tom Tyson's *Rynosseros*. That famous National ship and the equally-renowned menage vessel of high-captain Ajan Bless Barratin were separated by less than seventy metres. Mostly it was chance, fate, pure destiny, but part of it, an important part, was a mix of careful planning as well, part of a scheme about to reach its end.

Naturally there were crowds at first, hundreds of people watching the shapes moving on the decks as the ships shut down, hoping to catch a glimpse of the strange lifeforms from the middle of Australia, some trace of the menage exotics who crewed these severe functional teratonic vessels.

When a rhinoton in a long desert cloak lifted its distinctive profile against the charged and restless sky, there was a muffled cry — of awe and wonder, even revulsion, if the truth be known. Then the creature donned its wide-brimmed shore hat and went about its deck duties, and the crowds slowly dispersed. In Twilight

Beach, nothing holds crowds for long except fire-chess and the breaklight, not even the vivid microcosm of Ajan Bless Barratin's four Exotic ships driven in from their menage mission by what some oldens still called an act of God.

Scarbo turned from the rail smiling.

"There's at least one rhinoton in the crew, Tom," he said, gesturing across the flat sand at the closest ship. "Probably come up to see his namesake."

Tom sat under an awning with Shannon out of the afternoon heat, watching the advancing wall of cloud. He smiled. "You think so? Me or the ship?"

"Your guess," the old kitemaster answered. "I just wonder if their captain will pay respects. It's Barratin, the contract-captain."

Tom watched *Gyges*, studied the strange plated hull decorated with weather-faded suns, mandalas, profiles of totem beasts and animal fetishes like some antique carnival ship recently used for war. The vessel was devoid now of kites and cables, a box of half-seen wonders closed and sealed but for the shape of the occasional crewman moving about. "I can do without it, Ben."

Scarbo struck the rail with an open hand. "Too late. Here he comes."

"Alone?" Tom asked, getting up to see.

Barratin was not alone. The tall dark Ab'O high-captain walked along the docks, accompanied by his bizarreman, Monsanto, and one other, another tall 'man' wearing a cage of black battle mesh. A menage warrior. A lab-made exotic.

Tom watched them approach.

Boan watched them go. Belowdeck on *Gyges*, standing at a starboard port in Barratin's cabin, he saw his tall fine Captain carrying something, holding a package under his arm, with Monsanto the bizarreman, the one Boan feared and hated above all others, and — amazingly — that new thanatophon, the new-form thanatis, the death exotic in full mesh armour. They were moving towards the fabled ship of Tom Rynosseros — looking like shadowy lords of the storm now, picked out in sepia light under that wide and wired sky.

Boan glanced back at the duelling face he had been cleaning, placed it in the case next to its mate, closed the lid and snapped the clasps shut. He *had* been cleaning them, he recalled suddenly, trying to re-trace the sequence of events, the line of thoughts, part of his cabin duties interrupted when the weather turned bad.

The sight of Monsanto with his new toy had unminded him, terrified him, much much more than the rhinotons and androspars in the menage crew ever had when he first joined *Gyges*.

He put the case back in the locker and went up on deck, to look first at the angry sky, sharp with ozone, stitched all over now with lightnings, then across at *Rynosseros*.

Now *there* was a ship. Boan imagined apprenticing on her, working with Blue Tyson, Scarbo and the rest. A fully human crew. Not like being among exotics. *Rynosseros* was an all-lander, too, though a National ship in spite of that. Barratin had been the only registered high-captain prepared to take a tribal apprentice, a low-captain trainee.

And Boan did well enough. In the nine months since turning seventeen, he had grown to respect, even love, the contract-captain, certainly to love his ways, his patient care. With Barratin's guidance, Boan would one day have his own command, low or high, would rejoin the Sandive as a low-captain elect in its fleet, possibly a high. If he worked hard. Given Barratin's guidance. Provided Monsanto favoured him.

Mak, the oldest rhinoton on *Gyges*, the big deckmaster with the blue blue eyes and the notched ear, had warned him of that, of how Monsanto was a dangerous one, builder of living weapons, powerful Clever Man too, no friend to Ajan Bless Barratin despite appearances.

Mak said the lab-techs spoke of it back in Cana, of how it really was. Syr Chamin Monsanto had been appointed to Barratin's fleet by a menage faction eager to upset the balance of power. Old Mak couldn't remember details, and he didn't say those exact words, but he knew that much, Mak did.

Surely Barratin would know of it, Boan had decided, had said it again to Mak at the start of this mission, when the Glass Woman was brought aboard. A seasoned master-captain should be able to read Monsanto easily enough, expect such actions.

Old Mak shook his large head and had no opinion. He had once heard the Cana lab-techs speak of it was all. And there was still deck-talk among the androspars.

Boan decided he would find some way to ask Barratin about it, as soon as the unending protocols of fleet operations made it possible and Syr Chamin Monsanto's attention was turned elsewhere.

"Captain Tyson, you know Syr Chamin Monsanto, I believe," Barratin said, introducing his menage fleetmaster.

Monsanto inclined his head in silent greeting, no protocol there. He wore dark fighting-leathers as his Captain did, but elaborately quilted at shoulder and hip. His shaven head was marked with the broken chevrons of his menage sect. The eyes came at you, Tom decided. The eyes of a man you could never imagine resting. A man used to watching for opportunities.

"And this is his latest levitive. Nemwyr."

"A thanatophon?" Shannon asked, identifying the creature by the mesh. He had read the scientific briefs put out by Cana.

"Not quite," Barratin said. "A thanatis. A new variant. A prototype. Being perfected for Sandive operations against the Astani. We are very proud."

"Full mentality?" Tom asked, intrigued by the man-form inside the black cage.

"Yes, Captain." Nemwyr answered himself. "Cognitive and viable, not a sport like our zoomorphs and tangentals."

"Capability?" Shannon asked, though Tom had been going to.

"As the name suggests. I am a killer."

"Care to tell more?" Tom said.

There was a smile inside the filigree. And Monsanto smiled and opened out his hands to speak for him. You see how it is, those hands said, spread wide. Confidential. We've said enough. I'm sure you understand.

Barratin was impatient with it all. "We are field-testing always. Not something we wish to have known in Twilight Beach." He cocked an eye at the clouds crowding the western sky, drawing ever nearer. "When that turbulence clears, we go."

Then why bring it to show, this deadly variant, Tom wondered, as Scarbo no doubt did, and Shannon too. With people still watching on the docks, why did Monsanto allow this new creature to be seen? Why did Barratin allow it, choose to pay respects like this, traditions or no?

Tom studied the high-captain, wondering what the package contained, wondering why this veteran sailor chose to run an Exotic fleet in the inner deserts, wondering whether or not there was some family obligation, some karmic debt being discharged here, something more than the money and prestige of it.

The menage crews were crazy, the missions of the Exotic ships beyond accounting. One sometimes passed them on the desert Roads, saw the strange man-forms toiling on the decks, sweating ephlors and androspars, rhinotons, basics, pisacs and calibandros. Everyone wondered at the commitment to filling the desert with such bestiaries, following logics and philosophies no-one tried to explain. The high-captains who drove their 'zoo-ships' were the best the teratonic tribes could get. On those decks they ruled totally. The attending bizarremen worked their malformed crews, at home their fellows laboured to make such creatures — for display, for strife, for the unfathomable prestige.

"Exotic ships don't usually reach as far as Wani, Captain," Tom said then, trying for an answer, doubting there would be more than a smile and the outspread hands once again from Monsanto.

Barratin surprised him. "We are engaged as couriers-of-honour, Captain Tyson. We carry the Glass Woman from Pereche to Cana. Basically it's diplomacy and religion. Your usual mix."

"I'm sorry, Captain Barratin. The Glass Woman?"

"An effigy. A life-size figure."

"Menage relic," Monsanto said. "A great honour for us."

Barratin acknowledged that with a brief nod. "I should not have come this close. The storm brought us in."

"Nonsense, Ajan," Monsanto said, reasonably. "You saved us a day using the Grand Lateral. The sats never read turbulence. Not weather like this."

But Barratin glanced at Tom and then at the lowering sky, as if searching the storm for what he would say next.

Boan liked being with Mak. Apart from Barratin, who was firm, detached, often cool, always scrupulously fair, the old rhinoton was probably his only true friend on *Gyges*, sometimes irascible and complaining, but generally placid, tolerant, pleased to talk.

Boan found the exotic sitting under a deck awning out of the last of the sunlight, watching the play of lightning moving in from the west. Carl, the scarred old ephlor and Mak's friend, dozed nearby, nose twitching at the charged air.

"Mak, they took the thanatis to *Rynosseros*." Which was a question from Boan. As head of the ratings, Mak got to talk with the Captain.

"I saw," Mak said, flicking an ear in the breeze pushing before the storm. "Very strange."

"But why, Mak? Nemwyr's been a secret levitive all this time. Why display him now?"

Mak watched the lightning approaching Twilight Beach and shrugged his big shoulders. "We shouldn't be here," he said, but softly, to himself really, not to Boan.

"They had him wearing armour," Boan said, trying to keep Mak's interest in this, wanting to know what it meant. "They didn't even try to pass him off as man-crew."

"Bo, you ask the Captain when he gets back," Mak said. "I can't figure it. He hasn't told me."

Conversation ended, that meant. The blue eyes were on the storm; the dim (so Mak often wanted you to think) levitive mind on other things. Quiet Mak, so fierce-looking, so powerful, a hundred years old or more and nowhere near as dull as he gave out. He wanted Boan away from him; Boan accepted there were reasons.

The lad went to the poop and watched the small group on *Rynosseros* standing with the wired sky at their backs, now and then like so many puppets on sudden jerking strings of fire.

"No, Captain," Barratin said. "No refreshments. We must be ready to move out. I wanted to meet you. And Monsanto wanted to show off his new man."

And Tom saw Barratin and Monsanto exchange the briefest flickering strike of glances. They met only at the eyes, it seemed, and there as enemies, that much was clear.

Yes, warring eyes, Tom decided. These men hated each other. Or rather, recognized the state of conflict between them for everything it meant.

Then Tom saw the smile inside the black cage, the eyes watching *him*. This was the deadly one, this Nemwyr.

"We understand," Tom said, wanting to be out of it, shying from that deeper play of the tribes, these caste and status conflicts.

But there was more. For then Barratin handed over the package he was carrying. "For you, Blue Tyson. For the honour of a meeting at last."

Tom unwrapped the heavy bundle, uncovered a gleaming Broomhandle Mauser C96, modified, oiled, fitted with homotropically-biased Grunweld sights, fully restored, gleaming in a leather holster and waist belt. Tom was left speechless.

"A true captain's gun," Barratin said. "From the days of Sun Yat Sen and Chiang Kai-Shek. From the days of the October Revolution and the Kuomintang. A good officer's weapon. Will you accept this?"

"Yes — yes. Of course. But, Captain..."

"Nemwyr was Monsanto's reason. This is mine. Wear it now." And Barratin smiled. "Next time you see *Gyges* or a deckload of teratons, think of me." The words echoed with their hollow fateful hint of meaning.

And he turned and departed. Monsanto and his thanatis, caged and deadly, caught just that bit unprepared, were left walking to the rear.

Tom interpreted that too. He stood holding the antique ballistic, reading all that had happened. It was a tangled net of half-known, half-sensed things, and watching the group moving along the docks, Tom realized that Barratin had just now told Monsanto he knew something about the bizarreman's purposes. Barratin knew, and Monsanto knew, and Nemwyr did. Tom could not fathom the workings of advantage played out there, but he too knew something crucial. He knew he had just been given Barratin's own gun.

"Here he comes now," Boan told Mak, though the rhinoton never turned from watching the thunderheads piling up over Twilight Beach, dragging in their dry fitful lightnings. "Without the package."

"Got your duties done?" Mak said, almost absentmindedly, not looking at him.

"Done. I'm going to ask him, Mak. I'm going to ask him about Monsanto. Tell him what talk says."

Now Mak's blue eyes swung down from the cables of light stitching the deep folds of ale-coloured cloud. "You go easy, Bo," he said, friend and deckmaster both. "Something's going on and you keep clear of it. Barratin has Monsanto's measure. Trust that."

"Yes," Boan agreed, and remembered what his father had said, approving his traineeship decision, much the same thing. Contract-captains play the factions like anybody else. Not blood-related, not kin-related at all, but in service to those who are. No open contracts for Barratin, his father had said, though Barratin could certainly have pressed for one. He chose a particular menage college and gave himself to it, a loyalty more in the man than in any signed document. Now he paid for that. Divide and conquer. This new levitive...

"He'll know," Boan said. "The Captain will know what to do."

But Mak was looking at the sky. It annoyed Boan, this seeming indifference from Mak, and puzzled him. The rhinoton had countless reasons for hating the bizarreman, far far more than Boan had, being on *Gyges* from well before Monsanto came.

Now seemed the right time. Boan wanted more than ever to talk it out, to worry at it and get it safely known, to even things out.

And because he didn't have Mak, he recalled not his father, but Rass, first his teacher, later his assessor at the traineeship adjudications, something she had said in class. "Watch what people do with their envy," she had said. "It fuels the pride and the terrible fear of not mattering, of nihilism and nemo. It leads to all strife in human affairs, that fear, that envy. It is part of humanity's eternal song. It shapes the dance." Her words.

There had been dialectic requirements to argue that during class, but Boan remembered sitting there entranced with her seeming simplification. It helped him now to fathom some of it, this idea of the unending dance. He thought of this present part of the song, this manifestation of its unchanging music.

He was glad for the memory of Rass, fancying then that the lightning made question marks to the unasked questions waiting in him.

"What was that all about?" Scarbo asked when the menage visitors were back on *Gyges*.

"He gave me his own gun," Tom said. "Look!" He indicated the worn brass escutcheon on the grip.

Scarbo frowned. "Who was the one in the suit?"

"Barratin's enemy, I would think," Tom answered. And noticing movement on the poop of *Gyges*, he belted on the weapon, in case someone watched, someone other than just a curious teraton rating admiring ships. "I don't know what this means, but it's more than bridge respects."

"Can we find out?" Scarbo asked.

"How, Ben? Those are sealed ships. We deal with them only with their consent, just as we cross the menage principalities on official Roads. You don't pry into Exotic affairs. Tell me how we learn more?"

"We can't go through the tribes," Shannon said. "That'll get us nothing."

"So?" Scarbo asked.

"I wear this for the next hour or so for whatever it means, till the sky clears and they leave. We stay up here where we can be seen watching. I think I've been seconded."

It was an hour later, when the fretful sky was starting to ease into long loosening cordillera filled with sepia light and the play of electricity at the horizon had diffused into dim flashing shoulders against the land, with only an occasional brilliant thread, that the Glass Woman was found shattered in its padded container.

A quick investigation revealed fingerprint evidence and halation trace belonging to menage-attachment, low-captain trainee Boan Guise Treloiyan.

Three of Monsanto's prime androspars came for the boy where he sat on the deck with his teraton friend, watching the angry sky become easier. Without a word, they dragged him across the commons to the poop, where Barratin, Monsanto and the fierce-looking Nemwyr stood. Like a train flowing behind them came the crew, Mak and the others, muttering with concern to see gentle young Boan treated this way.

There was no reading the faces staring down at him. Monsanto and the still-meshed thanatis were simply eyes, wide and beholding, no emotion or purpose evident in the rest of their faces. Barratin's face, on the other hand, for those in the crew with sufficient wit and cognition indexes to judge it, was set in a strange display of intense concern and resignation. The same mix of qualities hung on his words.

"Explain it, Bo," he said, gripping the rail, and those with sense enough — Boan one of them in spite of his distress — saw that the high-captain no longer wore his sidearm.

"I can't, sir!" Boan cried, forgetting that fact altogether. "I remember none of it. I couldn't have done it. I wouldn't!"

"Your traces, Bo!" Firm, scrupulously fair, but weary, a few of the more gifted androspars noticed, and one ancient blue-eyed rhinoton, deckmaster, head of ratings.

"But why, sir? Why would I? What possible reason..."

"He's right!" Mak cried. "What motive?"

Monsanto's eyes marked whose voice that was. Old Mak, you are done, those eyes told them all. You will be pulled from life, from these skies and deserts, I swear it.

"Sandive plant. Or Astani," Monsanto said lightly, softly. "Someone's advantage. Faction play. We can get facts."

"No!" Barratin said. "This has shamed *me*. Not my college. Me! This needs settlement." And it seemed to a very few, to quickening, watching Mak for one, that this was to spare the boy.

"He is junior..." Monsanto began to point out, but Barratin's hand slammed the rail, denying the bizarreman adept this.

"No! Bring the faces!"

"Trouble on *Gyges!*" Scarbo said. "Look! They're crowding the commons. What's going on?"

Though they could see the commotion well enough at seventy metres, Tom went to the mounted scan, turned it on the Exotic flagship where before it had conspicuously not been trained.

"Some sort of convocation," he said. "A judicial matter. A trial!"

Shannon had the other scan going. "Barratin has Monsanto and that meshed creature with him. The crew look angry."

They did indeed, and more than ever Tom felt the significance of events, of the visit, of the gun he had accepted and now wore. What — in that simple veiled gesture — had Barratin given into trust? What?

There was silence on Barratin's vessel when the duty-steward, a nervous bright-eyed ephlor, brought up the duelling faces. She opened the case, revealing the battle masks set smooth and gleaming in their recesses. All eyes — and Nemwyr's very fiercely — watched as Boan took up one in numb fingers, held it in terrified confusion, staring at it until Barratin came down from the poop and snatched up the other, set function, and pressed it to his face, sealed it there.

Then, like a sleep-walker, a dreamer responding to the uncompromising absurdity of his own dream, Boan activated his mask too, raised it to his face, made the contacts secure.

The crew, caught in the same web of dreamlike unreality, moved back to the rails, giving room. Only Monsanto and Nemwyr seemed to obtrude out of the dream, dramatically, coldly, studiedly aloof, too carefully uninvolved for the relentlessness of the dream-sense to touch them. Again, again, they were reduced to eyes.

Their detached acceptance of events, so one old blue-eyed crewman decided, showed their guilt.

"It's a duel!" Shannon cried. "They're wearing faces, the captain and some boy."

"That thanatis creature figures in this," Tom said, peering into scan. "Monsanto brought him along, wanted him here."

No-one crowding the scans spoke. They watched, listened.

"What, Tom?" Scarbo said finally, prompting.

"See it as raising stakes," Tom murmured, watching two figures on *Gyges* circling one another, the crew clustering right back, the other two figures on the poop, visible without scan, easily, but clearer with the enhancement, tellingly calm, Tom thought. "Barratin announces he will visit. Purposes there. Monsanto decides to join him and brings his death exotic. In mesh. Because Barratin has his gun wrapped. Why? Just a gift? No. More. He brings you a weapon. I bring you a weapon. Purpose?"

"A man in a trap," Scarbo said. "Trying his best."

"Yes," Tom said, staring at the faces circling, shifting, and at the two watching faces above.

Barratin's mask flashed, a pulse of energy which seemed to bring some of the final lightnings out of the sky and cram them, blazing, into his eyes, then sent a blade of it tearing across the deck to strike the insulated surface.

Boan's was a panic response, pure reflex rather than wilful attack. He flashed a lightning of his own, a blinding glancing bolt which struck the rail where Barratin had been and left shattered wood, fibre ceramic and plating.

Barratin came out of his roll, onto his feet, but his next glance had only a fraction of the death contained in the first. It struck Boan squarely and sent him reeling, a screaming cartwheel, into the crowd of exotics.

But he lived. He ached, was burned, badly in one or two places, but he stood. And again, from the panic, from sudden pain and sheer terror, an involuntary act with that face on his, Boan sent death at his Captain, burned him dead where he stood in his betrayal, in a sabotaged mask, sent him lightning-struck slamming dead, dead, dead into the companionway beyond.

In that same instant, even as all that — *all that* — happened, Boan knew he *had* done it, broken the Glass Woman, yes, damaged one of the duelling faces, there in the cabin, watching them leave for *Rynosseros*.

He had forgotten it, had had it forgotten for him. Clever, clever enemies.

Now he looked at Nemwyr, locked in his fighting mesh, psych-armour, a mentalist revealed. Yes, easy target for a mentalist, me, Boan knew. Pick the right mask before. Forget the statue you have broken. Tamper with the settings of one face.

And Nemwyr, there in his mind, stopped the lightnings Boan had ready, yearning to use, to send at Monsanto and his mentalist toy.

There was no answer there, Boan knew. But he had anger, desperate unsorted grief, and tears streaming from his eyes, blurring his dead Captain, hiding him, and he ripped the duelling mask away, sent it spinning aside.

He saw *Rynosseros* too through those tears, asylum, his only answer now. Possibly a way for justice, and something, something to reach for.

Boan ran to the rail, leapt it, slammed into the sand and rolled, got up running and aching, weeping, full of agonies, and one, one agony too many to bear, not ever, not in any life he could see.

Behind him there were shouts, cheers, commands. Behind him Monsanto and Nemwyr moved to the starboard rail, smoothly, easily, and watched Boan run, and watched the crew of *Rynosseros* watching them.

Away from scan, Tom saw the boy running on the sand. In a flash of reflex and confusion, his hand freed Barratin's gun, raised it, took a tropic sighting and aimed.

At the boy running for his life!

All that before Tom discovered the action, saw it properly as an act of his, realized why Nemwyr had been brought to *Rynosseros*, ploy and counterploy, understood the planted command and fought it. Saw on *Gyges* Monsanto with a gun of his own, raised and aimed. Heard the sharp report of it, saw the running figure stumble, fall, rise, stagger and fall again. Finally.

Discovered how little it took to raise Barratin's weapon that much higher. Then the crashing report, the jolt in the arm, Monsanto falling too.

And more, more. The shape of Nemwyr held aloft struggling in the arms of a rhinoton, determined and doubly-driven (though Tom could not know it), lifted high in those powerful arms and thrown to the bruised and bloodstained sand below those last few stabs of light, coming at them now like unanswered questions from that sad and troubled sky.

Stoneman

He sometimes pretended he could remember a time when there was a living belltree at every kilometre mark on the greater Roads, and a thousand k's meant a thousand trees, and you could see from one to the next, just like they said it was with ceremonial posts in the olden days.

The lesser Roads had one in five or ten or fifteen; on those barely used an infrequent one in fifty, if you were lucky; and weren't those Roads lonely to walk with so few stations on the way.

It was probably Rocky Jim's one professional lie to those who got him talking. But in twenty years as a stoneman on the desert Roads, he had probably seen a thousand belltrees die — 'seen' as in found them dead when he returned to the lonely stretches where they stood, sacred iron arrows aimed at the sun, emptied of whatever strange life they had once held.

They were meant to be self-sustaining, these roadpost AIs, many people had told him that; they were meant to last for as good as forever. Which to Rocky Jim was what twenty years as a stoneman seemed. Where was the problem? some stonemen said when he stopped at a lonely depot for a tech check. All things lived and died: true life, artificial life, dreams and memories. All fleeting. All part of the round.

But it worried him, and deeply. As he walked his lengths and stretches, mile by mile, tree by tree, he'd come upon yet another one no longer functioning, inert, no signal registering on the scratched plate of his small scan unit, with only the wind sighing about the tall shaft and sensor spines to give even a hint of life. It troubled him.

It was his other task, after all, part of his life as stoneman, visiting the roadposts, checking on them, reporting the changes (eventually reporting them), making status notes in his log. And if he lingered too long at a kilometre mark here and there, who was to know? His stretches were always free and clear; he paced out his lengths and tossed aside any rust-red gibbers or broke them with his cracker. Rocky Jim's Roads were always smooth for the great tribal sand-ships that came running in sudden thunder under their mantles of bright kites. No-one had cause to complain.

If he lingered by the trees and tried to coax their fragile identities forth, tried to make conversation, who was the wiser? If he talked to them and broke tribal law by doing small acts of maintenance, who really cared?

He did his job, walked the inner deserts, paced out his allotted Roads. He made sure he scanned each post, tossed aside every dangerous conspirator stone that might trouble a passing ship, or be thrown up to harm a roadpost belltree lost and musing inside itself.

But he always tried to talk to them. That was the powerful secret life of Rocky Jim who had once — thousands of belltree stops ago, many thousands of walked and re-walked Roads, in another life it seemed — been Rocco Jim, and before that (how many hundred thousands?) Morocco Jim, first a seller of camels, then partner in his own five-building caravanserai outside Mider.

He had fallen a long way into this secret life — because of speculations gone wrong, because of a woman he loved and a man she loved, and drink and the grief. He wished the story were better, less a commonplace story, but he never embellished it, never to himself. At forty-six, an eighth generation African in Australia, he had fallen out of considerable tragedy into this secret life of his, and he would never climb out of it again.

At 1040 on that hot quiet morning, in a waste of red stone and scorching sand, under a white-blue sky that never drew a veteran stoneman's eye in the middle six hours of any day, Jim came out of his pace-reverie, the final lines of a collapsing mantra, and considered his Road.

In his pack, long-handled cracker angled over his back, more than ever he echoed the Bedouin ancestry someone had whispered into his genes — pass it on! pass it on! He became aware of the weight of his gear, of bedroll and supplies, of the small scan case hanging down his front in the shadow of his broad-brimmed hat, of the crunch his boots made on the graded surface.

Now it was no longer the automatic stoneman's litany (Watch the Road! Look for stones!). Without the mantra to lock his thoughts into easement, he was alert behind his eyes. He interpreted what he saw. Now, only now, outside the litany, he calculated the distance.

An hour at most, Jim decided, and Lateral 913 met Long Line 20. This desolate B-Road had its final offerings, JS-A421-9 and TF-R143-6. Then it was down Long Line to Bay Ruggen probably by month's end. Tech check, log-in and gossip. Interiors other than his own deep cool mind.

Watch the Road, look for stones, the pattern went. But conscious now, unaccompanied.

What had that National sailor said — what? — six months ago? About a search he was on, about medieval alchemists searching for the Stone that turned things into gold — or symbolically, ultimately, into fulfilment and personal meaning? The Philosopher's Stone. It made a sort of sense, as most things came to do given time enough.

It was his role, his name as a pacer of Roads that had made that sailor stop, made him pull aside his rented skiff under its five modest kites to discuss that power in names on his way out to some desolate and forbidden destination, one of the old arcologies he had said.

Stoneman.

A name. A label that locked things in. Defined but invariably suggested other things beyond the definition. There was never an end to it; such was the power in names.

Jim paced out the rhythm, hunching up his pack and cracker

(which you did when conscious, feeling strains and positionings, yet never did inside the litany trance). Well, he was welcome to the stones he found, that sailor. People talked about such odd things, whatever got through, whatever became urgent and needful in this all-accommodating land. The light did it, or the distances, something. Words and names did it too.

The Stonemen shared their stories. That sailor on his way to Turker Fin was nothing. There were cameleers, lone tribesmen, privateers, mystics and crazies; once there was a hundred-foot charvi parked beside a Road, kites in, and a tribal captain calling down, challenging him to a contest with slingshots. A deserted ship, no crew in sight. Just the one man in mirrored fighting leathers, a Clever Man. They had named a target; Jim had won the best out of ten and walked on, never looking back, accepting the interruption, the intrusion of it as he did most other things, without a word to anyone about a lone figure on a deserted ship. Not for many months anyway, and only, then to a few at the depots.

Stonemen, the intimates of so many rough red gibbers and glossy black austrolites, became skilful peltasts by a sure and subtle process. They tossed stones aside, or they fitted them into their slings and cast them at makeshift targets, barely breaking stride. Some dared to knock eagles from the sky, or lizards from rocks where they sunned themselves; some surely risked everything and targeted the diligent canisters of already dead (pray God so!) belltrees.

It was a rare stoneman who did not keep his hand in, who did not punish offending stones this way during the long stretches of 'highway dancing'.

And Jim knew something important was locked up in this, like that National sailor had said. He knew that whenever you consciously did a thing more than once — locked it into a structure where time passed and light changed, that it acquired its other meaning, its numinosity, its symbol meaning.

What souvenirs do you keep? What matters, tell me? Where do you belong? Stoneman's questions. Not special to think on at first — just like anyone else's questions. Except that stonemen kept coming back to them.

Watch the Road. Look for stones.

Conscious of it and calculating, Jim moved on.

The hundred-foot charvolant, *Hajan*, ran at 90 k's down Long
Line 20, that important ship, that neglected Road, as part of a
dalliance, a self-indulgence on the part of its captain, Chy Anda
Relenprise.

Relenprise stood at the polished, laminated poop rail in his
own totally binding, totally defining reality, so different from
Rocky Jim's, thinking of the stoneman who had once beaten him.

He made calculations of his own, decided he knew where his
unsuspecting opponent would be at that moment, in that other
time-frame, given his schedule. The Ab'O smiled.

It was reckless doing this, yes, but as well as being one who
made hard decisions and controlled lives, Chy Anda Relenprise
liked to think he was someone who was keenly aware, more than
most, of intersecting, colliding realities. He savoured the myriad,
simultaneous perceptions of life as a philosopher might, as a
senior lifewatch commander should but rarely did these days.

He was fascinated with how that stoneman would react,
seeing him again, the Clever Man on the 'dead ship', here to cast
stones once more. A man rarely given to recreation or frivolity,
let alone self-indulgence of such a public kind, Chy Anda
Relenprise realized with amusement and not a little pleasure
how he would enter stonemen legends through the stories this
man told — become a mystery of the Roads — and he liked it.
Like taking on a new identity, part of an unsuspected self.

He smiled thinking of it, thinking of the irony of it. "Have you
met that Clever Man yet?" the stonemen would say. "The dead
ship parked in the middle of nowhere? He'll cast with you.
Doesn't say much. It's very strange."

Thus did he merge realities, bridge the gap, enter another
world and its mythos.

Relenprise gripped the rail, enjoying the smooth finish, the
touch of varnished, laminated wood. He watched the straining
kites above and before, glanced back at the cloud of red dust
behind, savouring the different worlds.

Here, inside thunder, he existed with others who knew that

constant sound so well that any change, the slightest variation, carried meaning quickly deciphered, who often found its absence, the resulting silence, a strange, even disturbing condition. People who looked at the sky in the middle hours because the great kites were there, and because (like Relenprise himself and Janice Roa belowdeck) they had choices and interiors other than their minds, places to withdraw to without mantras and pace-rhythms.

There, beyond those low hills, probably those very ones, that stoneman — Jim was his name, something Jim — would be pacing his Road in what was never really silence because it was a fine-tuned mosaic of small vivid sounds, what — Relenprise fancied — was really meant by 'deep' silence. That steady tread, breathing rhythm, mantra-layered (he knew almost everything about stonemen, but as learned knowledge), creak of leather, shift of powered cracker on the back...

Relenprise believed he knew.

It was more than some contest between peltasts. It was a confrontation of different, likely irreconcilable realities, and Relenprise loved that with an astonishing, possibly unprecedented passion. In a sense, with his sling and stones, he too became a stoneman, the highest of the low, in an instant — part of the ongoing legend life of the Roads.

And it was really quite inevitable that while Relenprise saw his indulgence as the result of a passion, he never once saw it as a weakness. He caressed the rail and smiled, loving how his mighty ship slipped between the twin time-perceptions, the somehow mutually excluding and re-enforced mundanes that governed how truths and body-senses aligned, were in fact made.

Jim lived in mantra silence, in far-distance, deep silence, interrupted by the slow sliding thunder of ships. Relenprise inhabited thunder and transit wind, swiftly changing vistas and cyclorama sweep of horizon. Stepping down from these things into Jim's silence and the unmoving heat to cast stones was a remarkable, quite unreal thing to do, almost uncanny, a precise and unprocessed ritual.

Loving the excitement, Relenprise struck the rail with his left hand. Janice Roa would continue to remain furious. But she would play the game as surely as he did. She would co-operate to create the 'dead ship' he wanted. She would sit belowdeck with her formulae and samples and wait. Grant him this indulgence.

Hitler painted water-colours. Napoleon played chess poorly but with an incredible passion. Sarah Bernhart slept in her coffin. Chy Anda Relenprise threw stones with stonemen. *A* stoneman.

Feeling *Hajan* run in thunder under his hands, he gripped the wonderfully smooth rail that marked his reality so simply and so well, and smiled.

Jim probably kept at it because of the trees. The original program had sought to put roadposts on all the Roads — simply because that was where the modest AIs were happiest, inhabiting the great silence, communing with the land, relishing the winds and uncomplicated sun. Holy law determined that, Djuringa knowledge. But, as Jim had learned from depot staff and sandsmen, there were problems. The tribal life-programs had once flourished, had grown ever more ambitious and complex. In a sense, they had become too successful, more and more provocative, more the subject of contention. Too much had been done too well. Restraint was needed, rationalization, serious reconsideration of objectives. Jim learned of the cutbacks, how few new trees were being made, and those only to test some new refinement — no longer the largesse of populating the Roads, of making life for its own sake. Even God knew when to stop.

Jim flung a gibber far into the waste — stopped, fitted, flung, barely breaking stride. As he often did, as all stonemen did, he thought of ships. That was how the cycle ran. Cast aside a stone. How did it get there? A passing ship, too close to the edge. Slipstream in-pull. Or — the old fancy — someone deliberately casting them in (a phantom army of anti-stonemen, counter-stonemen, working in an opposite way, marring the Roads).

Ships were the bright pretenders, never part of this, not really. Painted, bedizened wood, metal, ceramic, fibre-glass, packaged power and light, comp and circuitry, moving points of startling otherness that did not quite fit, never quite belonged, or if they did, only as the occasional desolate wreck, broken open and re-made.

They were barely allowed to exist in Jim's world. They skimmed by in their false register of time and space with some tenuous yet vital link to stones — flashing between Road and sky, squeezed into some relentless, often illusory, sometimes infuriating between.

Jim maintained that fleeting unreality, sustained the lie, helped make the vital illusion possible. He served that strange interplay.

He grunted once, his normal laugh these days, these years. Of course stonemen failed to transmit such rough keen wisdoms. In the depots, to the technicians and staff, how could they not sound quaint and wrong-headed. Ships don't belong? What nonsense! Kinship between ships and stones? Oh, yes? But those techs didn't understand the final reality: that stonemen did not start out as quiet men with their eyes fixed on the ground and not the horizons, just as they did not start out as peltasts.

Jim, fully conscious, outside the litany, grunted again. The land gave you its face, made you after its own image. No stoneman wisdom that. Much older, and never more true. And Jim smiled, but it was not some odd uncommon ghost of a smile hopelessly out of sync, chasing the vanished bark of his laugh. Sixty metres ahead stood JS-A421-9, its eighteen-foot shaft canted at 85 degrees on the left-hand verge.

Jim felt elation, true heart-racing pleasure — bent, scooped up a small smooth stone hardly worth the effort, fitted it into the worn seat of his sling, flung it far out into the waste. The act was an exuberance, almost one of celebration. Before the stone could make its tiny impact cloud, Jim had his sling back at his belt and his scan up and working.

He read everything then. Impact cloud. Pilot light of the scan. Absent life signal.

Absent.

Stonemen rarely hurried, rarely changed stride inside the litany or out of it. Jim's pace quickened, itself a phenomenon of great moment. His heart did. His eyes narrowed behind his shades; his free hand became a fist he completely failed to notice. He felt the anger again, sweated with the anxiety of it. He reached the belltree, stood in the narrow spoiling shadow it made across his Road, and held the scan up to the diligent canister.

Nothing. No blip. No pulse. He had been here, at this very spot, seventeen months before. The tree lived then. It had talked, been coherent for almost a full hour in fact — an hour! — had murmured to him, given him day-old windsong from its dim-recall rods. It had tried.

Jim ignored the peeling paint he might have sanded back and spray-sealed again. He ignored the few poor weeds around the base. JS-A421-9 was gone.

Desperate, he hunched up his gear and hurried on. One did not hurry into such late-morning heat but Jim was out of rhythm, oblivious to stones. He hurried along the Road, boots kicking up dust. One thing mattered now. Only one thing.

In the thunder, in the gritty transit wind, Janice Roa stood with Relenprise at the rail, watching the cyclorama shift of the changing, changeless land. She had not yet been told his plan, not all of it. She knew only that Long Line 20 put an extra day on their trip, and that the biotects at Maldy were going to be kept waiting because one of their senior lifewatch commanders wanted an unscheduled sampling of stoneman efficiency.

"One in fifty, Chy," Janice Roa said. "Why risk this?" Relenprise was splendid-looking in his suit of lights, one of the few men who could make her doubt herself.

"It's because he's the one in fifty, Janice. They're the ones I need to observe most of all ultimately. The psychology alone would make it worthwhile."

"By you in person?"

Janice Roa could endure that glare because of her shades; Relenprise could endure Janice Roa because she was smart and quick and made him appear relentlessly efficient, and because he did not often have to look at her eyes.

"I've chosen this one before. I want to confirm observations made then."

"Sanfer says you cast stones with this man."

"Sanfer is correct." She was becoming tiresome.

"Then..."

"Yes, Janice. Saman could do it when *Amiad* comes by next

week. But I want to do this myself, do you understand? And I'll be calling for closed ship."

"What? Sanfer told me..."

"Janice! Closed ship. In about one hour forty minutes. You see to the rosters. Tell Sanfer and the others."

"Yes. Yes, Commander."

His lungs were burning when TF-R143-6 became visible, his tread less sure than it had been in ages. Dust billowed around his long legs, an explosion of dust each time he drove a foot down. One fist punched the hot air, the other gripped the worn case of the scan. He wavered as he walked, and blinked to make sure of what he saw, for he found himself looking down a gentle gradient at what was suddenly a vast panorama.

There, with his first glimpse of TF-R143-6, came the sweeps as well — the intersection of Lateral 913 with Long Line 20 and the long gentle curves that overlapped about the junction and allowed speeding ships to turn in smooth practised manoeuvres from one axis to the next. Because of the nature of intersections and ships, stonemen spent quite a while on the sweeps, doubling back and forth like indecisive mendicants, finally selecting a course along which to go.

As if for the first time, because it startled him then, Jim noticed the colours: the dusty variegated red-golds of the Roads and the sweeps, the red of the wide land itself. He noticed the afternoon sky, the ailing fretful blue of it, but brought his gaze quickly back to the tree. It stood like a dark thread — no, like a solitary nail struck into the edge of this great haloed cross laid upon the bloody land.

A final nail angling in, mis-struck.

Jim squeezed his eyes shut behind his shades so sweat ran down his cheeks like tears. He hunched up his cracker and pack (part of a new urgent pace-litany) and stumbled on a stone he did not see and did not try to seize and may have imagined. It told him truths he quickly put aside. Not now. No stones now.

With the tree in sight, he strode down his length of the closing crucifix, no mendicant, rather someone obsessed with the prospect of salvation, though certainly not his own, with the fervent hope of something like redemption.

Just once, close to the tree, sixty metres, and seeing himself as he must have looked, he grunted, his laugh. Stoneman humour was durable; the symbol life of the land usually that strong. Hearing himself seemed to confirm it; he almost smiled. He saw how it was, and for once it was true. Symbols could cease to matter. Already in Hell, Golgotha had no meaning.

Hajan stood on the starboard verge of Long Line 20, free-kites and parafoils down, great photonic inflatables tethered low like so many captured clouds.

Sanfer and his five-man crew were making final checks, sealing the ship for this repeat drama. Relenprise was back on the quarterdeck with Janice Roa beside him. Lookouts would spot the stoneman in plenty of time for them to complete 'dead ship'.

"Why here?" Janice Roa asked. "Surely the crossroads..."

"I want it as close as possible to how it was last time. And the posts tend to distract him. I want maximum effect."

Relenprise was gazing straight ahead, out over the stern rail and not at her, but Janice knew better than to let any of her real feelings show on her face.

"There are three choices of direction, Chy. Four if he decides to turn back."

"He has log and tech check at Bay Ruggen. This is the one he will use."

"I may be out of line..."

Relenprise turned to her. "Janice, you are. You have this scheme of yours, these wonderful plans you want to see implemented, but all that can wait. The Maldy projects can wait. More important by far is how we resolve our present program. One thing at a time. This is my..."

She actually interrupted him. "With respect, Commander. Phasing out belltree AI is beyond dispute. Your program works so well it is self-maintaining. Your death-ship has other things it can do. Ten years, Verage says, twenty at the most, the roadposts will be finished. It is the other life-projects that need urgent attention now, before opposing lobbies form: the Trale relicts, the rogue andromorphs and tangentals. Your expertise..."

"And your plans and samples, Janice."

"...your trained crew. *Hajan*, the death-ship..."

"They really do call it that?"

She noted his sudden abstraction and was intrigued by it. "Everyone with sufficient clearance calls it that. Those who know do, yes. The great Relenprise. Slayer of belltrees. Scourge of Artificial Intelligence."

"Janice..."

"Not flattery, Commander. Ask Sanfer. Really do ask him. Ask your other crewmen. Make them tell you. You have managed to do what Bolo May never could, things the Princes and tribes cannot. All the dilemmas, all the ethical debates are disregarded. You with your secret mission bring order and sense into the recklessness and unchecked exuberance of your overzealous predecessors.'

"Then let me tell you, Janice, that there is more to this than sampling the views of a stoneman. A personal thing. I ask your indulgence. We'll get to Maldy when this is done. You can display your necrogens and latest toxologies. If you can convince me between now and then, I promise I'll support you at the preliminaries. In return..."

Janice smiled. "This never happened."

"Exactly." Relenprise watched the Road again, a single straight line of red-gold ochre, deserted in the blazing afternoon sun. "Get your presentation ready. When I have cast stones, I'll give it my closest attention."

"Thank you, Commander. It's all I've ever wanted."

Jim's hand shook as he held up the worn black case. Only here, at the foot of TF-R143-6, did he touch the switch, allow himself to see what showed on the tiny screen.

A pulse. Positive. *Alive.*

Jim dumped his pack and cracker, moved in so he touched the sixteen-foot shaft. The totemic paintwork was badly worn, almost gone, and the sensor spines were bent and brittle-looking. The diligent had been scoured at some time (struck by a falling austrolite perhaps), the dim-recall rods in the base were partly exposed and dented.

The post had never been a favourite, too vague, too undefined and rhapsodic, not like poor JS-A421-9, who answered questions and asked about the Roads and places other than the one where it stood on Lateral 913. Different interiors than its own centre.

This one, TF-R143-6, was living, barely living the signal said, since the definition reading scarcely reached the red, and right then — with JS-A421-9 gone, lost to him forever — this one was enough.

But failing too. Plainly failing.

Jim needed to urge it forth, bring out the entity fading inside the worn diligent canister and long shaft.

"Are you there?" he asked, his voice cracking and making an awkward bray of his words. He said them again. "Please answer. Are you there?"

No answer. Too far down. Too far in.

Jim forced himself to be calm. Try something else. Sometimes precise questions worked — a different kind of precise.

"What have you seen in the last five hundred days? Ships?"

"Few ships," the faint voice came, strange and unclear. "You."

"What? What's that?"

"You. Coming again."

"Yes. Clearing away stones. Checking the posts. What about others? The ships?"

"Yes. Marking us off. I've seen your death-ship, *Hajan*..."

"What's that? What ship?" He thought he knew the name. *Hasan. Hanan. Hajan.* Something like that.

"Just now," the tree said. "Crossing there. *Hajan*."

The word drew thoughts together. He remembered casting stones with the Clever Man. *Hajan*, yes.

"Do not die! Do you hear? I'll find the ship."

"Of course you will," the tree said, its voice very faint.

Jim hunched up his gear and hurried on, his cracker athwart his shoulders so his shadow made a cross again, made him a tiny crucifix moving upon the vast emptiness of another.

The ship was there, standing by the Road exactly as before, like something that did not belong, something discarded from its own reality.

Hajan.

The same ship. The death-ship. When it ran by, belltrees withered just that much more, shrank back like recoiling anemones, like snail's eyes, pieces of their lives snatched away on the sudden wind, drawn wire thin on the long slow thunder.

Here it was, taunting him, testing him again. Same black hull. Same kites — quicksilver inflatables — barely stirring in the still air, herded together like trapped angels. The dazzling man on the quarterdeck. No-one else.

Dead ship. Death-ship.

Brilliant Death called down to him. "Best out of ten, stoneman."

"What's happening to the trees?" Jim called up. "What are you doing to the trees?"

The dazzling man might have frowned; Jim thought he saw a frown above the dazzle.

There was hesitation.

Relenprise was furious, found himself momentarily disarmed by the question, by this violation of expectation. He considered abandoning the whole thing — imagined Janice's face, Sanfer's, re-felt his other need. Relenprise hated being trapped, and he felt trapped now.

"You tell me, stoneman!" he said. "You monitor the trees for the tribes." Relenprise hated the need for the words — they were too immediate, too intrusive and numerous; they ruined the magic. Soon he would give it up. Very soon now.

"Too many are dead, Lord," Jim called through the hot air. All his years of walking, slinging stones, making entries, finding new silent spaces in the great vastness, finding another one gone. It all made sense. "Too many are fading. One spoke of this as the death-ship."

Serious words, Relenprise wanted to shout down, warning him. Dangerous accusations. But that sullied the mythic thrust of the encounter even more. Damn the fellow. Damn him spoiling it all.

"Best out of ten. What do you say?"

"Yes," Jim said.

Good, Relenprise thought. We can save it. He moved from the stern rail, drawing his sling from his belt.

Jim saw dazzling Death climb down the hand-rails like any other man, step over the travel platform down onto the Road, come mercurial across the red dust, darkness underneath the dazzle, mirror glass sewn to black fighting leathers.

"Target?" Death said.

Jim pointed fifty metres away, out to where the westering sun struck Clever Man glints from veins of quartz in an outcropping. Make Death cast at emblem-Death. Play the symbols.

"That one," he said.

"Agreed. Your cast."

"Wager," Jim said.

"Like what?" Death was smiling and frowning at the same time.

"Kill no more trees. Swear it by all the honour you have."

Honour? Relenprise thought. Yes. That was the proper currency here. And so few words. Good.

"I will kill no more trees."

"Your ship will not." Nor anyone on board, Jim was going to say, but didn't. This was Death. *Hajan* needed no crew. He studied the blind ports and empty decks, the silver phantom kites barely stirring on their lines.

"Agreed."

Jim nodded, pleased, locked in his reality, dimly aware of shutting out another. "What are your terms? I'll swear to be your man..."

"Not necessary. You are that already." This was perfect. Relenprise couldn't have wished for better. "No. You will tell others of this meeting, but only when the time is right." Relenprise smiled. This stoneman would dice with Death in his thoughts and dreams for years, till finally it came spilling out, all of it, confirmed then in the tales told by other stonemen, on and on. Either way, win or lose, Relenprise would have it.

"Agreed."

"Your cast then." The words were all perfect now.

Jim cast and struck a handspan to the left.

Relenprise smiled and cast. Too short. Dust leapt up a man's-length before it.

Jim selected a stone, fitted it, made his next throw.

A hit. But no smile; Jim was too desperate for satisfaction.

Relenprise understood that. Perfect. He fitted a stone of his own; he cast and hit.

So it went, each getting his hand in. The scores became matched. Death was calm and smiled, unable to lose, never trapped by wagers and honour, needing only myth. Jim sweated tears from the black glass of his eyes and put his soul in every cast.

One throw would do it.

Jim made his cast, struck the stone like he meant it to burst.

Death smiled and barely tried. The final stone missed by a cable-width, spun dust into the air like old blood.

"Done!" the Ab'O said. "You are the one in fifty. You have my word." And he turned on his heel and left Jim panting in the heat and dust, climbed the rails back to his deck and resumed his silent vigil.

Jim hitched up his gear, bewildered, uncertain what to do. He stood watching the dark ship and the kites arranging and re-arranging themselves above the man's head in subtly changing semaphores till he could bear the gaze and the silence and the hint of smile no longer. Then he started down the Road because there was nothing else to do till *Hajan* finally came running by, bound in thunder, safe in its deadly place between sand and sky, itself like a stone cast from a mighty hand.

Word of honour, yes. But who ever won with Death? Not even one in fifty.

Jim kept walking as the sun fell down the sky and the shadows of the outcroppings lengthened, and his own shadow grew more and more insistent as the cruciform shape all stonemen knew.

Death's smile did it. A smile when he played, a smile when he lost. But he would kill no more trees. *Hajan* would not.

Jim thought hard. He grunted, a bitter laugh. What did he know of smiles?

That infuriating woman was on deck again.

"He's more than five k's away. Can we go, Chy?"

Damn her impatience, her lack of understanding. That most of all. She would get nothing from him, nothing.

But he calmed himself, became reasonable, made himself play it out. He needed her yet.

"Yes. Tell Sanfer. Loft kites and move on. But leave me at the helm alone. No-one on deck. Dead ship (death-ship, he loved it!) till we're well past him." He made himself add: "I appreciate your co-operation, Janice. You will see."

She nodded, her own hard smile softening. "Thank you, Chy. I'll tell Sanfer."

Jim trudged on, head down, dissatisfied, his stoneman's cross — cracker athwart pack — thickening, lengthening out into the shadow edges of the Road now, becoming the early night of the land.

He thought of Death. The smile was a ghost right there before his eyes. Words ran upon it.

"Marking us off," TF-R143-6 had said, in almost the same line as it mentioned *Hajan*. "You are that already," Death had told him. Already his man. The one in fifty.

The words ran. Had the tree been blaming him for what the death-ship did, whatever it did to slowly, surely, murder the trees? Did it see him as part of that crew?

All he did was check on the posts. Log changes. Use his scan. *Mark them off.*

And Jim stopped, crucified upon the land.

One in fifty, the Clever Man had said. Not *Hajan* at all. Stonemen.

He moved then, even as the slow sliding thunder grew at the edge of his world where the red sun stood like a burst heart, but first — first he flung his scan far out into the pulsing, roaring darkness.

Hajan ran at 80 k's before a tail-wind, kites bloody with sunset.

Jim crouched on the verge, marking the ship with his eyes, not daring to blink. He watched it grow, rolling on, roaring, barely in his world now, with Death as dazzling sunset at the helm. He imagined the smile on the man, on the ship — all one.

And as that totality moved past, he stood, he cast. As Death's crewman he let fly, saw Death struck, tumble, saw *Hajan* waver under the impact and leave the Road, shuddering, careening, unable to escape. Heard the new thunder, saw the death-ship turn about itself in a closing final attempt to withdraw.

Then he did not watch. He hurried. To find stonemen, others he could tell.

Lucky throw, he thought. Lucky stone.

And he might have thought of Goliath then and the bringing down of the mighty, but his cross had become one with the darkness, and symbols and realities had merged, unknown and nameless, into the urgent black wind on which he ran.

Privateers' Moon

Usually the house sang. It was built to make music out of the seven winds that found it on its desert rise. Vents in the walls, cunning terraces, cleverly angled embrasures in the canted terrazo facings drew them in; three spiral core-shafts tuned them into vortices and descants, threw them across galleries, flung them around precise cornices and carefully filigreed escarpments so that more than anything the house resembled the ancient breathing caves of the Nullarbor.

Which many said was Cheimarrhos' intention, that his great granite and limestone pylon was nothing less than an inverted network of caves set in the sky, chimneys and vaults and inclines in a structure such as Sumer must have seen, or Ur of the Chaldees, or Teoteochan of the Toltecs.

Paul Cheimarrhos called his house Balin, and on the day he finally showed me the roof-field there was a stillness on the red sand beyond the large deep-set windows, a lull I could not help but take personally, knowing Paul as I did, as an omen of some sort, as if my presence had caused it to be.

And, accordingly, as if unable to bear that terrible quiet, the middle-aged, incredibly vital Three-line tycoon talked about winds. Obliquely but inevitably. As we walked along the polished limestone corridor of Gallery 52, Paul rounded on me yet again, fixed me with his piercing blue gaze.

"When was the last time, Tom?"

"Only the once, Paul, three years ago. You used to come out to the coasts. I was here for the Anderlee hearings, but never got this far up. There were too many of us."

"The Anderlee thing, yes. I'm sorry." The polite show of regret quickly vanished from his eyes. He was too excited. "Then this makes up for it. Today is unusual. We usually get one of the four. The brinraga reaches this far north, and leftovers from the angry red-sky larrikin. I tune them down to gentle house-guests, mere palimpsests. Balin can do it. I'm so glad you're here."

We reached a corner window and looked out on the desert once more, but on a new vista entirely, stretching red and empty to the horizon.

"We even get spill-off from the sanalatti at this latitude, can you believe it? The experts say it's impossible but I know better. It's why Tyrren and I chose this spot, this exact place. I know the Soul when I feel it. Those scatterlings are unmistakable."

We stood looking out on the empty desert and I couldn't help but wonder how he did view my presence. Portentously, no doubt — the visitor who had arrived on the first windless day in four months.

"Are you familiar with the name Memnon?" he asked.

Knowing Paul Cheimarrhos' interest in antiquities and the ancient Mediterranean civilizations, I welcomed the change of subject.

"One of Alexander's generals?"

But of course Paul had been talking winds. He laughed, throwing back his thick mane of silver hair so it shifted like a magnesium shower along the shoulders of his cobalt house-robe.

"You are thinking of the general who led the Persian Greeks at Granicus. No, I mean the Colossi of Memnon, Tom. Two seated statues of Amenophis III on the Nile banks near Thebes. Some still believe they were designed so the sunrise and sunset winds made them sing..."

"Sing?"

"A plaintive hooting song, yes. But that was an accident, nothing more than a freak thing. Others claim the Great Pyramid sang before it was sealed, that the engineering equations covered that. Some say Djoser's pyramid at Saqqara did the same, that Architect Imhotep was master of the micro-zephyrs, expert in a whole secret art of hierocantrics. These tales are apocryphal. Balin exists and does all this. David Tyrren worked with me on it."

I made a sound of acknowledgement to show him I knew what pretty well anyone did, that the great architect had worked on the house, pylon, monument — though I knew that Paul had done all the initial layouts himself. It was his own design, despite the careful elaboration that had made the design a reality.

We were walking again because that filled the silences, turning up into Gallery 55-B, working our way to the final upper levels, to the elaborate totemic roof-field at the pylon's crest where the wind-banks stood and the rows of strange acroteria were laid out like memorial pieces in a graveyard in the sky.

I needed to see that field, to find out if Paul Cheimarrhos had in fact done what David Tyrren suspected, and had — after much agonizing — revealed to Council at long last. It seemed I was in time.

Gallery 55-B was blind, no windows there to show the desert and sky in its twin infinite registers of red and blue, just cool limestone and granite — part of a wind-race when the vents and conduits were aligned and operating.

The whole truncated pyramid of Balin was a wind-trap, a man-made mesa over three hundred metres high, full of cave-chambers — every one part of some cunning, precisely reckoned equation — and with a 'cemetery' field on its flattened crest. With its canted sides, its cavetto cornice and taurus moulding, it did look very much like the pylon of some great ancient temple gate never completed, never given its companion pylon or connecting wall, with no temple precinct at its back.

We turned into the wide transverse apron of Gallery 60, and there it was, laid out before us under the hot blue sky: the summit field set all over with shimmering, totem-like acroteria, tall blank ceramic and stone pillars, some elaborately painted, others bone-white and glaring in the sunlight, pierced with fibrile openings, set with airfoils and sonic wires.

It was exhilarating to see it all at last, and deeply disturbing — for at the very centre was a shallow basin, like a radar dish thirty metres across, and at the middle of that, so I believed, so Tyrren had confirmed, Paul Cheimarrhos' great act of sacrilege.

The twenty-six wooden burial poles were ancient, without doubt the undeclared cache stolen from the Vatican collection decades ago, smuggled back into Australia in ones and twos, hidden in black market havens, finally incorporated into Balin, perhaps the ultimate purpose of the place, though I quickly put that fancy aside. It was hardly likely — the idea was a measure of my own reaction to being here at last, to seeing the forbidden relics set up so boldly on this vast open deck.

Each post had its special ceramic cap, making it safe from orbital surveillance. Tribal comsats scanning the site saw nothing more than a shallow dish set with one more group of aerodynamic wind-posts. The angle of curvature of that depression had to make oblique scanning impossible as well.

Paul stepped down onto the flat roof-field, looking for all the world like some notable out of antiquity with his blue robe and silver hair, a Chaldean prince or an Akkadian merchant atop a ziggurat in ancient Ur or Sumer. Or again — allowing my fancies free rein, trying for the composure I needed — some of the acroteria, the totemic signs carved on them, took me half a world away — from Mesopotamia to Meso-America, and I imagined I was an Aztec priest in jaguar headdress and cloak of human skin stepping out to officiate at a ceremony to Chac Mool. Balin invited such notions.

I was hurrying ahead now, heart pounding, so that Paul was following me, making no attempt at all to keep me from the depression at the centre. He did want me to see it.

Only when I remembered what hung in the sky high above us did I slow my pace, force myself to look less eager, more the casual visitor overwhelmed by this magnificent display.

Slowly, more slowly, I completed a gradual arc towards my real goal, giving Paul time to catch up. Then, together again, our footsteps ringing on the limestone flagging, we made our way to the very edge of the dish and looked down at the cluster of poles at the centre.

"Every now and then," I said, quietly in the vast expanse of air and light, "a National does something like this. Luna Geary. Tony Wessex. Dominic Quint. If we're lucky, Council learns of it before the tribes do. And I hope we're lucky this time, Paul, though I doubt it."

"The tribes who made those poles died out long ago, Tom. Bloodlines lost, only revenant DNA trace, languages forgotten. This is as fitting a place for them as any."

"How we see it isn't important, you know that. It's what they think. Every act like this — even suspected acts, rumoured acts — harm Nation."

"The tribes can't blame Nation for what I do. It's like privateering in the sixteenth century, the sea-captains operating on a special brief from the Crown. Drake, Hawkins and Frobisher were not official agents of Elizabeth Tudor but they acted for her."

"A handy rationalization, Paul. They held letters of marque. They *were* legal agents."

"No, Tom! You miss my point!" One hand cut the air, a dramatic sudden gesture, a measure of the force of his feelings. "It is exactly what I say. It's like Iran-Contra once was and the Special Operations Division of the CIA..."

"Secret agenda. Deceiving the populace."

"No! No!" Again the hand cut the air. "We are both privateers, Tom. Me with Balin, you on *Rynosseros*, keeping back details from all but a trusted few..."

"And having them kept back from me."

He took the reproach calmly.

"Who told you? Tyrren?"

"No. We asked for the plans. There's been a tribal satellite tethered above Balin for a month. That's what really brought me here."

"Ah, yes. My Star above Bethlehem."

"A very deadly star. It can't be simple reconnaissance. Not coincidence. I'd say a warning."

"Tom, I've had those poles for twenty years..."

"They're from the Vatican catalogue. The ones they didn't give back. Part of a *cause célèbre*."

Paul Cheimarrhos said nothing for a moment. His clear blue eyes flashed in the sunlight.

"You're well informed."

"You know I work with Council."

"Exactly what I mean! A privateer!"

"All right, a privateer myself. I didn't bring *Rynosseros*, but my coming here will have been monitored. That roadstop you specified, seven k's out..."

"Sabro."

"Sabro, yes. There were tribesmen there. No questions were asked; the continent-crosser dropped me; it was a routine transit stop. But I made no attempt to conceal my identity either. That *would've* alerted them. It's why I wrote instead of using tech. The invitation had to come from you."

"I'm glad to have you."

"Despite the omen of no wind?"

Cheimarrhos laughed. "Despite that omen, yes!"

We were silent for a moment, each of us alone with our thoughts, gazing down into the dish at the small forest of shapes clustered there. The glare from the hollow and the surrounding field made it easy to shut my eyes, to escape the ancient painted posts masked from the sky by their insulated caps. Paul's voice startled me when he spoke.

"Tom, I will tell you something you will not know. What Three-line is, or was. Thirty years ago I invented a device which could measure haldane force around individual Clever Men, show which ones could access the most powerful vectors."

I couldn't believe what I was hearing.

"Council knows about this?"

"No. Secrecy was a condition. I tell you only because of our guest upstairs."

I resisted the urge to look up. This was incredible.

"The tribes couldn't allow such a device to be used," Paul continued, "especially by non-Ab'Os. They bought the Three-line patent, demanded it, the plans and prototypes, made sure it remained a lost invention. They gave me this concession, on tribal land because the winds fell here, with enough funds and tech support to build Balin and establish a fortune in service companies.

"Those gave me a certain limited political power, as you know, which I've finally managed to pass on to my sister. Some of those companies help me acquire antiquities for my collection.

The tribes permit them to operate. Ironically they made it possible for me to get these Vatican posts."

"But you've kept them," I said, my thoughts racing, wanting more than anything to ask more about the device. "You haven't given them back."

"As I say, Tom, the bloodlines no longer exist. Or if they do, only as revenant imposters. Who makes the claim? Who truly can? I do nothing more than collectors of antiquities and *objets d'art* have always done. For my pleasure I accumulate and keep safe objects which even their makers and inheritors might damage or ruin. It's the paradox of antiquarians and special collections everywhere." He looked into the sky. "My own Star now. I've been watching it. I have an antique Meade LX6 over there. It does the job."

"A laser strike at any moment, Paul. Balin might not survive it."

"What do they see, Tom? Nothing."

"There's more," I said. "Earlier this month, authorities in Rome finally confirmed that a special collection of burial posts — part of a personal gift to the Popes — was stolen in the years after Balin was built. An antiques smuggler was named; he named someone once attached to Three-line who has since disappeared. Nothing definite, all very tenuous, but your Star suggests how they're seeing it."

Paul surveyed the silent glade before us. "I've had them twenty years. I'm for this land, Tom, for all this. I'm the right sort of collector..."

"How they're seeing it, I said. You didn't even try to trade for such relics."

Paul laughed. "Oh, I made enquiries. But why haven't they confronted me? Sent in a search team, demanded entry, interrogated my staff? Why no formal investigation?"

I hesitated. He seemed perfectly serious, as if the obvious answer had not occurred to him. It made me cautious.

"You tell me, Paul, assuming you can trust your staff here, assuming they're not serving outside interests. I can only guess that it's part of the deal you made — what? — thirty years ago? This Three-line device you created would seem by its nature to weigh in as something between a holy artefact, something pertaining to the Dreamtime, and a National crisis. I'd say they made a deal with you at the level of their belief systems. Gave oaths, never expecting this. Now they have a dilemma requiring careful deliberation."

Paul turned away from the small forest of posts.

I followed him back across the roof-field, not wanting to ask my next question under the naked sky. Gain-monitors could never reach down so far, but scan could, and how did we seem, I wondered? Like conspirators? Very much Paul's privateers?

"One more thing," I said as we reached the open gallery that would lead us back into Balin's great mass. My heart was pounding as I said the words. "Did you hold back any Three-line knowledge? Plans? A duplicate prototype?"

"Of course not," Paul said, and was as closed to me then as a new moon, as the invisible satellite was — his Star, that sinister moonlet locked and turning with the world, geo-tethered by its micro-filament to the parent facility over the equator.

Paul Cheimarrhos smiled. "So serious, Tom. Come. We must not be late for lunch. Sarete is Three-line now. She might never forgive us."

"Paul, I have to know. The device..."

"Later. Come now."

There were six of us for lunch, and the others were already seated at the long cedar table before a breathtaking view of the western desert: Sarete Cheimarrhos, Paul's reputedly formidable sister, her dark-skinned Islander assistant, Naesé; to her left one of Paul's actor friends, the renowned John Newmarket, looking splendid in the Edwardian finery that was his Todthaus trademark, and next to him, white-suited, so urbane, the economist, James Aganture, agent for one of Three-line's longstanding European clients.

Sarete had been overseas during my visit to Balin three years before. I had heard a great deal about this celebrated woman; even Tyrren had issued several cautions. Now here she was rising to greet me.

If the flamboyant and expansive Paul could be likened to a messianic Beethoven cast in silver and blue, then his calm and elegant sister, with her black gown, long dark hair and sombre, appraising gaze, was something from the shadowed spaces of the El Greco that hung on the room's northern wall. She was ten years younger than her brother by all accounts, but the smooth untanned skin gave her a timelessness, a twenty year range of possibilities at least.

There was a smile, a generous one, but it never reached the eyes, and in the instant I knew that this pale, severely pretty woman intended me to see this duality of response. I was Paul's guest, the luncheon no doubt his idea. Just as Balin was completely his domain, the administration of the Three-line holdings was hers, and this had to be taking precious time out of a very busy day.

Rather than feeling affronted, I was glad of the hard honesty. There were probably enough lies in this great house already.

"Captain Tyson," she said as we shook hands. "I believe you and John know one another." I nodded and smiled at the actor. An answering smile softened those famous gaunt cheeks. "This is James Aganture, one of our European consultants." Aganture and I exchanged smiles as well. "And this is Naesé, my secretary."

A fitting assistant for her employer, I decided, an Islander woman, quite dark, middle-aged, with small eyes and small fleeting smile. Naesé rose, gave a slight bow of the head. I did the same.

We took our places. I was seated next to James Aganture at Sarete's right, opposite John Newmarket and Naese. Paul spoke a word to Anquan, the major-domo, and joined us, immediately taking charge of the dinner conversation by asking James Aganture to bring us up to date on the situation in Europe.

The svelte, white-suited European did that until the food arrived, when the business of eating gave me an opportunity to study Sarete and the others, though I found it harder to do than I expected. Thoughts of what Paul had said about his invention kept crossing my mind, and I was glad when the meal was over at last and I could adjourn to my quarters for siesta.

Around 1500 there was wind.

I was drawn from sleep by the deep swelling song, went to the windows and looked out, used house tech to bring different vistas to the wall-screen, one cycling after the other, every angle but where the posts stood.

It was thrilling to see and hear — the outward signs of Balin coming alive. The pennants and long windsock drogues at the corners of the roof-field stirred on their poles; the helium-filled outrider kites floating high above the house started shifting in the sky, inditing their signatures on the bright air. Spinner caps turned, the most sensitive of the sonic acroteria began to sound. Like some great ship advancing through time, trailing cloud-wrack and windsong, Balin was on its way again.

Tolerances were adjusted: within ten minutes the field was thrumming and whistling, within twenty howling and keening. From further down the great sloping mass came a deep moaning that meant one or more of the induction vents were cycling open, the spiral cores engaged, that power-cells were regenerating and airflow was being guided through the mighty house. There were corridors now where my casual passage from one room to another would vary pitch and tone, add a subtle difference to the house-song. This was Paul's great legacy. This!

I must have stood there for fifteen, twenty minutes, reading the land, studying how this structure stood upon it, considering what micro-climates might exist in its shadow. Then the phone chimed, drawing me back, and it was Naesé's face in the glass.

"Forgive the interruption, Captain. Sensors showed tech use in your quarters — we assumed you were awake. If it's convenient, my mistress would appreciate your calling on her in, say, fifteen minutes?"

The request did not surprise me.

"Certainly," I said. "I'll be ready."

On Balin's sloping west wall was a small open place like a col or cirque on the side of a mountain, and in the sun-trap made there was a walled garden, little more than some lawn and a grove of dusty orange trees.

A house-servant, Cristofer, led me there, opened the low bronze door and let me out into the tiny grove. The westering sun warmed the spot; the sloping planes of the wall-face came together above me in a gradual point, with stone wind-masks spinning on their pins in the vents.

The wind had strengthened, I noticed. The pressure systems over the desert had shifted — it was probably the brinraga which struck the parapet of the garden, stirring the fruit trees, whistling up the granite face to the vents above, where extruded murtains randomized the flow, altering its direction, tailoring it to the house-song.

Tyrren had built well. The massif of Balin sang but the garden was a pocket of calm, not only a sun-trap and a wind-haven, but also a place sheltered from the vast music forming all around us.

Sarete was sitting on a white wooden bench amid the trees, wearing a gown of dark green polysar and speaking softly into a comlink at her wrist. Though Three-line's Chief Executive, she apparently did much of her work from Balin, away from the coasts, privileged with the com tech that required. I marvelled at such easy luxuries. Near her, on another bench and using a lap-scan, sat Naesé.

Both women looked up when I approached, but Naesé turned her attention back to the scan display almost immediately. Sarete gave a polite smile and switched off the link.

"Thank you for coming. Paul considers you his so I won't keep you long."

I went to make some appropriate remark, but thought better of it. This audience was wholly on her terms; she had reminded me as much.

"We could not discuss it at lunch, but tell me frankly, Captain, what does that comsat mean?"

"They're geo-tethered, as you know. The logistics of moving them, aligning them..."

"Costs."

"Yes. They use them that way all the time, but it means filing deployments, getting clearances, logging variations. It's a busy sky."

"So I've discovered. It tells us how seriously they regard this."

"It does. It may be a routine shift, simple reconnaissance, coincidence..."

"Council sees it as a warning."

"Strong probability."

"Because David talked."

"No, Sarete. Tyrren told us nothing, simply confirmed what was already available through channels."

"Ah, channels. And do you think there is an agent in our midst?"

After Paul's empassioned evasions, again I found this directness refreshing.

"Can you doubt it? I would have thought infiltration preceded a tech commitment like this." And I glanced briefly upwards. "Given what Balin is, I would assume infiltration occurred a long time ago. This is unique."

"Agreed."

"How large is your staff?"

"Here? Seven including Naesé. All trusted. All here a long time. Some rarely go above. We keep house secrets, Captain."

"Your guests?"

"Possible. Unlikely. They will not see the...relics either. But what can that station do? I've been given general configuration data but I'd like you to tell me."

So you can make a decision, I realized. Make policy for Three-line.

"We read lenses deployed. It's probably *irijinti*. Given twenty minutes it could effectively demolish Balin."

"Which took eight years to build. Twenty minutes."

"Depending on intensity and duration. They sometimes move deployed like that..."

"Target the roof-field?"

"Easily. To a square metre, possibly less. But hardly their intention." I glanced at the Islander woman sitting quietly among the trees. "They'd want to commandeer the...relics."

"Naesé knows everything, Captain. Should I leave?"

It was such an unexpected question that I hesitated.

"You understand that I'm still making up my mind about all this?"

"Of course."

"All right. Then as Three-line you should. But only if it's a regular routine to do so. Anything could seem provocative now.

Do you leave Balin often?"

"Occasionally. You like Paul, don't you? You're like him."

'Like' and 'like', both words revealing more about Sarete and her relationship with her brother than perhaps she intended.

"We understand something in common, something difficult, probably irreconcilable in our affairs."

"Ah, your role as privateers."

"Paul's word, Sarete. I suppose it suits."

"What would yours be? Patriot? National? Romantic?"

"Privateer will do."

"You have no satellite over your head."

"I do now. And for all I know I may have one for every Ab'O Prince I've ever dealt with as Blue."

Naesé looked up suddenly, made a hand-sign. Sarete raised a hand to excuse herself for a moment.

"Yes?"

"Foreman has entered the Manada."

"Excellent. Send on that." And to me: "Your advice?"

"In what capacity?" I said it to remind her of the levels that separated us, wanting the distinctions to matter. There were different values at work here; Naesé's interruption, this allocation of time, had shown me that.

"As a State of Nation man?"

"Persuade him to give the poles back. Or leave here immediately."

"As the Blue Captain?"

"The same."

"As Paul's friend?"

"Sarete..."

"As his friend?"

"I'm still deciding, but I'd say stay. Risk it."

"Really?"

"If Balin is struck and the reason is given as sacred relics, there are many who will not believe. The tribes are seen as ruthless aggressors, hostile to Three-line, to Nation, to all non-Ab'Os, displeased with past concessions because of a device Paul invented long ago..."

"Nation knows about the device?" It was the first time I had

179

seen surprise on Sarete's face. The eyes first widened, then narrowed. Her mouth drew into a line. Alarm, disappointment, annoyance, I couldn't tell.

"No. Paul told me before lunch."

Sarete nodded. Her head lifted a fraction. She glanced out at an errant drogue — orange, red and bright blue — cutting the wind forty metres away. I could not be sure, but I believed she did it to conceal something contained in her gaze — or perhaps missing from it. More than ever she resembled the El Greco madonna above the cedar table.

"What will you do?" she asked finally. "As yourself?"

I smiled, watching the kite as well, seeing it as some complex bird-equation worked out upon the registers of air, left to find resolution, to create its own fragment of meaning. It occurred to me, absurdly, very fondly, that Paul would probably have names for his kites. This was his house, his ultimate statement. Everything belonged, made for the homeostasis Paul Cheimarrhos needed, externalized in kite and corridor and wind-chase. In the burial poles in that shallow dish.

No wonder he had been glad to relinquish the operation of Three-line. Dreamer, idealist, monomaniac, he wanted none of it. Who knew what wonders, what pieces of self, Balin's vaults and chambers contained? This was more than a vast schema of the Nullarbor's Breathing Caves, those hundreds of miles of underground conduits, chambers, tortuous chimneys. This was a living extension of the man, every corridor, each framed vista and spinning wind-mask. Seeing it any other way just didn't begin to give the truth.

He had to continue, remain just what he was. He had no choice.

The kite, set upon its wall of air, mindlessly navigating, brought that in, gave that answer. Just as he had set it there, given it that brave and futile task, serving, being, till it was finally destroyed and replaced, he had put Balin upon the land, raised it up for its time. His statement. His stand.

I watched the woman whose lift of head, whose gaze had led me out to the kite, realizing, imagining what she too had been through, the years of dealing with this reality of Paul's.

She had seemed hard and alien before. Now she seemed

trapped and committed, caught at the moment of deciding. Caught in the choices of others. As I was. As Paul might yet be.

"I will remain here till that satellite moves away," I said. "If my presence can deter them, provide another reason for not striking, then good. Do you mind having one more house-guest, Sarete?"

"It's not my place..."

"I'm asking you anyway."

"Not at all, Captain. It was good of you to see me."

Again the safe courtesy, the illusion of my having gifted her and not the reverse. She was alien again in that moment, and I found myself hating it, hating what she represented, this seeming lack of connection, the cool pragmatism, the failure to read or simply accept one set of equations because she had equations of her own.

I left the garden but did not return to my quarters. Instead I climbed the escarpment, gallery by gallery, to a viewing lounge close to the summit. There I stood amid the low ochre-coloured furniture, safe behind the thick glass, watching the sturdy outrider kites hanging in the sky and the long streamers of dust and cloud which boiled off this stone massif and converged at the horizon as lines in an endlessly moving yet strangely constant perspective.

The house-song was clear but at a comfortable remove — like an orchestra tuning somewhere else. I began to see the great structure as something to be maintained in that other sense, and wondered which of the staff members — Anquan? Cristofer? Deric? — might abseil down these vast faces, clearing wind-wrack from the vents, carrying out service checks, replacing fixtures, tuning the structure in fact.

I recalled the meeting in the garden. Could Sarete not see the virtue in this vital reality? It was an eternal act of defiance, this great demesne, a continuing statement of identity, personal for Paul, but for Nation too, a crucial affirmation.

Or was that just my bias?

I tracked clouds to the horizon and considered equations, found myself coming back to the new integer, probably the ultimate issue in all this.

What a device Paul must have created to be allowed such a thing as Balin.

I sensed someone at my back, turned to find the calm figure of James Aganture standing near me, the cultured, white-suited gentleman from our luncheon. Like me, he was gazing out at the desert, deep-set brown eyes filled with admiration.

"Amazing, isn't it? It just goes on forever."

"Yes."

He moved in beside me, stood watching the sweep of the land, the boiling ribbons of red dust streaming past, gloriously capped now with low cloud, trimmed with gold by the afternoon sun.

"You lose a sense of such scale in Europe," he said. "It might be said that here you lack density, weight of identity, but that surely is changing. We stand upon a great symbol. Another waits above. It is a testing of symbols really."

During lunch I had imagined what conversations I might have with someone like James Aganture, had wondered what talk there could be with that avenging moon fixed in our sky, steadier by far than those trembling outriders at the ends of their cables. That he had almost read my thoughts startled me.

I nearly smiled as he worked his way into what he wished to say, Sarete's question, no doubt Paul's. My own.

"Will it strike?" he said.

"Will it strike?" I answered him.

"Pardon me?"

"I ask you the same question, James. And I wonder why you remain when the risk is so great."

Aganture's well-shaped mouth turned down, his dark eyes widened. "A visit planned weeks ago. I did not know until I arrived."

"Of course. So will you leave soon?"

Aganture did not answer. He waited a few moments, bringing his long hands together before him, then came to it again. This time he was even more direct.

"What will Council do, Captain?"

"Excuse me, James, but I'm still not sure what you mean."

"I know you are here as a representative of Nation," he said.

"I know about the posts. It is why I was sent."

"Sent? By whom?"

"The Vatican, Captain Tyson. I am Monsignor James Aganture, the instrument of the Cardinals Elect and the Holy See."

"Hm. Your interest here, Monsignor Aganture?"

"Please. It is James. And it is merely a visit to negotiate for full restoration of the posts."

"How did you learn of them?"

The man smiled. "Our own investigators. There are those who saw to the actual handling who could later be bought. Thieves prosper in this. Once they had disposed of the merchandise, they still had information to sell. Once we had the principal's name..."

"Cheimarrhos would be an expensive name, I imagine?"

"Expensive enough. We had made reasonable guesses. Balin is world-famous. Our host is known for his collecting. And he is hardly subtle. Once he even enquired about direct sale; he is on public record as a 'liberator' and 'protector' of relics."

"Does Paul know?"

"Not yet, Captain. I have not lied, simply withheld. I am a senior operative for a legitimate corporation dealing with Three-line in other areas. It was easy to come here. My first loyalty, however, is to Mother Church. I thought it best I learn of Council's intentions before declaring myself. And, yes, we know about the satellite. It will settle eveything, ne?"

I met the churchman's gaze. "I hold Blue. I have full executive authority where Council is concerned in matters like this."

"I suspected as much. Will you order him to return the posts?"

"Order him? First you ask what will Council do, as if it can do anything, and now this."

"Captain, please. You will understand, I hope, when I say that you are not altogether the best choice here, ne? You are Paul's friend, you are a champion of National interests. Is it not provocative to have sent you?"

I fought down my anger. "Sent, Monsignor?"

Aganture frowned, clenched his hands again, though elegantly, without force.

"But...forgive me, Captain. I naturally assumed that was how

183

it was. I know you can travel where you will..."

"James, go and declare yourself. Make your official representations and get away from here. That is a very deadly star."

James Aganture nodded, studied the striations of dust and cloud beyond the glass, the sharp and startling perspectives of the sky.

"Yes. But this is as delicate as it is urgent."

"You are here as a businessman as well as a friend."

"Exactly. We mean to buy them back if we can. Make them a gift to the tribes."

"Ah, I see. All good business, Monsignor Aganture. Curry favour for the Church."

"Captain, it really is not that simple."

"Of course. It isn't for Council either. They can't help themselves. I like to think I am here for simpler reasons."

"I see that now, of course. May I ask what they are?"

"Paul is an old friend. At a distance, it is easy to take positions, have the luxury of serving ideologies and some greater good. I came to make up my mind. I needed to know."

"Yes. I'm glad we've had the opportunity to speak. And please..."

"Your identity is safe for the moment."

"Thank you, Captain. You must understand that I cannot afford to jeopardize my organization's trade dealings with Three-line. It is difficult to know what to do for all of us."

"Keeping options open just in case."

"Very awkward, yes."

"You have spoken to his sister?"

But I saw at once that he had, that this was Sarete's answer too, and more of her questions. James Aganture was here at the invitation of Sarete Cheimarrhos, I was suddenly sure of it. I left him no time to answer.

"You ask for confidentiality. You impose upon my duty to my friend. I now ask you to tell him who you are. I give you until, let us say, dinner this evening, Monsignor, yes?"

"Yes. Yes, Captain."

And I left him, found my way down to my quarters on Level 42, welcoming the option of silence and opaqued windows, needing the time to consider what really had to be done, thinking of the Three-line device and wondering what my real reasons now were.

At sunset we saw the view that made Balin renowned across the world — the Inferno, great boiling lines of cloud plunging towards the horizon, meeting in the pit of the sun, drawn like great rivers, like tattered banners, cohorts, cables of molten gold laid upon the sky, the angles of a mad geometer hauled and hurtled into the blazing, settling point like a rehearsal for the end of days.

Even Sarete and Naesé were there for it. We sat and stood about the lounge and could not find enough words for conversation, no moment when the few comments made did not do more than force silence again.

There was only the sky, the whole world drawn to that single ravenous point. And finally, as if in scorn, the sun closed its mighty eye in one slow blink, denying the clouds their lustre, turning them to lead where they sailed, streamed, panicked in the sky: you are too late, too late, little brothers, I turn my gaze from you all.

We subsided where we sat or stood, muscles loosened, sighs sounded above the rolling, healing frenzy of the house-song. John Newmarket tugged at his collar; James Aganture slowly shook his stately head. Naesé sat with what seemed like a rapt expression on her face, considering the changed world beyond the glass. Sarete saw me give a deeper unsounded sigh, allowed the faintest trace of a smile to touch her pale lips.

Paul turned to us all, stood with his back to the glass.

"The world has many great identifying winds, enabling winds, precise expressions of the pneuma. The simoom, the sirocco, the khamsin, the meltemi, the monsoon and the santana. Pieces of the patchwork.

"I accept the reality; I accepted the challenge as Imhotep did. Here is the codex that lets us read what it tells us: not understand, never understand, but know. Just take in and know. The wind moves upon the land. It completes an equation in the soul, resolves itself through only those devices nature has raised up, precisely designed, to read what such things mean. Us. *We* are the world's way of apprehending itself. We complete all that out there.

Our affirmations, our emotions, are the lock for that great key. This house reminds us."

I smiled. Paul had uttered similar words at the Anderlee gathering three years ago. I was an easy convert; I used my own ship to affirm such truths in myself, such a rich and simple knowing.

"Tomorrow," he said, "there will be towers of cumulus and laze-lions all day, nothing like this. This is justice, Tom, for Fate having served up a windless man, trying to build some new Tarot here. So you never add this to your legend! *Comprendez?*"

"I do, Paul," I said, laughing. "I'll hobble you with eclipses and minor comets from now on. Nothing less!"

"Apology accepted, gracious man. And you, James?" Paul was exalted, magnanimous; it was a pointed gaze, laden with irony and fond reprimand that he gave the clergyman. James Aganture had no doubt confessed.

"We have riches, an embarrassment of all that humanity has wrought. Cloisters, scriptoria, great art collections, antiquities, centuries of sophistry and clever talk, the doctrines and arguments. Now I find the simplicity of my God here. I remember that my eyes are the windows of the first and last cathedral I shall ever know."

"Accepted. And you, Honest John? You've seen it before. Anything to add?"

I was interested to see that lean, spirited John Newmarket also looked abashed.

"I lost words for this ten years ago, Paul," the actor said in his rich full voice. "This must endure at all costs."

Which reminded us all and stole the edges from Paul's smile for a moment, though just a moment. Our host was not to be discouraged.

"Tonight we hold a starwatch in honour of our uninvited guest. We dress warmly. We go above. We find our personal monkey-moon and regale it, drag it up close, count its legs, tell our fortunes on its parts. I'll name every wind that troubles us. Yes?"

There was general assent, but I caught quick unguarded glances from Newmarket and Aganture towards Paul's sister, then

186

found myself at the end of Naesé's own coolly appraising gaze.

"Dinner is at 1900," Sarete announced, and led the way out of the lounge.

Paul held back, like some captain reluctant to leave the bridge of his ship, and I held back as well, not surprised when his expansive mood fell away like the gold of the departed sun.

"Do you know what Aganture is, Tom?" he said when we were alone.

"A churchman."

"He told you!" Surprise and suspicion sat in Paul's eyes for a brief, flickering instant. "Well, he hinted at trade cutbacks. Direct dealings with the tribes. Circumventing Three-line altogether. All veiled, of course, the spineless fool!"

"What will you do?"

"About Aganture?"

"About your Star?"

"They'll do it, you think?"

I shrugged, not mentioning the device, determined to keep away from that topic for the moment. "You said it yourself earlier today. The bloodlines are gone. They may not care about the poles at all. What you are becoming is a very useful example. If they strike at you, it's a warning to everyone else. They may need a precedent."

"Do you know who Newmarket represents?"

The question surprised me. "Newmarket?"

"A Tosi-Go subsidiary, a Three-line rival. A mercenary actor, Tom. *My* friend. Leave the posts where they are but sell them to Tosi-Go so the tribes dare not act. Not why he visited, oh no. Just happened to have been approached; thought he'd mention it like a caring friend."

"So what will you do?"

"No offers, Tom? Nothing from Council?"

They were bitter words, from a man who was trying hard to reconcile different realities. Forcing himself. Again.

"Nothing. I told Aganture. I cannot be who I am and come here without representing Council, but I do not follow their specific wishes."

"And what are their specific wishes, do you think?"

"I imagine to see you continue. To see Paul Cheimarrhos and Balin and Three-line survive."

"In that order? Well, two of those I heartily agree with, though I'm not sure I believe you. I'm no longer Three-line. It's an alien thing."

"You know what I mean. Council can't order you. They want you to remain as a symbol. That's your great worth to Nation. The posts matter because they put you and Balin at risk. That's how I think they'd see it anyway."

"Hm, well thank them for that. That much I can accept."

I discovered it *was* what I wanted, Paul believing that I was here for reasons of my own, out of friendship and personal esteem, for reasons ultimately as elusive and mysterious as his own. Learning of the Three-line invention had complicated the issue; I found myself needing to ask about it, realized how partisan I now felt, would be the moment I asked the questions that had tormented me all afternoon.

"What would you advise?" Paul said.

"What I told Sarete earlier. I'd stay."

"Good. The poles?"

"Hardly the issue."

"No?"

Perhaps I could ask about it. Paul had mentioned the device to me. Knowing my background, of my time in the Madhouse, he had brought it up. But again I hesitated, knowing that the moment I did ask, I was no better than Newmarket or Aganture.

"It's what I was leading up to earlier when you showed me the posts. It's the Three-line holding itself that concerns them. Not the company — this great house of yours. The concession was given a long time ago and it's become too celebrated, too newsworthy, too steady a slight. I would think getting you to admit to having the poles will be used as counter-propaganda to discredit you in National and International eyes, making you appear as someone plundering, stealing away art treasures for his own material gain. Pirate rather than privateer, Paul, the critical difference. Just one more exploiter and opportunist. I believe the satellite is meant to force your hand."

"They won't strike?"

"They'd possibly destroy what they're overtly trying to save, if that matters. It seems an unnecessarily dramatic thing, using a comsat."

Paul nodded, finally asked the inevitable question.

"Why haven't they mounted a land assault or at least done a search? Sent Kurdaitcha in?"

"Because they already have."

"What? Who?"

"Your guess. I told Sarete this afternoon. I would assume it was done long before they moved that station."

"But who?" Paul was genuinely amazed; it obviously had not occurred to him at all. Again I could see that the dream was being spoiled. "Our staff has been here since Balin was built. Cristofer and Deric came in from other Three-line holdings..."

"Exactly how I would have done it. Planted someone when Balin was being built. Before then, if I could."

"Kurdaitcha?" Paul was making himself accept another way of thinking, a hated spoiling pragmatism.

"To keep an eye on Three-line initially, yes. To make sure no new inventions came along. To keep an eye on acquisitions."

"So what happens when I don't frighten?"

"A land strike, I'd say. They must already have verification that the poles are here, so it depends on how willing they are to sacrifice a handful of relics. If they can't neutralize what Balin represents by embarrassing you, they could use the posts as an excuse to destroy it anyway. A regrettable casualty. But whatever this is, Paul, it's the final stages of some carefully planned action."

"Yet...you came."

"One Coloured Captain may suggest all Seven Captains are involved. And the other Captains will come if you ask. It may stay their hand. You're a symbol, Paul, just as we are. Not Balin, *you*. There can be other Balins, other ways of doing this. It's you we can't replace. And that's my comment, Paul, not Council's, not the Captains'."

"Yes. Yes. Thank you, Tom."

We watched the streaming, shadowing chains of cloud racing for the edge of the world. The words of my handful of desperate questions were right there, held back, barely held. It might have been the sight of Paul that stopped me. His hands were fists at his sides. He sighed.

"Tom, I have changed my will. In view of circumstances. Regarding Balin. Will you be notary to it, take the signed original back to Council?"

"Paul..."

"Whichever way it goes, I want it officially lodged. Yes?"

"I'll be glad to take it."

"And see the terms are carried out?"

The fists, the tension across his shoulders, were more vivid than words, than any other persuasion.

"Yes. If I can. Yes."

"I'll give it to you before dinner. Before we go above. Come to me in my quarters at 1840."

"At 1840."

And he left me standing there with my questions, with sudden relief and self-reproach, and before me the rushing, frenzied, cloud-wrack chasing the sun, lean, iron-grey conquistadores seeking gold but succeeding only in building night in the far hidden places of the sky.

After showering and changing, by the time I knocked on his door at precisely 1840, I had put my curiosity aside, determined to wait, trusting that he would reveal more later.

When the door slid back, I entered and found Paul sitting on a divan by the windows, the last of the day a tattered ruin of light behind him in the western sky. He was examining a Canopic jar, one of a set of four 18th Dynasty pieces resting on a low table to one side, replacing the jackal-head stopper. He set it down as I approached, took an envelope from inside his black and gold house-robe, and handed it to me as I sat down.

"A formality, Tom. I've involved Council. It's fair they know my position."

I put it in a pocket of my sandsman's fatigues and went to tell him again that it was a pleasure, but Paul spoke first.

"Tom, why were you in the Madhouse?"

I tensed immediately, feeling the barest edge of panic, residual reflex fear. It never failed to surprise me. This was the question no-one asked, that was only rarely answered if ever, that now permitted my questions to him. Paul asking it mattered. I didn't give any of the usual replies.

"I don't remember. They would not tell me."

"They?"

"Tartalen. He was in charge. One day I'll return. I'll ask."

He kept at it. "You should."

"Why, Paul?"

"There is a mystery about you. You're a National *and* a sensitive. The field is strong..."

"The other Captains..."

"No. I've met them. They've all been here at one time or another. You're different."

"Paul!"

There was a knock at the door.

"Dinner and starwatch," he said. "This will be Sarete."

"Paul!"

"Gain-monitors, Tom. We may have an audience. Later."

We went to the door, found Sarete and John Newmarket waiting there.

"We go to study our demon," Sarete said, pleasantly enough. "The others will be waiting."

"On to the feast!" Paul said, and together we headed along the corridor, the house adding our variables to its ongoing song.

Dinner was an easy affair, first Paul then John Newmarket telling stories; James Aganture giving his views on the future of Mother Church in view of new tech embargoes recently imposed.

Finally the dishes were cleared away, and the six of us started our climb to the summit. In the Gallery of Record, Cristofer and Deric gave us jackets; warmly dressed, we stepped out onto the dark windy field.

It sang under the moonless sky. Under our feet, the house moaned deeply to itself. We crossed the plateau, the acroteria looming beside us like funerary totems, bleached bones keening in the cold brinraga. We made our way through the restless shapes, keeping well clear of the central depression, heading for the northwestern corner where Anquan had set up the old Meade telescope, its short thick barrel pointed at the sky directly overhead.

"The refreshments, please," Sarete told the old major-domo, raising her voice above the rush of wind so she could be heard, and Anquan went off with Cristofer to get the evening's collation.

Paul sat on the low stool before the telescope and used the eye-piece, made some quick adjustments.

"I have him," he said, his voice strong above the air-flow. "Very wicked-looking deployed like that. They really do know how to use psychology. Who's first? James?"

The churchman moved to the stool, settled himself and peered through the eye-piece. Paul stood beside him, looking straight up, silver hair streaming in the wind.

"See it?" he asked loudly so we could all hear. "The red lights are mainly tactical — 'barrican stars' to frighten us. Tom will confirm it. They're supposed to light up like that just before a strike."

"Really?" Aganture said, moving clear of the stool. "Is that true, Captain?"

"Yes," I said, studying the small group as best I could, dark shapes, blowing shapes, wanting to ask Paul about his comments earlier, concerned that we may have been overheard and interrupted deliberately, deeply worried by what that might mean.

"Your turn, John," Paul said, and the actor took his place at the telescope.

"It does look angry," was all he said.

Paul laughed. "It wants us to think that. It's trying to be hot and raging up there, but in reality it's a very cool thing, very calm."

Newmarket rose and moved away. "I've seen enough. Captain?"

"Sarete?" I said.

"No, thank you."

"Naesé?"

"No, Captain. Thank you."

I positioned myself on the stool, and after a split-second of auto-focus saw the *irijinti*, saw it again in actual fact, since I'd seen the displays Council had at Twilight Beach, began matching its configuration with other comsats I had seen up close this way, started when Paul whispered at my ear.

"The Canopic jar is a second prototype. Get it away from here. Say a gift!"

The wind sang about us. Possibly no-one heard.

I made myself stay calm, my heart racing as I peered up at the evil red lights.

It explained everything. Not the posts. Not Balin. Not just those things. Far more serious, much greater danger. Paul had broken faith.

The jar, a duplicate. *He had used it to read me!*

"Paul...?"

"Finished already?" he said, speaking for the others to hear.

I rose from the stool. "Let me get my configuration list. I still say *irijinti*, but I want to type it. I can almost make out its markings." My voice sounded steady above the wind.

"I'll try for a better fix," Paul said, calmly enough, taking his place at the eye-piece once more.

I hurried from the field, entered the Gallery, ran down the ramps towards our chambers. My footsteps echoed on the polished stone, set a desperate percussion into the air-flow.

The palm-lock to Paul's rooms had been keyed to me, no surprise at all; the door swept aside at my touch. I crossed the softly-lit interior, immediately went to the four jars on the low table: monkey-head, falcon-head, human-head, jackal — seized the jackal-head, removed the ceramic cap, saw the dull black tech that gave it its extra weight, the recessed contacts and displays.

What had it shown? What?

"I will take that, Captain."

I turned at once. Naesé stood in the doorway, a laser baton in her hand.

"I'm sorry. This is a gift to me from Paul. Ask him."

She raised the baton, aimed it at my heart.

"Captain, I am Kurdaitcha in the final moments of a very long, very old mission."

"You..."

"Colour, Hero status, mean nothing compared to my brief, do

you understand? Without that jar and the contents of the envelope in your pocket, I will be sung. I dare not fail. Save your life."

"The envelope contains Paul's will."

"No. His will was lodged with Nation long ago. What you have contains blueprints for what you hold in your hands. Look and see."

I placed the jar on the divan, brought out the envelope and opened it, saw words and schematics.

"Yes?" Naesé said. "They are mine. Paul's life might still be yours if you hurry."

I threw the plans onto the divan and ran for the door. She let me pass but called after me. "Captain! Wait!"

I ignored her, running for the ramps, needing to get Paul from the roof, away from the telescope and the field and the line of sight of that deadly watcher, aware that it already had all the commands it needed.

I saw the result of those commands as I leapt out upon the field, a thread, a wire, the tiniest filament of dazzling light connecting Balin for just an instant to its attendant moon, then the tearing scream of its brief and deadly anger above the keening windsong.

I did not need to go out to where the telescope had stood. There would be time later. I waited by the door as the three figures came to me across the windy field, Sarete in the lead, head raised, cool and detached, resolved as ever, yes, leading them, John Newmarket and James Aganture to either side, eyes downcast, ashamed.

As I watched them approach, their faces lit from the doorway, I heard Naesé at my back, panting lightly from her run. She did not have the jar or the plans; she no longer held her weapon.

"Your mistress has done well," I said.

"She has saved Three-line and Balin," Naesé replied. "She made a difficult choice. An only choice."

"What did Paul read, Naesé?"

"What do you mean?"

"With the contents of the jar?"

"That you are a sensitive. That's all."

"Nothing else?"

"Nothing else."

"I don't believe you."

"I know."

Sarete and her companions reached us, stopped before the doorway. Her words might have come from Naesé, from a script of exculpation they had jointly devised.

"He knew the consequences, Captain. He made a choice, without considering anyone, never consulting others. Something had to be done. I made a choice too."

More words than I would have expected. Still James Aganture and John Newmarket looked in different directions at the night. Only Sarete and Naesé met my gaze.

"It wasn't the posts," I said, so nothing was hidden. "There was a second Three-line device. A duplicate."

Aganture and Newmarket both looked at Sarete.

"Nonsense," she said calmly.

"Naesé has..."

"Nonsense, Captain. There was never a duplicate."

She knew. Of course she knew. Naese did not say a word.

"I see. Privateering."

"What, this?" Sarete asked.

"All this."

"I suppose so. Not your kind, but yes."

"Not my kind, no. Never my kind."

I went out onto the field then, went to the where the old Meade telescope had stood, came back with the lines of blood painted on my cheeks.

Sarete grimaced with distaste when she saw them. "Captain, is that really necessary?"

"Tell her, Naesé."

The Kurdaitcha frowned. "He is Blue, Sarete. He has made vendetta against this house."

"You're joking. I am this house now."

"No, Sarete," I said. "I think you will find that Paul has bequeathed it to Nation. Years ago. Naesé can check."

"Ridiculous! That can be negated."

"Naesé," I said, drawing rage and loss into that small hard

word.

"You don't understand, Sarete. Those signs. In front of witnesses, he has sworn vendetta. He can strike at anything to do with Three-line, at any ships coming here. Through him, Council can. You must leave here. All of you."

It took only moments for the implications to be understood.

"This is not the end of this," Sarete said.

"No," I was able to say. "It is not."

On the desert near Sabro, there is a mighty house, a vast pylon set against the sky. Though left to Nation as a final bequest from the man who caused it to be, it is deserted now, neither National nor tribal, a monument at the interface. The great vents stand open; the structure howls and sings and braids the winds into endless tapestries, strange proclamations of desire. At the crest is a field and a shallow empty dish thirty metres across.

Once a year, seven ships go to that great house, the only ones who can since it is reached by crossing tribal land. The crews climb aloft and reach that field. While the crew-members do small acts of maintenance, the Captains sit in the depression and talk.

Sometimes there is a ritual of watching sunset, sometimes a starwatch. Kites are set upon the air, new pennants added to the dream.

At such times, coincidentally, no satellites ever cross that sky. The comsats studiedly avoid the place as if contemptuous of something all too futile.

The Captains smile in the windy darkness or in the flowing riot of the dying sun. More than anyone, they know the worth of dreams.

They know it is never that.

Dreaming the Knife

Stiletto night. The moon itself a sharp narrow blade curving close to the dry hilt of the land, rising, being drawn ever further into its bed of stars.

Tynan Lees stood at the starboard rail of the speeding sandship and felt the beginnings of the Knife.

"Ah. Is this it?" He spoke the words aloud, as if he doubted what it could be; there was no feeling like it. "Is this my dagger I have before me?"

Old words. Probably Islamic, Omar Khayyam, he thought as he said them, and what did he really know of Islam? Just the origins of his name. Assassin.

He found the deep focusing again. Yes, the concentration was definitely there. Soon, soon he would have it. Instinctively, barely noticing it did so, his right hand closed to receive the haft, another old custom, as old as haldane Kurdaitcha, possibly older. His other hand gripped the rail.

Tynan Lees smiled at the wonderful irony. As an Ab'O aboard *Rynosseros*, the only Ab'O, he had made this night voyage possible, exempting the vessel from the usual strictures imposed by the tribes. His presence allowed this powered run into the sheath of night — no need for kites and wind, though there was wind aplenty whistling about the superstructure, pouring over him from the bows.

And by midnight, much sooner but midnight would be right for it, when there was no colour to him, when he was darkness too, the Knife fully formed in his sharp clear mind, then he would send it into the heart of the Blue Captain. At just the right time, everything perfect, the dagger moon at zenith.

Tom Rynosseros would be dead at last, the debt paid in full.

"Mr Lees?"

The Ab'O turned, his right hand first tightening before relaxing from its grip altogether.

But it was the old man, the bald leather-skinned kitemaster, Scarbo, there beside him at the rail.

"I'm standing down now. Tom has the next watch. He wants to know if you'll take a cup of tautine with him."

Drink with the enemy first, yes. He'd refused the old man's invitation earlier, waiting for this.

"Tell Captain Tyson I'd be honoured."

"You might do that, sir. I'm going for'ard myself."

Lees felt his body tense, felt the rush of anger at this casual insolence. But no second Knife for this one, not ever. Scarbo was not the sensitive his master was. No Knife would take him.

Perhaps a strike of a more temporal kind though — a quick sword-thrust between the ribs. Let the whole ship go down with its Captain, he thought, though Tynan Lees knew he would never do such a thing. It was just his anger, his contempt for these ignorant Nationals. He had long ago become a man of honour, useless exalting male honour. As his Lady Sa once reminded him: only men fought duels. And the helplessly patriarchal Lees saw his own folly laid out in those words — the feeling of having to go outside exalting nature to be so wise. He could never do it.

He watched the kitemaster depart, made the quick motion of his hands that meant unworthy, then found the shape of his quarry at the helm, mostly silhouette, just the tiniest part of him illuminated by the lights from the companionway and the soft glow of the helm's own readouts.

Night, when everyone is dark, lit only at the eyes.

Lees crossed the commons and climbed to the quarterdeck.

"Captain Tyson, good evening."

"Good evening to you, Blade Lees. I'm sorry we did not meet earlier. We're undermanned at present; I was using the somnium after a double watch."

Lees made a gesture — probably unseen — to show it was of no consequence, but his thoughts were racing.

Blade Lees? This National knew him for a non-Kurdaitcha assassin, a man from one of the private households. It made Lees check the underline: the psychic stratum where the Knife was turning about itself, newborn and wonderful.

"Captain, the honorific? You know us?"

"I know you, Blade Lees. Of you, I should say. I knew the Lady Sa."

He speaks it from his own mouth. Good. But how? How could he know?

It was as if Blue Tyson read his thoughts. "Scarbo recognized the house sersifan you wore when you came aboard. The Lady Sa's sign. He told me."

" 'May her face be carried in righteous glory before the eyes of heaven,' " Lees murmured.

" 'May her heart be itself a lantern in the dark places of her passing.' "

Another shock. "You also know the *Amduat*, Captain?"

"I know that your Lady Sa cherished the *Book of the Dead*. Will you have tautine or tisn?"

Composure was what Lees needed. Part of his Lady's sign, there on the sersifan he yet wore on his chest, was the crescent moon that now rose above the desert fastness, that had in fact determined the day and hour of this strike, Lees timing it just so.

"What I would really like, Captain, is kites. Can we spare some, even for a powered night run?"

Perhaps his enemy smiled, he could not tell. "By coming aboard at Maldy you have saved us a day's run to Sollellen. It will be a pleasure, Blade Lees."

"Tynan, Captain, please." He could not stand the honorific here with the Knife forming, safely lodged in the fierce dark of its becoming.

"Tom, then," his enemy said, leading him into further unwanted intimacy, trapping him.

Fortunately Blue Tyson was touching controls, sending commands to the cable-boss, releasing the inflatables from their deck sleeves, the only automatic barrage *Rynosseros* carried, four helium-filled parafoils that ran up on their lines, deploying against the vivid stars in curved squares of intense black.

"Your signature kite?"

"Furthest out."

"Not closest in? Heart of the shapes?"

"I prefer the tribal way. 'The brave man leads'."

"Ah." Now the Bayas *I Ching* as well. Lees imagined the insignia, blue animal head on ochre. Yes, he thought, and quickly found the Knife defining itself, solace in that, power and purpose too. "Thank you. You can tell I am one for the old ways. It does not seem complete without a canopy."

" 'The truth of her form curves in beauty above the land,' " Tom Tyson said, quoting again from the ancient Egyptian funeral texts.

This was unexpected. Lees never doubted the Knife once it had been summoned, but nor could he resist finding it, cherishing it as a miser would a favourite jewel.

"But drink." The voice summoned him. "Then tell me how you came to serve the Lady Sa."

Back to it. And with such a request.

Lees took the cup of tautine and surveyed the night. As he sipped the sharp refreshing liquid he looked upwards, savoured the clear cool wind shearing away the few clouds, listened to it singing in the cables, saw how the kites spread, the separations intact and satisfying, dark as they were, found the one he thought carried this Blue Captain's sign. Beyond the shapes, the moon was rising as surely as his minding did in him, and close behind, no more than a few kilometres now surely, the recovery ship, *Kulta*, was riding in *Rynosseros'* dust trail, its Clever Man captain, dependable Merdes, tuned to Lees' mind-line, waiting to be called in for the pick-up when the act was done.

Kulta was special, Soti-made but Kurdaitcha outfitted, a favour to the new Soti Prince. *Rynosseros'* systems would never find her.

Lees smiled. What to tell his enemy as his Lady's sign rose and the Knife formed? All of it? Bring his beloved Lady Sa alive for this time of justice? Speak her out, more than keep her in memory? Oh yes, if Lees himself could stand it.

"Captain..."

"Tom."

"I have been the most blessed of men. I was out-of-family, a bastard son abandoned at birth, without pedigree. Before I came to be a household man, part of a retinue, before I knew I had the gift, I was destined for the Samanta levies. You know them?"

"Yes."

"It would have been a small life. I was sixteen years old, in the muster, actually lined up for the selections, standing in the dust outside the Chirason Gate, when my Prince came by. What a day that was."

"Stoutheart Tiberias Kra."

"Yes indeed. Before he died at Heart-and-Hand. Before he was..."

"I was there, Tynan. I saw him die."

You did, Lees said to himself, but my Knife is not for that.

"I was told you did. With Kra this day was his sister, the Lady Sa, and the Clever Man, Medenty, Kra's close friend, often a valued adviser to both of them. She was in her fifties then, but still a great beauty, and a powerful administrator with powerful enemies of her own.

"They regarded the dozens of us for Samanta, the ones not taken by the techmakens and the Colleges. The three of them spoke together. Suddenly I felt them at my mind, Kra and this Medenty, at that time assigned to my Lady's staff. They tracked my mind-line, found my origins and the latency. Kra went about his business. I was taken aside and interviewed by the Lady Sa, then by her Clever Man, then by them both together. Right there in the levy office, with everybody watching. They offered me training and a posting to the Lady's private household."

Blue Tyson's voice came gently out of the darkness.

"And how many Knives have you summoned in her service, Tynan?"

"In ten years? Eighty-six."

Eighty-seven, he told himself, and found the shape again.

"She used you sparingly."

"Kra wanted me for his own, but there was a promise being kept: the next mind-fighter hers. She insisted on it. I wore her sersifan, took only her enemies. Eighty-six is not many, but if you had their names you would be amazed."

"You are a Clever Man?" the Blue Captain asked, inevitably.

"No, Captain. I carry only the Knife. I access no haldanes, read only a few of the dragons. But I know you have something of the gift." Lees had already scanned his enemy and knew how limited that gift was. One application only.

"Sometimes I see hero-shapes," Tom Rynosseros said. "No dragons."

"But you can follow mind-war."

"I see energies build and fade, nothing more. Few patterns."

"I was told that when Kra died at Heart-and-Hand you saw the patterns there."

"A rare occasion, Tynan. It's not always like that."

He tells that much truth at least.

"My Lady asked to see you because of it. She sent for you when she heard. Your account helped her accept what happened that day, let her see her brother had caused the strike against Heart-and- Hand, that protocols were observed."

"And so helped cause her death."

He admits it! Speaks it from his own mouth!

Lees fought to keep his voice even. "You brought the man Docri on your ship."

"Not my man. I knew him as a mercenary interested in a commission for Samanta. I was on my way to see your Lady Sa at her invitation. I did not know he had a contract against her."

Not what our Clever Men say, Captain Tom!

"You brought him."

"Paid passage, Tynan."

"You were told to observe closed ship."

"That directive came when we were an hour out of Maldy. I had already granted passage to one I took to be an approved contract-soldier."

"Always a man of honour," Lees said. His voice might have trembled just a little, though deep in him the Knife was sure.

"Like you, Tynan. More tautine?"

"No." The mind had to be steady. "Some tisn if I may."

So he could drink with his enemy still, with her sign rising beyond his.

Tom Rynosseros found the flask, filled two ceramic cups. Lees heard them clink; took one in his hand. Heard the words: "Help yourself to more." Drank in silence.

Ten minutes, perhaps thirty went by, Lees could not tell, not having the helm display. He had the night, the Knife, and he considered one in terms of the other.

It was easy to do with the scimitar moon midway to zenith. Sharp. Sweet. Precious. The wind rising, building into a stronger, richer roadsong.

All good. All soothing.

As a household man, Lees had not been on many ships — a voyage now and then when the Lady Sa travelled, sometimes alone when there was something to be done, occasionally an act of payback such as this was. But the ways of charvolants were always new and exciting.

Only the moon made it different now, made the pain new — her sign suspended right there. Sometimes the kites moved, and held it occluded for a moment. Then it was back, sure and sharp.

Bitter moon. Pointed. Poignant.

Poignard.

An hour or two to midnight. It couldn't be more. He reached out to *Kulta* riding like a shadow close behind, touched Merdes' mind, confirmed the form this would take. Nothing more than a touch of mind, a yes, no need of an answer.

Then a glance at the Knife. He held it as sure and steady as a shout. Quiet pride in that; he knew he had never made better.

His second cup of tisn had gone cold. It no longer warmed his hands. He became aware that he had been lost in thought, that a silence had been between them.

Still an hour at least. Long silences were the sailor's way, he knew, but more words would be needed soon. Something.

Blue Tyson spoke. "You were not at Chirason that day."

He keeps at it! "I was rostered elsewhere, Captain. Kra had left no sons. There were accession protocols and representations from all the houses. I was away from the household on my Lady's business to the newly-chosen Prince."

"Have you ever wondered at that?"

"What?"

But Tom Rynosseros kept silent, an almost fully-dark form at the helm, lit only in a small blue-green glimmer at the underside of the jaw, in a faint yellow wash at the right shoulder.

"What was that, Captain?" Lees asked, though the question had penetrated by then.

"Why would anyone wish to kill the Lady Sa?"

Again he dares! So casually. Anger filled him.

Lees forgot midnight. He brought the Knife into that state of readiness Kurdaitcha, Clever Men and Unseen Spears called *adaio*, the thrust or the cast, one moment before. At the same moment he reached out, scanned his adversary two paces away, read the inchoate mindfield this National had, the receiving field that gave the Knife its edge, let it be the way, reached back to find *Kulta* as well, said: Now.

And simultaneously, for all it took was an instant, he thought of Lady Sa dying, lying in her airy room in Chirason, fatally poisoned, sinking into death. Lees and his Lady alone, as astonishing as that was. Medenty and Merdes and the medics all sent away. Ordered away by a few imperious words from the dying woman.

"Jimi, you will heed what I say." Jimi, she had always called him when they were alone; her private name for the boy she had from the Chirason Gate, from the sure promise of Samanta. "It was not...this Docri...you understand. He gave the first-stage toxin. When he greeted me. The reagent...was given later. Jimi..." And she had arched up, died, just like that, not in his arms though one hand had reached up to claw at his, but there with his name — his other name — on her lips.

Adaio. The Knife spinning and flashing in the underline, filling it, target aligned.

"Tynan, tell me. Why the Lady Sa?"

Adaio. You saw her before I did. Spoke to her an hour before. You.

"Blade Lees, this is important! Why the Lady Sa?"

It was not the demand of an answer that saved the Coloured Captain then; it was the reflexive need of Lees' training, to betray nothing by how he spoke. That mental effort to control his voice for any kind of answer other than the truth took the strike from *adaio* to held-and-waiting again.

Wait, he told *Kulta* riding in the dark, moving in.

"I was told..."

"You were told? Who told?"

"Her Clever Men. Medenty and the others."

"Forget what they said, just for a moment. They may have been deceived too. Why the Lady Sa?"

Too? Lees did not answer. Could not trust himself to.

"You carry a Knife for me, Tynan?"

Thank the Ancestors for darkness; this tested all his composure. What to say? Midnight. He'd never reach it. The dagger of mind spun in its fire. Screamed there, ached there, targeted.

The Blue Captain was speaking.

"...think I caused her death, don't you?"

Yes, Lees wanted to say, to shout, glad to be free of secrecy. The best justice was known justice, guilt admitted, payback understood.

"Yes!" It took him seconds to realize he had spoken aloud, confessed his mission. Lees held the Knife very close to *adaio*, aware of the kites, the emblem moon, the wind in the cables, keenly alert for his enemy's crew in hiding, planted earlier in anticipation of this admission from him. But Lees read nothing, not a presence, not a chance. Why was this National telling him then?

"My final night," Tom Rynosseros said, "if you have a Knife for me. You might answer my questions. A discourse to the end. Midnight, yes?"

How does he know? Lees wanted to scream the words. Was he more the sensitive than they said? Could he read the presence buried in him, using the very skill that would doom him? Could he see *Kulta* riding in the night? Lees was used to reading the capabilities of his targets quickly, skilfully, so none ever knew he had done so, and he had found no trace of such an ability. It was not possible. It just wasn't.

Lees did something he had not done in eight years at least. He recited the accession mantra to himself, used it to become the atavism again, the calm centre, the Hand-with-the-Knife, the distillation of impassive force. He considered the land, unseen, rushing by out there, wove that into his silent song — read ship and stars and stones, tapping, trapping their imagery. The Lady Sa did not intrude, nothing unwanted did. He even used the old word-stations: home to hone, cry to kris, stillness to stiletto. He read the land as knives. Night to Knife.

He was himself the form he carried when he returned to the cold cup crushed in his hand, to the wetness of tisn mixed with blood, to his silent enemy watching him. Some eyelight told him that.

"It is now," he said, Knife said, the only thing possible. Knife spun, ached in him, *as* him.

"Do it on a question," Blue Tyson said. "One answer."

"Yes." Barely.

"In Chirason. At the tribal court. Pretend it was not me, though I swear I did not do it. Why would anyone want to kill your Lady? For a moment pretend. Why would anyone else?"

"Advantage." So difficult to say.

"Yes? Something more?"

"Inheritance." Difficult. More than one answer too, but Lees stayed with it.

"Yes, Tynan. Inheritance always through the female. Who chose the new Prince?"

"Clever Men. Convocation. A corroboree."

"Why him?"

"Medenty? Closest blood. The closest."

"Who opposed?"

"No-one." Agony.

"Who opposed in secret and dared not speak?"

"What?" *Adaio*.

"Who opposed? Who might have?"

"No-one."

"Your Lady did."

Adaio! Adaio! Knife shouted. But he had to ask. "How do you know?"

"Was she asked to wed the new Prince?"

"Formality. Asked, yes."

"Tenure, Blade Lees. Sanction. Permanence. You hurried back to find her almost gone. I believe she could not tell you all of it. Tynan, someone delayed the message telling me closed ship. Who told you it was me who finally killed her?"

"Her best. My teacher. Our new Prince."

"Medenty."

"Most loyal. Yes."

"And your friend? Merdes?"

"Yes. He said so too. Others did."

"What is Merdes' line?"

"What?"

"His line, Tynan!"

"Anjan through Jurinju. Medenty's true son..."

"The new Prince of the Soti. Your Lady had no sons?"

"No."

"No secret sons?"

"No!"

"Tynan, I was with her. She was dying. She had already been given the reagent. She asked me to find you. You arrived when I had gone."

"You lie!"

"No, Jimi." Incredibly, Blue Tyson spoke *that* name. (Could he have lifted it from his mind? Could he?) "She loved you. She asked me to search. You were no casual find at the Chirason Gate. You are her undeclared son and she wanted you saved. Possibly you as Prince of the Soti. But she had powerful enemies. She dared not say. It would have been your death."

"You did not say before. You let me continue."

"You had drawn the Knife."

"No! No! I hadn't then. You could have met me when I came aboard at Maldy. Tell me!"

"Then it must be some other promise to your Lady. Not my way but hers, yours."

Lees' hands were fists, the Knife barely held, the force too great. He had never rejected a summoning before, never withstood one, never even tried. He had never been wrong. "What?"

"Not yet. It must be done your way."

"What?"

But he knew. He understood the simple truth of words spoken long ago. You learn by doing, Jimi. Only men fight duels. Men who learn the other way, the female way, calculate and avoid, use subtlety. He had never been that kind of man, but others were. His own friend and captain, Merdes. Oh, Medenty, can it be? Powerful *Kulta* riding in the night, Merdes there, coincidence?

Lees turned from the helm, ran to the great stern vanes where the rooster tail of dust boiled up in its roaring spray. He turned the form within him, re-made, re-shaped it, a thing never done before, gave the bright blade another face, sent it hurtling back at the hungry shadow.

He did not need to know it had found its mark. He did not need to know that twelve crewmembers would speak forever of a force rushing through them out of the night, finding their captain.

The place in him was empty and calm, the last of Jimi put aside. Now he moved back to the helm.

"Will you come with me into Chirason?" he asked the quiet figure at the helm.

"I promised your Lady I would. As witness. There may be one more Knife."

"Yes."

Fifteen minutes later, *Rynosseros* swung away from Sollellen onto Lateral 246. Neither man said a word, but Lees found the kite of the Blue Captain where it rode on the darkness, looked beyond it to where the sharpest vendetta moon rose bright and hard on the face of heaven.

A dagger, yes, definitely that. But a smile too, he decided, as her shape rose to the darkness of his, Knife to night.

Definitely a smile.

Totem

Everything has its message.
Nothing tells us nothing.

– Andrew Mallin

The life dump on the outskirts of Tell is not the only one the tribal biotects have used. During the secretive years, the heady early years of the AI quest, the Ab'O scientists of Australia took the cast-offs and spoil from their life experiments out beyond Wani, far beyond Bullen Meddi to the shore of the lonely sand-sea at Trale and left them there. It was the dumping place before respectability came to Tell, before the exciting decades that ended with the True Lifer riots and the cut-backs.

Trale today is unique in all the world, though so few go there or dare speak openly of its existence. Officially it does not exist. It is taboo as both idea and fact.

Today beach totems stand along the blazing shores, strange teratoid constructs of bismin, citilo and tri-sephalay, a thousand variants and hybrids as unsettling to see as an unresolved trompe l'oeil or a suspected false perspective or a stairway to nowhere in a half-demolished house. They are called — fittingly enough — Abominations by the tribes, more disturbing than Fosti with its Living Towers (that life project had global acclaim and tribal endorsement at least), more by far than the thousands of belltrees scattered across Australia, left as roadposts beside quiet desert Roads, or set up as tourist novelties on the terraces of the coastal hotels.

The Trale totems seize the eye like a new colour; they stand in the heat of the day like bright stone flowers, or glitter under the moon like wet iron or the subtle dozen midnights in an insect's back, inviting apposite names only art critics and classicists could love: trochars, onagers, spinnerets, magganons — the list goes on, an ambitious attempt to rationalize what simply is. Failed experiments run riot. Abominations.

There are seven distinct shores at Trale, reaching out from a low pentagonal headland that is nowhere more than six feet above the surrounding desert, yet high enough to give a gentle gradient to the long beach slopes where the totems stand, a point of distinction: beach, sand-sea, headland.

On the flat, heat-baked promontory itself is Fender's Folly, what probably started as a testing station (or worse, a killing vault, though who would admit to that?) before it was abandoned and the cast-offs left to flourish unsupervised in their own strange fashion. The Folly became the obvious pied-à-terre for anyone permitted into the region, or for those who took the dreadful risk, eluded surveillance and came anyway: walls to shelter behind from the cold night winds, ledges under which to hide from the mid-day sun, a condensation post and bore rig feeding a cistern.

It is like a sephalay masonic form itself, or a construct left behind from Eniwetok or other test sites from that time of global strife. For me, the blank interlocking causeways and revetments have always suggested that sort of thing, as if a World War 2 gun emplacement had been wedded to the ancient observatory at Jantar Mantar in India. But that is all. It has never spoken to me as it has to some.

Warboy called it an angry place, or rather a place for anger, true to his arguments about locality. He found its pointlessness infuriating.

"Look!" he cried, too loudly in the terrible heat, striding up from where we had moored our Dimity sand-skiff. "It's a locked cipher, Tom. It does nothing, tells nothing. A controlled nullity!"

"Forget it, Michael," I replied, entering the Folly by the worn path. It took me behind the first of the high canted walls into the shadows just now forming at 1116. The slender band of darkness was infinitely precious.

Warboy strode along the top of the wall, a vigorous grey-haired man in his early fifties. The anger he read in the Folly came from him, from too much stored too long behind that hard florid face. He stepped from one concrete bastion to another, waving his arms like a mad Bedouin chief.

"Mallin says he has decoded this! This!"

I sat leaning into the shadow edge, pressing back against the wall, imagining that it cooled me more than it actually did. All the way in he had been like this, raving about Mallin and his informational theories. Nothing about the totems and Mallin's work there — he accepted that readily enough. Only about the claims made in *The Beach Gazette* or in some humble three-page feature in an issue of *New Land*, that the Folly had itself become an encoding by association, an accidental but integral rosetta for something, because of the totems, because of the focusing.

I would have called him down, reminded him once again that we were here to solve the mystery of a man's death, but I cherished the thin shade, the time alone without the wearying intensity of him. I still believed that he would make an effort when I gave him my news. I told myself that Michael was completing a valid transaction of his own, that he would be of no use till that was done.

It took half an hour, no more. I was drowsing in the shadow margin when he returned, stretched out on the concrete like the effigy of a crusader knight. He came down the main ramp, turning into the section of gallery we were using. I looked up at him standing there, wondering not for the first time what his eyes looked like.

Warboy believed in the eyeline and the dangers of eyelining; he would never remove his sunglasses, nor would he allow me to remove mine.

"You know what, Tom?" His voice was easier, thank goodness, the echoing harshness gone. "There's a new one on Beach 4. Not far from where Jacobi died."

He always spoke as if I had more than a cursory knowledge of the Trale site.

"Have you typed it?"

"No," he said. "It may not be locked yet. Could be a dexter variant, but with a trumpet bell opening two-thirds up. Something new. I'll write it up, send a copy to Mallin."

"You won't have to," I said, sitting up, deciding to get it over with.

"What?" Some of the habitual anger again. Mallin's name was that kind of negative talisman.

"Andrew is coming out too, Michael. He'll be here around 1300."

It was almost worth it to see the dropped jaw and open mouth (I had to imagine the widened disbelieving eyes), to hear the incomprehensible sounds he made as words wouldn't come, then the harsh cry: "What! But he's out at Mandana!"

"Not now he isn't. He's on his way here. It's what the tribes want; both of you involved. Jacobi dead on Beach 4 with all the symptoms of heart attack — or an eyeline death — is reason enough, wouldn't you say?"

"You don't..."

"Please, Michael. Hear me out. You saw the pictures. You saw that look of bewilderment and terror, the staring eyes. You saw the clenched fists. Fingernail scarring. Extreme stress. No other human trace; there was no-one else here. The tribes did the forensics and found nothing. So they call us in. They specified you and Andrew. I'm just scrutineer. Accept it, will you? It's going to be hard enough. You were colleagues together — two of you still are, like it or not."

The thick canted walls were open to the sun, to an infinity of blazing emptiness, but Michael Warboy looked like a man caught in a trap. His eyes were shut away behind black glass, but his silence and sudden composure were more than just calculating. I was used to the ravings that had marked our voyage, the characteristic vituperation against faculty colleagues and projects other than his own. His lack of response now was frightening to see. Finally he spoke again.

"Who's bringing him out?"

"Lisa Maiten."

He knew of her; she had done lab work for Life Studies in her postgrad years at Inlansay.

"Hmph. Probably another Mallinite by now." He might have spat had his throat been less dry. He made the motion. "Can I say something?"

"One more thing, Michael," I said quickly. For all I knew it might be my final chance. "I want to get this done as smoothly as possible, so we Nationals look good out of this. We've got less than 24 hours till the watch-ship picks us up, that's all. I'm not sure why you and Andrew are such enemies..."

"It's complicated, Captain." There was new distance between us. Captain instead of Tom. But at least he was calmer; maybe being at Trale did it, having the chance to do first-hand research again, any kind of first-hand work himself.

I decided to pursue the matter. "Coming out here you said it's his ancillary encodements, his notion of extended contexts. Do you think it might be simpler — that his disbelief in eyelining upsets you?"

"I've got till 1300 you say?"

"You see both points of view are vital now? Three months ago Jacobi came out to update the index — that's what I was told — and he died of fright. They kept us away all that time, no Nationals allowed in."

"An eyeline death needs another set of eyes, Captain. Another soulframe to launch the intention. He had no-one with him, the old fool. The tribes would have cleared him for an assistant, but no. He came all this way alone."

"He wasn't wearing glasses when they found him, Michael. They were in his pocket. What makes a man take off his sunglasses at mid-day?"

"What are you saying?"

"It's what the tribal investigators are saying — that it's not an accidental eyelining at all, that it's deliberate encodement. A totem *told* him to die. They need to know if they have created some death-look analogue. That's why they specified you. And Mallin, since you were both attached to Jacobi's staff. But they need you, Michael. They respect your eyelining theories, your published work."

Warboy's impassive chitinous gaze held mine. He knew all this, and the idea intrigued him. This was his area, the informational legacies of unsuspected things. He was no doubt considering Mallin's imminent arrival and counting his losses. It was a curious withdrawal to watch, as if he were dampening a self-indulgent mode of conduct and superimposing another.

"It would have to be a mover."

"Explain that." I needed to be sure.

"Mutable. Only partially locked. You know that most of them are solar-powered, but I mean more than just aligning to the sun throughout the day. It had to change its configuration in some catalysing way — approach, reach and probably depart from a potential ideomorphic crisis, a freak or intended conjunction. Like a baited trap. Forget the sergeant-majors, the xoanons and the sandwives; they're almost always locked forms. Something lured Jacobi in close; he removed his glasses to see it a different way; the configuration reached culmination, then probably evolved away from it. No trace now that we could find."

There was a hollow boom from somewhere down the shore, then another, and another further out. The 'noon guns' were going off, the magganons releasing their stored-up gases into the overheated air. You could hear the tinkle of glass as the payloads burst free of the fragile chimneys.

It was the active part of the day. All along the burning Trale shores, the unlocked and mutable totems did whatever it was they did. The trochars siphoned up their tainted artesian spill; the orreries shifted their bright fossil lenses; the spinnerets laid fragile cable that shot forth to dry, turn to powder and blow away on the afternoon winds.

More guns sounded, dozens of sharp detonations now. Michael and I waited till the last of them had discharged their loads. Then I stood and took one of two identical envelopes from inside my djellaba.

"Here's all the tribal authorities gave us. It's not much."

He took it, slipped it inside his own sand-robes. "Just keep Andrew out of my way, all right? I'll use the hour I've got." He turned and left the Folly.

I sat in the concrete gallery another ten minutes, then decided that as scrutineer I should be keeping an eye on what Warboy did at Beach 4. I climbed onto one of the baffles, followed its course around to the north so I could spot the scientist.

The shoreline shimmered in the heat; the hundreds of intervening totems seemed to shift more than their functions allowed — the air above them glinted still with suspended silicon particles from the noon firings, though the guns were finished now. The beaches were quiet.

There was no sign of Warboy at all, not at 4 or 5, not beyond at the furthermost sites out near 7.

I immediately looked southward to 3, 2 and 1 — no sign of him there either, and a quick glance downslope showed he wasn't collecting gear from our modest Dimity skiff.

In this strange landscape, it was easy to feel irrational panic. I found my binoculars and tried again. Through the instrument the images settled down, steadied. I moved across Beach 4 quickly — from the swollen onion base and tall organ-pipe chimney of a re-loading magganon, on to another, on to the shifting light-boxes and smoothly-cycling lenses of an orrery, across to a splendid rorschach, its distended butterfly-wing platelets lifted to the sun. Downslope then to a sergeant-major standing alone at the very edge of the sand-sea like an elongated Mayan stele.

He wasn't there. I was about to move on to Beach 5 when a trochar split in two — or rather a crouching figure stood away from it. Warboy had been behind it, doing what Jacobi had probably been doing, noting close detail. I saw the shrouded figure put his glasses back on, stand back from the totem, studying it.

"Damn you, man!" I said, feeling incredible relief, annoyed that Trale had gotten to me this way. I left the high walls of the Folly and hurried to him.

The trochar he examined sat like the carapace of a tortoise made from dirty stained-glass, ribbed and frosted in dull mottled shades, mostly ochres but also green, dark purple and bronze. There was the dusty six-foot spire of a percept tower lifting from one end, fitted with sensor spines, these upturned slightly and locked at the noon hour. The only movement came from the subterranean moisture cycling sluggishly behind the cloudy panes, bubbling through the conduits, drawn out of the earth, heated by the sun and fed back to it laden with volatized amino acids and exotic enzymes. Not for the first time, it occurred to me that there were secret places beneath this forsaken sand-sea only the trochars knew.

"Anything?" I asked.

"Nothing here, no," Warboy said, turning away from the trochar, facing where the body had been found. "But Jacobi might have staggered over to the kill-site from here."

We crossed the long slope to the spot itself, tagged with its yellow peg. Jacobi had been on his back; he could have fallen away from any of the three totems standing close by: a locked coralline dexter, a mature spinneret, and a primed and straining onager, a sport in that, curiously, unlike its kin, it was turned away from the sand-sea, facing half-upslope instead. Its armature was curved right back, its ladle full.

Or as Warboy had said, Jacobi might have staggered down the hard smooth slope from any direction. The winds that scoured the Trale littoral would soon rake the sand clear of footprints.

I imagined the dying, sun-blinded scientist spinning away from some lethal bioform, arms flailing or pressed across his eyes as he wandered among the totems to this eventual dying place. With nothing for company but Abominations, possibly a magganon firing a final salute, a bubble of gas bursting free, showering him with flecks of glass, or an onager ratcheting its arm, kicking its lump of organic waste out onto the sand-sea.

Or nothing as dramatic. Nothing at all. Just the thick fluids bubbling through the trochars, just the heat and the silence.

"Can you do tests?"

Warboy grunted. "I can duplicate a few," he said, sounding distracted. "But why bother? Tribal investigators did all that. My job is to observe the bioforms. Speculate, since that's all I can do."

"Buddy system, Michael. One of these has probably killed a man."

"All right. Our job. Don't worry, I'll work with Andrew. But I intend to do my own work too."

"I understand." And I returned to Fender's Folly, not letting myself look back till I was among the low walls and could use my binoculars. I felt guilty doing it, but I hoped to catch a glimpse of the man's eyes.

Andrew Mallin arrived at 1310, his thirty-foot Maud skiff appearing as a coloured spectre out of the south-west. Lisa jockeyed the seven kites with a skilful touch and brought the craft in next to ours.

Andrew Mallin didn't make it easy for her. In his eagerness to reach Trale, the tall hawk-faced man stood in the bow, wearing his glasses but without sand-robes of any kind. His leather scrap-jacket was open, the bright circles, squares and triangles of the simulated mission patches made him look like an airman from another age rescued and brought here, in no way the colleague of the earnest figure out on Beach 4.

He jumped from the low deck and rushed to shake my hand.

"Tom! Lisa said you were chosen for this. Good to see you again. A single day but better than nothing. Where's Michael?"

"At the site," I said, indicating a point on the shimmering shoreline, then went to help Lisa unload the skiff. Together the three of us carried their equipment into the Folly.

"He must be furious," Mallin said when we were among the walls. He smiled as he used binoculars to locate his colleague. Lisa Maiten and I exchanged smiles of our own; she had been the only sailor the Department of Life Studies could call on who had sufficient accreditation to qualify for Trale, a former postgrad in her thirties, red-headed, palely pretty, an experienced sailor dying of Colourman's Disease, at the end of her third remission. It was always good to see her; I applauded her unspoken reasons for wanting it this way, doing what she loved so much. No doubt she had endured Mallin's tirades travelling here as I had Warboy's.

When Mallin left for Beach 4, tribal file under his arm, I walked with Lisa down to the skiffs.

"What's the real problem, Tom?" she asked as we checked the brakes and chocked the wheels against the afternoon winds.

"Getting them to co-operate, to see this invitation as more than just the formality it probably is. With Jacobi gone, they're more faculty rivals than ever. I'm sure Mallin will have told you that

Warboy is an eyeliner, if you didn't know it before. Keep your glasses on. He'll tend to stay away from the rest of us."

"I was in Physics but I knew Life Studies had one on staff," she said. "I suspected it might be Warboy. Is he the whole thing?"

"Oh yes. Eye-contact programs the unconscious. Looks can kill, casual glances trigger malaise or death-switch or angst."

"Or elation. Or love."

"Or schizophrenic imbalance."

Lisa shook her head at the wonder of it. "How does he get to teach?"

"He doesn't. Purely research. But he publishes constantly. Makes the Department and the university look very good."

"But doesn't often walk the streets, I bet."

"True."

"What's the word?"

"Psychoactive. Human eye-contact is psychoactive. You get looked at in a crowd, a quick meaningful glance at dinner, meet someone's eyeline in passing — I suppose you have exchanged something, a naked moment. Soulframe to soulframe. I'd hate to think they're right."

"Is there valid research I should be keeping up on?" Which might have been a first oblique reference to Colourman's.

"Very little that's empirically sound. Mainly testimonials. 'I was deflected from personal resolution on 4th May.' Claims of faith healing and shaman magic, crucial historical encounters; the choosing of known and potent evil-eye emissaries to foreign courts, Christ's laying on of hands actually being an eyeline ministration of great power. This is provocative and top secret because tribal AI is being accused of soulframe status. It was a traumatic death..."

"Heartstop caused by shock."

"Blood analysis suggests that. The scarring on the palms. One of these constructs does seem to be a killer."

"Ersatz life, Tom..."

"Don't say that, Lisa. These *are* lifeforms. I have to keep telling myself that too. Congruence is missing, that's all. No meaningful exchange. The tribes are very nervous about it — Jacobi was here at their behest, checking the variants. Accusations have been made in the media that he found things the tribes wanted hidden, that they meant him to die. Eyelining is not nonsense for them, but they'd like it confirmed or refuted one way or the other. Have they unwittingly created death-look?"

"I certainly don't pick easy ones." She looked beyond our moored skiffs, watching the empty desert. Perhaps it was another reference to her condition, though if so it was a comment too pointed to acknowledge. The sand-shades hiding her eyes made it safe and easy, a true blessing; Colourman's changed the eyes, told observers that a strange and beautiful brain death was occurring, slowly taking a personality down into the infinite corridors of self, leaving it trapped there in increments of disconnexion. A day would come when Lisa would not return from one of her assignments; she would have gone sailing off into the desert on a journey to nowhere, trapped helplessly within herself.

As we walked back to the Folly, I allowed myself to brush against her, sleeve to sleeve in the old way, a sailor spiek for 'with you'. She smiled under her hidden, dying eyes.

"Yes," she said. "I know."

It was tempting to think that Warboy and Mallin had reached an understanding, and that their walking back together boded well for the mission; but it became obvious that in these initial hours at Beach 4, this was probably the first time they had spoken more than in monosyllables, and that it was Andrew who was trying to persuade Michael Warboy to take it as a compliment to them both and something owed to Jacobi's memory.

It was just after 1700 when they returned. There was still plenty of daylight left, yet all along the shores the totems had almost completely shut down. The spinnerets had shot cable and were inert; nothing could be seen moving behind the trochars' panes; the orreries were locked tight in the different houses of their zodiacs. Silicon lids had formed in the magganon chimneys earlier, that happened soon after the noon firings, at the very height of their vigorous heliotropism; now they silently fermented their gases and did whatever it was constituted this part of their cycle. The cauchemars glistened, sweated their sweet resinous ichor; the onagers which hadn't launched missiles of waste would not do so now till first light. Their ratcheting, thudding ejections would wake us.

And now the wind came blowing in upon Trale from across the sand-sea, the thermals giving way to the cool brinraga, a much kinder wind than its unruly cousin, the larrikin. Even as Michael and Andrew reached the Folly, the few warning gusts gave way to a sudden steady airflow, full of stinging sand, scouring the slopes, causing the temperature to slide into the twenties, eroding the spinneret tracks and the small hummocks of onager waste down to nothing.

Sheltering behind the thick walls, we were probably breathing totemic material: the last of the magganon particles, spinneret and onager dust, though none of us donned the light filter masks provided by the university. The water in the cistern probably contained oil of trochar or worse. It didn't bear thinking on, and I didn't mention it, afraid that Andrew might seize on the portentousness of such things and alienate Warboy even further.

My one concern was nursing them through the night as allies, making it possible for them to work together tomorrow. For me it was Nation's interests at stake here.

I tried my best, and Lisa did, unasked, eager to make my job easier. When night came to Trale, moonless and windy, with frosty stars blazing overhead, we set our cooker going and planted dim telltales to mark the cistern and the skiffs. I prepared a meal, but Michael said he wasn't hungry and excused himself, saying he had eaten something at Beach 4.

It was while we were eating that Andrew gave in to the excitement he felt, his delight at being at Trale again, even for so short a time. He probably thought that Michael was off somewhere, that he couldn't hear; he stood with his head exposed above the parapet, enjoying the airstream on his face.

"The brinraga is a true shastric wind," he said, rhapsodizing. "A communication wind. Unlike the larrikin which has no music, no pulse, and is rightly called the heresy wind by the nomads."

"Shastric wind!" Warboy snapped from the darkness. "Can you believe this? Heresy wind!"

Sand shifted, gravel spilled on a slope as Warboy jumped

down into the gallery where Lisa and I sat around the cooker, and Andrew stood leaning against the parapet. At his arrival, we immediately averted our gazes, donned our glasses, and turned his way.

"I didn't know you were listening," Andrew said truthfully, but it sounded lame. He looked like a schoolboy caught out mimicking a teacher, though his words had been from simple zeal.

"We agreed to avoid this sort of craziness," Michael said sharply, seeing it his way. "I'd hoped to be spared, here of all places. Spared this!"

Andrew tried again. "Michael, it's so close to your soulframe."

"You always say that, Mallin! *The* soulframe! Not mine!"

"All right. But it's so close. It is! I'm a sensory interface inside and out. Everything designed for meaningful input. I have breathed molecules — inhaled the air here, the magganon fumes, residues of trochar spill and cauchemar sweat. Physiologically I process and decode. I am designed to do so and to respond — in ways I'll never fully know. At the psychic level, the same; I translate the shapes about me — this Folly has to be a psychoactive nexus, no less than what is out there. We read it in the emotional residues we feel, responding to the light here, the scents, the countless mnemonics cueing memory, just in recognizing empathy when it's felt for all that it is."

"That's enough now! Really enough! I do grant some of that; you know I do. But the totems are different. They are new, with new semiotic payloads, separate from these surroundings."

At another time I might have voiced my suspicions about a changed land, about reciprocity in the arrangement between the totems and this lonely place where they stood. But this was their argument, and Michael rushed on to make his point.

"The rest of what is here at Trale is base normal. We are designed to accommodate it as minimal."

"You can't separate the parts, Michael," Andrew said, trying his best to be conciliatory but slipping into old practised arguments too. He no longer sounded contrite. "The totems are *here* in *this* psychoactive locus. It's a psychoactive whole, a gestalt. They relate to those base normals and stand in

225

significant harmony, contrast and opposition. This has become a nexus for the total of that — a connected information tree we may spend lifetimes misunderstanding and decoding."

"No!" Michael was adamant. He spoke now as if to a dull and obstinate undergrad. "We desensitize to those base normals, we always do. We only process them when we travel between them and then temporarily. We do process new and unfamiliar things like these bioforms. The base normals *form* our bias, the xenophobic handicap we must overcome. Not part of the message any longer."

"Jacobi's dead," I said then. "And the Tell specialists are watching how we manage this."

Just get them through the next seventeen hours, I kept thinking. Working together. Get them both points with the tribal directors at Tell. Something for Nation, anything.

"And this is a different task entirely, gentlemen," Lisa said. "You're professional enough to see that. The truth does not care what we separately believe."

It was an unexpected and oddly artless comment. It could not have worked in the common room at Inlansay, but here, from Lisa, it hit home.

I had underestimated Michael as well. Just when I expected him, expected both of them, to tell her to keep out of it, warn us both off, he heaved a sigh and moved to the corner of the open gallery, looking out through the entrance to where our yachts stood in the windy dark. Trale was having a potent effect on both of them.

"Very well," he said in what might have been resignation. "Very well." And he moved out of the Folly into the uncaring wind.

"I'm sorry, Tom," Andrew said at last. "It was thoughtless of me. It's so good for us to be away from the university. And Michael tries, God knows, but he's sensitive about the eyeline. He believes he's had colleagues die from eyelining, valued friends. The notion of unhuman equivalents doing this disturbs him greatly, virtually forces him into areas usually left to me — and to Jacobi, of course, when he was with us. It has to be of paramount importance in everything he does here."

"He'll work on his own research then?"

"He's better than that. He may surprise us. His work is very good."

"The watch-ship will pick us up around noon. We only have half a day. If he won't work with you, Andrew, you must do what you can alone."

"Yes," he said. "So let me find him now. I was thoughtless. When we're out here it doesn't seem right to push theories too much anymore, yet everywhere is subject matter to provoke them anew. I may be able to do something."

Mallin left Lisa and me crouched around the glowing cooker.

"Thanks," I said when we were alone. "You did it better."

She smiled and removed her shades, exposed her incredible languishing eyes, the irises so pale, almost colourless.

"They're after the same thing. They want to discover what simply is, but at the same time they need to be meaningful to themselves first, desperately self-fulfilling, like any of us."

Which was a metastatement for us then, something to sustain the revelation of her eyes in the flickering light.

"Thanks anyway," I said, and her smile softened, changed, did something to re-make the pale weathered face. The pale, downgraded irises shone.

"You'll probably laugh," she said. "But I'm hoping for another remission. Tell me if you mind, Tom. I don't think I'll harm you, but you might do a Christ healing for me. Who knows?"

"A Christ healing! Just promise you'll tell no-one."

"Done."

I took both her hands in mine, and by the warm glow of the cooker gazed into her eyes, for the good it did, or the ill, for the easy kinship of ministering.

I woke to the far-off snap and thud of discharging onagers, to discover Lisa comfortably close beside me, saw the empty sleeping-bags near ours and so slipped out of mine without putting on my shades.

The sky was suffused with an uneven pearly light, a milk-glass blend softly opalescent at the dawn edges in the east.

I climbed onto the wall and surveyed the beaches, all that Trale was — or visibly seemed to be, saw an onager release itself, heard the sound of the torsion cancelling, the thud as the arm closed on itself, watched the tiny payload complete its arc. There was a soft impact cloud followed by the sound of a strike, faint but distinct in the wonderful silence.

I went to the parapet, focused my binoculars, quickly found Mallin and Warboy at Beach 4. They stood together near the three bioforms I had visited with Michael the previous afternoon, and seemed to be conferring. Neither wore djellabas; the fanciful and open-ended patches on their scrap-jackets made them look like ancient astronauts seconded from missions never completed, tasks hinted at but undisclosed. I saw cameras and testing equipment at their feet and felt relieved. Maybe something could be done before the Tell ship arrived.

An hour later, the scientists came wandering back for breakfast, and Lisa set out a morning meal as sunlight snatched away the first shadows and began baking the land again.

"We believe we've confirmed the contact site," Andrew said.

Warboy nodded. "Where Jacobi was...programmed to die." He did not say 'eyelined'; he was trying, both of them were. "Near the three pieces we noted yesterday."

"Can you be sure?"

"Three months after it happened, no we can't be sure. We believe one or more of the three may have been attempting a congruency."

"Not with Jacobi," Andrew hastened to add, then looked warily at Warboy who seemed not to have minded the interruption. "With each other. We assume they are cognate beings, even if tangental. We must allow they could do it all the time."

Warboy clasped his hands before him, almost as if on a table, the mannerism of a man who often spoke out at faculty meetings.

"They had geared up for a congruency in terms of citilo and sephalay. Jacobi triggered a communication package not meant for a human percept system. He blundered into an intricate AI conversation net and it killed him."

"How sure can you be of this?" I said.

"Never sure. I must repeat. How could we be certain of something like that? But it's consistent with the proximity of the three totems to each other, the fact they're angled in that way. The potential for psychoactive signalling among them would be very high."

"Then it actually could have..." I hesitated.

"Yes," Warboy said, without looking at Mallin. "I suspect it eyelined him, viable transaction, that it has a catalysing equivalent to the human eye. Kindred DNA somewhere, compatible aminos and molecule chains, whatever cues the soulframe, causes it to process a change. It may have launched as Hello, but it was as sure as a gunshot into his psyche."

"How do they do it, gentlemen?" Lisa asked. "How do they communicate with one another?"

"How can we answer even that?" Mallin replied, almost as if the two scientists had worked out a compromise and this was Andrew's turn. "Light semaphores from the dexters, organic thread from the spinnerets, tension patterns and angle in the onagers' throwing arms, you tell us."

When Andrew hesitated, Warboy continued. It was almost comical. "We get just enough about Trale to drive us crazy. We've some clues, but research has been so limited; we don't have DNA simulations or observation time to be certain of anything. Compared to the tribal experts, we're like children playing."

Lisa poured more coffee into our mugs. "So what now?"

"We go back to Inlansay," Warboy said. "We devise theories to accommodate all this — try to come up with a suitable range. We discuss them and discuss them some more. Sometimes we do stupid, desperate, all-or-nothing things like intercept communication nets not meant for us, if such things exist. We write up the guesses and hunches with amazing conviction and panache, and the tribal experts laugh as usual since they probably know exactly what it was they made in the first place."

"We only have till 1200."

Warboy snorted. "Just enough time to tantalize us. They can announce how leading National experts were given the chance to solve the mysterious and tragic death of their renowned colleague. They want nothing discovered here. No eyeline equivalent, no cause of death. Our only consolation is that they cannot know what really happened either, otherwise we would never have been allowed to come. Or left alone to look around."

"For all we know," Andrew said, "they may want to be able to blame us for something when we've gone. Accuse us of tampering, damaging the bioforms, sabotaging them."

"The ship will be here regardless," I said. "Do what you can. Please, everyone, you know the routine. Make sure you're clean. No samples, no souvenirs, nothing but photographs. They may not even let us keep those this time. And when it arrives, they could have gain-monitors trained on us. Speak in whispers, backs turned, or they'll know what we say."

Warboy laughed. "Who has anything to say?"

Perhaps we all thought of the totems then, for the silence that followed seemed very eloquent indeed.

At 1050, Lisa and I loaded our skiffs with what we could, then walked along the different beaches observing the totems. The cauchemars sweated resin, the orreries clicked and shifted like bone carousels, the trochars pumped away, the rorschachs lifted symmetrical platelets to the burning sun. Many of the big columnar bioforms — the sergeant-majors, the sandwives, xoanons and coralline dexters, even the spinnerets, looked dead and functionless, but we knew the unlocked ones turned imperceptibly like the hour-hands of antique clocks, angling slowly to follow the course of the sun.

Finally we passed the empty cipher of the Folly again, and crossed Beach 4 to find Warboy at the death site, matching his charts of alignment and configuration variations with continuity photographs taken a year before. Andrew Mallin was upslope a short way, standing near what I suddenly realized had to be the newly-formed totem Warboy had discovered soon after we reached Trale.

"What makes a man take off his sunglasses at noon?" I asked when we joined him.

Andrew smiled. "What indeed? And what makes an ordinary-enough coralline dexter grow a throat opening the size of a dinner plate?"

"I'd hate to think."

"But do, Tom. Do, both of you. All guesses are welcome here — it's what we traffic in in the absence of forensic data and adequate empiricism."

"How do they reproduce?" Lisa asked.

"Good question. Put it with: 'How do they communicate?' Without samples, with what the tribes let us bring, again we can only speculate."

"Speculations then," I said.

"Very well. A spinneret shoots cable, volatile for up to, say, half an hour. Another spinneret overlays that with thread of its own — they can angle and re-align over several days, actually choose targets. The overlay point could be the start. A simple cross-pollination analogue, but smile at the 'simple' will you? We all do."

"Sexes? Asexuality?"

"Not known, Tom. Not to us anyway. But random or conscious cross-pollination is one suggestion; there are others involving directional sporing, wind-blown thread residue, insect carriers as in the plant kingdom. The brinraga may do it all, blow trace elements, move insects sticky with cauchemar resin."

"The onagers?"

"We know there is angling there too, though their breeding cycles must take weeks, months, to complete. We see them facing the desert most of the time, but they can re-align and turn."

"Like the one at the death site?"

"Yes, like the one over there. That could be a breeder beginning or completing. They take quite a while to do it. The continuity photos will determine that. I was here last year. I know I would have remembered an upslope onager. It certainly wasn't like that then."

"Jacobi's death?"

"You see a connection too? Good. I'm giving that thought. It could be a wonderful connection."

"So how would the onagers do it?" Lisa asked. "Their throwing arms?"

"Yes, shot from the arm, I imagine. Michael agrees. A specially prepared matrix instead of the usual waste load. The waste may even be a supporting culture, a fertilization package with a built-in food or fertilizer store. The onagers shoot out onto the sea, the matrix erodes in the wind, the brinraga moves the payload to a point on the shore. Statistically it would succeed quite well."

Lisa nodded. "And the other one, the tall one?"

"The coralline dexter? Harder to say. There are those lens plates in the shaft like the trochars have."

"Heat windows?" I asked.

"Possibly. But showing no internals like the trochar panes do. Black mirrors. Light traps. The dexters may be asexual, or they may have the capacity to be self-fertilizing, or nearly so. There are those refractive surfaces; there may be alignment from one to the next to allow intense, focused sunlight to be lensed onto receiver plates in another coralline in the right mode. Activating codes of light. You can read it both ways: as clumsy or overspecialized, but how can we know? These have a designed cycle but they are rejects remember, aberrant forms."

"So we are told," I said. "They could be special projects."

"Agreed. Still, that way lies madness. So then, a photosynthesis for spores snatched from the wind would be possible and convenient, or self-fertilization incubated by controlled refraction. Those dexters choose to turn with the sun; they don't have to." He shrugged.

I studied the new totem before us, the smooth vitreous shaft, the dark shiny swellings of the lenses. "If we allow purpose..."

Andrew nodded eagerly. "Yes. These are potentially very sophisticated lifeforms judging from the Fosti Towers and the Iseult-Darrian belltrees. We've never had enough time here. Once or twice a year, testing hypotheses made in the labs all that time. These are generally slow, sun-powered metabolisms, with body-clocks geared to the same 24-hour day-night cycle as ours, but since their DNA was sculpted, they may possess a different perception-consciousness entirely, a different time-sense..."

"I think the tribal biotects would have wanted humans to be able to interract with them. Why settle for less than that?"

"But these are — apparently — rejects, Tom. Just allow something so fundamental as a different time-sense. It may be natural for the smarter totems to see humans as frantic, driven creatures."

"Would Jacobi have seemed frantic, do you think?"

Mallin laughed. "I'm sure of it. Look at Michael and me with the time we have. Jacobi pioneered this area if any National did. One of the first of us the tribes allowed near the place. Most of the earliest formalized taxonomies are his. You agree that he probably cued the killer totem?"

"It's what you said before."

"It is. He seems to have intercepted a communication net. Think, too, then, Tom, of what I said a moment ago. How do the totems perceive us? As rushing, random particles? As threats? We don't even know enough to know if there's a predation cycle here — something to feed on them, damage them. We can't do more than allow for defence systems — equivalents of our teeth and fists and kicking muscles. They don't have coarse motion to defend with."

"You'd expect secreted toxins and irritants, acids, poisoned barbs, lensed light. But a death-look eyeline?"

"You're saying it. Michael would certainly say it was logical. He says an eyeline surrogate, but conscious rather than random, and frankly even I prefer not to grant something so mindless as a defence system kill. I want to see volition here, purpose. An accident. A misdirected communication package by lifeforms labouring within different mind-sets and time-frames. Not murderers."

When I looked round at Lisa, I saw that she was standing close to the new variant, with one palm resting on the vitreous-looking citilo shaft. Her other hand was adjusting her glasses; I immediately wondered if she had just now been going to raise them — or if she had already done so and was replacing them.

"Lisa?"

But she addressed Andrew, looking thoughtful.

"Your problem is having too many things to do in too little time. Your own research first, right?"

"Well..."

"Favours for colleagues in the Department back home. Honouring promises. It must be like that. Thinking of what you can turn out to win appropriations."

"What are you saying, Lisa?" I could imagine the frown behind his shades.

"I can see room for overlooking things, that's all. Tom and I don't have your preoccupations. We're possibly more detached."

"Possibly. But you're not being very fair."

"Colourman's makes you like that," she said.

"Do you have something?"

"Have you tracked the axes from the three totems and projected them across the three months since Jacobi died? Plotted a likely focus?"

"Of course. There could have been an interface focused on the new totem."

"More, Doctor Mallin. Resulting in the new totem."

"What! No! They're discrete forms. Not compatible. How could they interbreed? It'd be like dogs and cats..."

"But you don't know that for sure," Lisa said, strangely relentless. "You want to believe these are cognitive forms. They could know exactly what they're doing."

Andrew pulled at his chin, considering the idea.

"And for all we know," I said, "the trochars and magganons have been priming the land around here. They've had over a hundred years to do it, salting in necessary elements. Built a compatibility horizon, even changed their own patterns. Modified their imperatives."

Lisa was studying the new totem again. "Allow the possibility for a moment. The spinneret sends out its thread..."

Andrew interrupted her. "I see what you're getting at. The onager contributes a combinant payload, the dexter lenses light, incubates. Then a new bioform, a congruency of forms."

"Is it possible?"

Andrew was silent for several moments. "Lisa, who can say? Anything's possible. But to what end?"

"I can guess," she said. "I'm sure you can. Call Michael."

At 1130, three of us stood before the six-foot dexter variant while Andrew paced out trajectories, pegging in the lines of string so we could see just how precise the convergence was.

The onager was in the process of turning back to face the sand-sea like its kin, but Warboy explained how continuity photographs of onagers always revealed an anticlockwise sweep. In three months, the death-site onager could very easily have aligned itself, delivered its part of the birthload, and started on its slow turn to a locked seaward position.

The spinneret, for its size, had the precise angle and the range capacity to shoot cable to the site of the new bioform, and to add increments into the throat opening located above the girdle of black mirrors on its trunk. The coralline dexter had the mirror power to focus easily on the target.

"The process may be more elaborate still," Warboy said. "If the parent dexter spores, it may use the wind to blanket an area with seed. The other totems need only align on a likely target. Or spores could be caught in a sticky discharge in the onager's ladle and mixed there, the spinneret aligning to add its contribution of cable. All done at the onager."

Lisa laughed. " 'When shall we three meet again?' "

"What?"

"Nothing. An old dramatic piece. The purpose?"

"I can only think along the lines you have suggested. The three intentionally or unintentionally killed Jacobi" — he did not say triggered a deliberate and violent eyeline response, but it had to be in his thoughts — "and now have worked to create this new form, this...jacobi, as an interface for a specialized contact with humans."

Andrew came striding back along his convergence strings.

"It seems certain," he said. "So what do we do?"

Michael surprised us all. "Remove our glasses in front of the thing," he said, and turned back to face the totem.

Andrew objected. "Let me!"

"No, Andrew!" Warboy said. "Remember Jacobi. I'll do it. Only one of us."

No-one argued. Warboy had more to prove than the rest of us: was there eyelining involved, did this AI possess an integral soulframe, whatever that was?

The four of us stood before the totem, facing the side where the throat opening was, black and glass-smooth above the dark mirrors. Radiating out behind us were the trajectory strings Andrew had set.

In the hush of the final morning hour, Michael removed his

glasses and peered into the black organic panes.

I pushed forward to see them better, and Lisa did, and Andrew, all of us crowding there at the point of the convergent strings, like the living heart of a comet, or the focusing node at the meeting lines in a giant's horoscope.

Absurd thoughts crossed my mind, fearful thoughts of conspiracy, of totems aligning behind us, slowly turning, silently loading, but I did not look away. I thought of the bubbles of gas already trapped in the throats of the magganons, pushing at the fragile lids; of the trochars pumping away like stained-glass hearts, sucking up the life of the earth, changing it, pushing it back into the hidden places; of onagers building payloads, crafting them; of spinnerets soundlessly uncoiling eloquent saline cable; of the orreries swinging and clicking in stately calm, making semaphores to the sky, answering the rorschachs, shouting to them in a silence full of significance.

The whole beach was a communication. A communication net spread out.

All the totems, constantly signalling; a shore of urgently declaring forms. Look at us! Look at what is here!

I knew it even as I discovered I had my glasses raised, staring into the black living mirrors just as Michael was, with naked eyes — being answered, being told. Communication is what we do, how we measure our lives, make meaning for ourselves and so make ourselves meaningful.

And in that glittering darkness was a light — a star! — a single star lodged deep within the talking mirrors, no, in my *mind*, projected there!

It took only seconds, moments, to receive that message too, to bring it back out of that secret night.

We all moved then, the broadcast completed; Warboy replacing his glasses, standing; Andrew clearing his throat; Lisa already walking down the beach, her hands raised to her face as if she wept.

And, foolish competitors, the three of us remaining at the site tried to speak, to make comment, but nothing came of it. For there, stretched out about us, were the labouring shores, the totems glinting and shimmering in the heat. There, too, already, a kilometre out, was the tribal ship, the black Tell watch-ship under its gorgeous Pan-Tribal kites, waiting to collect our skiffs and take us away from Trale.

We wandered down to our tiny vessels under the gaze of tribal watchers who surely had to be wondering what it was we had just done, who might now have monitors turned our way.

"Let me go out with Andrew," Michael said when we had loaded the last of our gear. He stood with his back to the Tell ship and spoke in almost a whisper so his words could not be easily monitored. "We'll use the parafoil. I can manage it. We need to discuss what we're going to say about this, about the jacobi."

Lisa and I nodded, and set the two men on their way — into possible danger, reprisal, payback. Then we went to the remaining skiff, got our own kites aloft, and started out.

Despite the transit sounds, we too spoke in subdued tones, mindful of detection.

"That wasn't his first glimpse into the mirrors, was it?" Lisa asked as we rolled along, closing the short distance.

"No," I said, realizing now what Warboy's personality shift really meant. "He found the jacobi yesterday. He would've done it then, I'm sure, whenever he could. Andrew too I think."

"You think so?" Our kites blocked our line of sight to the ship. We spoke softly yet urgently before they shifted.

"Yes. The totems needed these men to work together. It had to be one of the jacobi's very specialized tasks. They know the tribes have abandoned them here, ostracized them. They prepared a revelation that might get out to the world and start something better for them. Acceptance perhaps. Not just at the level of what we suspect is happening here."

"What do you mean, Tom?"

"I wonder if an eyeline can be programmed. If we have been made unconscious carriers of a subliminal message to others."

"To get past the tribes." Then, "Yes," she said, and I wasn't sure if it was simple agreement with what I had said or an affirmation about something else.

We were four hundred metres from the Tell ship, both of us distracted. There wasn't much time.

"Lisa, when you looked into the mirrors, did you see

anything? A star? Just the one?"

She frowned. "I'm not sure what I saw. Not really. Why?"

"I've been told something. Given something important. I have to go back to the Madhouse. I have to find out what it means."

Lisa nodded, then spoke, her words powered by a certainty matching my own. "I took off my glasses." She removed them again now, her pale eyes squinting in the intense light.

"So did I." I smiled and removed mine as well.

But Lisa shook her head; she meant something more.

"But I'm in remission. I know it."

I met the pale gaze, ignoring the helm, letting the off-shore thermals draw us along.

"Then..."

"Very specialized, you said. Eyeline. Soulframe. Your guess. I prefer to think cognate life doing whatever it does when it has the chance: considers itself and tries for more."

We crossed in silence then, our glasses off at noon, both smiling, me thinking of my star, my three signs, and of her last words too, wondering if Michael and Andrew, if any of us, could conceal what we knew, and if a message waited, locked away in each of us, a message the tribal biotects themselves might unwittingly carry forth when they examined the new totem. Lisa seemed lost in whatever certainty made her so glad now to show her eyes.

"Remission, eh?" I said, as the kites shifted to show us the tribal ship once again. "You know what I think?"

"No, what?" she asked, and frowned slightly, worried by what I might say in plain view like this.

"You might have at least given me the credit for it."

And we were laughing, still far enough away for the faces of the watching tribesmen not to resolve into eyelines, when from the shore behind us came the valedictions of that forsaken place, the first of the noon guns firing into the hot and patient sky.